Dear Reader,

When I wrote the first book of the OPUS series,
Just Like a Man, I honestly intended the character of
operative She-Wolf to have only a single book appearance.
I didn't even know what her name was at that point. But as
happens so frequently with us writers, she kind of took on
a life of her own and demanded a book about herself. Even
at that, however, the story I originally planned for her never
materialized. She was such a strong individual, she pretty
much dictated her own story. Naturally, she gave herself a
cool name like Lila Moreau, and—wonder of wonders—even
chose a different man than the one I wanted to pair her with.
I think she truly is the strongest heroine I've ever written.

And I'd like to thank everyone for their patience while
Overnight Male found its place in the schedule. I know from
your e-mails how anxiously you've been waiting to see the
book in print (as have I). I did have a very good time getting
Lila and her experiences down on paper. And I think I fell in
love with Joel right along with her. Here's hoping you do, too.

Happy reading,

Elizabeth Bevarly

ELIZABETH BEVARLY

overnight male

HQN™

ISBN-13: 978-0-373-77214-8
ISBN-10:   0-373-77214-9

OVERNIGHT MALE

For Wanda Ottewell,
who made every book better.
Thanks.

CHAPTER ONE

Darkness had always been Lila Moreau's best friend. Throughout her life she had used different kinds of darkness to aid her in different kinds of ways. As a child, she knew the darkness under a bed or in a closet could protect her from her mother's hurtful words. As a teenager, she felt the shadows of the city could shelter her from people, especially men, who wanted more from her than she was willing to give. As an adult, she used her shady character to keep others from getting too close. But this, the darkness that came with nightfall, was Lila's favorite. Nighttime was when all the best stuff happened. It was when the world—or at least her world—came to life.

"Hey, lady, ya got a hundred bucks to spare? I ain't been laid all week, and it ain't cheap in this part 'a town."

Lila growled her exasperation at having her profound—and kind of cool and gothic, if she did say so herself—musings interrupted. Okay, so maybe some of the life in her world was more of the low variety than it was of the high. She knew how to deal.

She turned from where she stood on the corner of N Street and Potomac in Georgetown and glared at the lowest-of-all-life who had emerged from the shadows behind her. He was maybe half a foot taller than her own five-four and probably outweighed her by a 150 pounds. Since he was dressed in double-knit sans-a-belt trousers and a shiny polyester shirt that was stained under each arm with perspiration, and since he clearly hadn't bathed in days—also considering the way he'd just greeted her—he was too poorly dressed and not articulate enough to be a pimp. So Lila concluded he must just be a big scumbag. This part of the nation's capital didn't usually attract people like him, since it drew such a large tourist and college crowd and was home to so many of the city's movers and shakers. (Well, okay, maybe there were one or two scumbags. Not to mention pimps.) But neither was it unheard of to find someone in Georgetown who wasn't exactly the cream of Washington society.

"Uh, I think you're a little out of your element here, guy," she said to the, ah, guy. "Bubba's Booty Barn is in Cheverly. But good news. You can take the orange line straight there and you won't have to switch trains at all. Metro station's that way," she added, pointing in the general direction of Foggy Bottom, and hoping he'd take the hint.

Of course he didn't. That would have been too easy.

Instead the guy grinned and said, "On second thought, sweetheart, maybe I won't need that hundred bucks. You look like the kinda woman who'd be up for just about anything."

Actually, dressed as she was from head to toe in black, complete with knit cap and gloves, what Lila looked like was a woman who was about to break in to someone's home. Of course, there was a good reason for that. She was about to break in to someone's home. Nevertheless, she hated it when men just couldn't get the gist of the most basic fashion statement. Duh.

Damn. She really didn't need a distraction like this right now. She had her schedule tonight timed down to the last second. There wasn't any available room in it at all for a maiming.

But she knew it would be unavoidable when the guy winked at her, nodded his head toward the alley she'd been about to enter, and asked, "Whaddaya say? Do a good job, sweetheart, and I'll give ya back half of the hundred bucks you're gonna gimme, too."

She smiled at him. "Oh, gosh, just keep the whole hundred, big guy. I mean, I *should* pay you for the privilege, shouldn't I? A great-looking, charismatic man like you? C'mon."

His flabbergasted expression in response to her enthusiasm was almost worth the interruption he was causing her. Almost.

It was a testament to his stupidity that he followed Lila into the alley without a speck of hesitation or suspicion. It was a testament to her skill that she unmanned him in even less than her usual five seconds. Oh, he'd still be able to father children someday. Unfortunately. After he regained consciousness. And, you know, found a woman who had the IQ of a piece of lint.

Now, then. Where was she? Oh, yeah. Darkness had always been Lila's best friend…blah blah blah…the darkness that came with nightfall was her favorite…blah blah blah… nighttime was when all the best stuff happened…blah blah blah…that was when Lila's world came to life.

Got it.

Brushing off the last lingering remnants of disgust at having come into contact with Mr. Scumbag quite literally, Lila looked around and assessed her situation. The alley between two rows of sleepy town houses was deserted this time of night, save the occasional unconscious—and un-manned—scumbag, and silent save the soft sigh of a late spring breeze that nudged a stray piece of newspaper from one side of the narrow pathway to the other. She gazed up at an unlit window on the third floor of one of those town houses—the one through which she would momentarily be crawling—confident that the occupant was by now fast asleep.

It would be a pretty standard breaking and entering, even though many Georgetown residents were protected by private security systems, this one included. In fact, this residence was even better protected than most, thanks to its owner's occupa-tion, and might prove a challenge to someone else. Someone who *wasn't* familiar with sophisticated protection devices that ran on arcane power sources.

Fortunately, Lila knew everything there was to know about sophisticated protection devices. And she liked to think that she herself was something of an arcane power source.

She flexed her fingers inside the snug black leather gloves, then tucked an errant strand of blond hair back under the black knit cap she'd tugged low over her eyes. The long-sleeved, skintight turtleneck and pants hugged her body like a second skin and served two purposes. Not only did they keep her warm in the cool April night—and, it went without saying, looked *fabulous* on her—but there was no part of her attire that might slow her down, tangle her up, or offer purchase for a pursuer.

Not that Lila expected to be pursued—never mind purchased—but one always had to be prepared for the possibility. Never, though, had she been caught. At least, not when she didn't want to be. She certainly wasn't going to screw up something like this.

Effortlessly and without a sound, she scaled the side of the big brick building, finding footholds by turns in the mortar between the bricks, the rainspout and the thick ivy growing up the side. Having already dismantled the exterior part of the alarm system in the front of the town house, she was lifting the window and pushing herself over the sill within seconds. She paused, standing motionless for a moment to survey her surroundings and ensure everything was as it was supposed to be.

Enough pale blue light emanated from big, illuminated numbers on the nightstand clock to reveal a man's horizontal form in the bed beside it. He was hunched deep under the covers, sound asleep, completely unaware of her presence. Had it not been for the low, regular thrum of his breathing and the steady rise and fall of his shoulders, Lila wouldn't have known if he was even alive. Well, had it not been for that, and the fact that she'd scoped the place out yesterday and had seen not a single corpse lying around.

She smiled. She was about to enjoy her favorite thing about being a spy: the takedown. Silently she retrieved a pair of handcuffs tucked into her belt at the small of her back and crept across the room.

It was only after she had launched herself at her quarry

that she sensed something wasn't quite right. Unfortunately, her body was in motion by then, and although Lila Moreau was a woman of many talents, defying gravity wasn't one of them. Before she could recover and retreat, the man who should have been sleeping was wrapping her in the covers, wresting the handcuffs from her grasp and snapping them— *chink, chink*—first around her wrist and then around the thick metal spokes in the wrought-iron headboard.

Immediately Lila began to fight, throwing herself completely into her assault. And even one-handed, Lila Moreau could wreak the havoc of ten men. But it quickly became evident that her adversary was more insidious than ten men, because he had her pinned to the mattress in record time. After more frantic struggling, she decided her assailant couldn't possibly be human. And after still more frantic struggling, she knew she was right. Because she realized then that what had finally brought überspy Lila Moreau to her knees—or at least facedown into a mattress—was… sheets. And a blanket. And a couple of fluffy pillows.

Damn. This was *not* going to look good on her report.

Eventually she managed to extricate herself—well, kind of, since she was still handcuffed to the bed. But even though a light had been switched on in the corner, she saw as she shoved the bedclothes off herself that there was no one in the room except her.

The furnishings were what looked like period antiques, but they seemed to be more functional than they were collectible, because all were clearly well used. Likewise, the Oriental rugs were richly colored but worn in spots, the hardwood floor beneath them polished but scarred in places. A fireplace on the other side of the room smelled faintly of burned wood, indicating it had been put to use recently. Its mantelpiece was crowded with models of wooden boats, and bisected floor-to-ceiling bookcases that were crammed full of old books. The remaining walls were hung with what appeared to be commendations of some kind and childishly executed works of art in baroque frames.

As masculine lairs went, this one was something of a departure from the ones Lila usually saw. Of course, most of the masculine lairs she saw had been decorated by men who were morally bankrupt, so there was a chance she wasn't really in a position to judge the decor. It was nice, though, she had to admit. It made her feel…calm. Until she remembered she was shackled to the bed frame, wherein she felt more than a little pissed off.

Wondering where her target had disappeared to, she reached down into her sock for the spare handcuff key she always hid on her person for just such an emergency and had never had to use.

And discovered it was gone.

Dammit. It must have fallen out while she was trying to subdue the counterpane in the ass. No way could anyone have lifted it without her realizing it. She began to search furiously through the bedclothes as far as she could reach, but there was no sign of the key anywhere.

Great. Now she was going to have to gnaw off her hand to get away. She hated when that happened.

"It's on the nightstand."

She whipped around at the sound of the deeply timbred voice and saw a man lounging in the doorway. Although they'd never met personally, she knew who he was. She didn't go around breaking in to the houses of total strangers. Who knew what kind of germs you'd pick up doing that? Lila only broke into the homes of her closest friends and enemies. And although Joel Faraday, code name Virtuoso, wasn't exactly either of those, she did know him—as an archivist for her employer, the Office for Political Unity and Security. He was also her captor, she reminded herself. Which might cause a bit of trouble, considering the fact that he was her partner, too. At least for a little while.

What he *wasn't* was what she'd expected. In all her years at OPUS, Lila had met only one archivist before tonight, but that one had been pretty much what she'd suspected all of the OPUS archivists were: a timid, wrinkled, eccentric little man she could sling over one shoulder. Joel Faraday was none of those things. Well, except for being a man. That part was obvious. Too obvious, in fact.

She guesstimated his age as mid-thirties, even though there was an air about him that suggested considerable life experience. His thick, dark brown hair hung almost to his shoulders and was shoved straight back from his forehead by a careless hand. Behind trendy, black-framed glasses his eyes were even darker than his hair, and the lower half of his face was shadowed by more than one day's growth of beard. Slumped against the doorjamb as he was, she could only guess at his full height, but it certainly topped six feet.

And every last inch of it was *very* nicely put together. Broad shoulders strained at the seams of an otherwise baggy white T-shirt, and black hair sprang from the deep V-neck. Loose, dark blue striped pajama bottoms ended in bare feet,

feet that were large enough to make her wonder about another fabled part of the male anatomy whose size was often compared to those, ah, appendages. One big hand was settled indolently on his hip, while the other cradled a half-empty snifter of something the color of rich amber.

"The far one," he added, dipping his head toward the nightstand on the other side of bed from where she was lying.

She turned her head to look where he indicated and saw the small metal key sitting on the farthest edge of the night-stand, just—

"Out of your reach," he said. Then he grinned. "They told me you always do this. So I confess I had a little advance warning. If I hadn't…"

He lifted a shoulder and let it drop, but left the statement unfinished. Not that it mattered. Had he not had his advance warning, he, not Lila, would be handcuffed to the bed. They both knew it. As he said, that was the way she broke in all her new partners. It was just her little way of letting them know up front that she would be the one in charge.

Not that Joel Faraday would be her partner for long. And no way would he ever be in charge. Well, not once the hand-cuffs were off, anyway. He would be on board for this par-ticular part of her most recent assignment only long enough to reveal some information, impart his evaluation and share her speculation. As soon as she had everything she needed from him, she'd be completing the rest of the assignment on her own. And then she hoped to go back to working with her regular partner—which largely involved flying solo, just the way she liked it.

As she jerked her wrist against the cuff snapped snugly around it, Faraday's grin widened. And the sooner she got back to flying solo, Lila thought with a silent growl, the better.

"I cannot believe I fell for this," she muttered aloud.

"You were overconfident," he said. "I've heard that about you." Very matter-of-factly, he added, "And overconfidence will get you killed in this line of work."

Yeah, yeah, yeah.

"What else have you heard about me?" she asked. Even though she was reasonably certain she already knew. Like checking one's credit report from time to time, it was always a good idea to ensure one's badass reputation was in order.

He gazed up at the ceiling, feigning deep consideration, swirling his brandy expertly in his glass without even bothering to make sure it didn't slosh over the side. "Let's see now," he said thoughtfully. "What have I heard about Lila Moreau, code name She-Wolf?"

He lowered his head to look at her now, pinning his gaze on her face in a way that made hot little explosions ignite in the pit of her belly. Interesting.

"Probably," he continued, "the same things everyone else has heard. That you're one of the best agents—if not *the* best agent—we have. That you were recruited by OPUS before you even graduated from college. That until recently, your record was spotless." When she opened her mouth to object, he quickly added, "Oh, but hey, that pesky attempted-murder thing has been all cleared up, and now you're back to tabula rasa."

"If I'd attempted murder, you can be damned sure I

would've succeeded," Lila said. "I never tried to kill anyone. Least of all *him*."

Him being the big man in charge of OPUS. Or, as he was pseudo-affectionately known in the organization, He Whose Name Nobody Dares Say. Mostly because nobody knew what his name was.

"Not that everyone in OPUS hasn't wanted to put a bullet in the guy at least once," she qualified. "But that whole attempted-murder thing was just a desperate, trumped-up charge they hoped would turn up the heat and flush me out."

"Yet still you managed to stay under their radar," Faraday murmured.

"Like you said. I'm *the* best agent OPUS has."

He grinned again. "I've also heard you're not modest."

"Modesty is overrated. Especially when it isn't warranted."

He neither agreed nor disagreed with her assessment of herself, and that bugged the hell out of Lila. What bugged her even more was that she actually gave a damn whether he agreed or disagreed with her assessment of herself.

"And I've heard that you're smart and focused and dedicated," he went on, sounding genuinely impressed, something that dulled the edge of her irritation. Which also bothered her. What did she care if he was impressed by her or not? "And that your number one goal in life right now is to bring Sorcerer to heel."

Sorcerer was formally known as Adrian Padgett, and at one time had been an agent for OPUS himself—before turning to the Dark Side and choosing a life of crime. He'd been on their list—and on the lam—for years, and Lila was only the most recent agent trying to bring him in. So far he'd eluded her, something that had only served to make her more determined, but this time he wasn't going to get away. Of that she was positive.

"And I've heard that if anyone can bring him in," Faraday continued, "you can. Because I've also heard that you don't quit until the job is done. And I've heard that you scare the hell out of most people. Oh, and I've also heard that you're arguably the most dangerous woman in the world."

"Arguably?" Lila echoed dubiously.

"Well, I certainly wouldn't argue with it," he assured her.

Smart man. "And do I scare the hell out of you?" she asked.

His eyes never left hers as he reminded her, "You're the one handcuffed to the bed. What do you think?"

She opened her mouth to reply with a quick retort, then realized she wasn't sure how he'd meant his remark. Was he saying he'd cuffed her to the bed because he was terrified of her? Or was he saying that since it had been a piece of cake for him to cuff her to the bed, she wasn't scary at all?

Wow. A man she couldn't get a read on. Lila couldn't remember the last time she'd met one of those. In fact, she wasn't sure she ever had.

"So you've heard quite a bit about me," she said, deciding to ignore his last comment. For now. Considering the way he'd listed all her attributes, she figured her badass rep was still pretty much in place. "Do you believe it?"

This time his gaze drifted from her face and sauntered down her entire body, all the way to her toes and back again. And every last inch of her began to tingle and grow hot under his scrutiny. Wow. It had been a long time since she'd felt that, too. That immediate shudder of sexual awareness that started in the pit of her stomach and exploded outward, demanding satisfaction.

Damn. This really wasn't a good time for her to meet a man who could do that to her. Especially one who could do it so quickly after meeting him. And do it with such amazing thoroughness.

"Well, handcuffed to my bed like that, you don't look too dangerous," he said. Ironically, there was something in the way he said it that made him seem very dangerous indeed.

Lila shoved her errant thoughts and feelings and tingling sexual awareness to the back of her brain and smiled at him. And she hoped like hell it was a convincing smile, and revealed none of the nervousness still quivering in her belly. "Good. Then why don't you come over here and unlock me?"

He laughed softly as he lifted the brandy snifter to his mouth for an idle sip, taking his time to draw the liquor into his mouth, and savoring it for a moment before swallowing. Lila watched fascinated as he completed the action, wondering why she found such a simple gesture so provocative, and why it suddenly felt as if she, not he, was the one who had consumed something that seared her insides with heat. He didn't answer her question, but when he remained rooted in place, she gathered that was pretty much all the response she was going to receive from him.

"I'd offer you a cognac, too," he said, "but I've also heard you don't drink. However, I stocked up on decaf green tea in anticipation of your, ah, arrival. If you're interested."

"Maybe later," she said, thinking news traveled fast. She'd voiced that no-drinking policy and preference for decaf green tea at her sister's house only a couple of weeks ago, and only in the presence of one other OPUS employee. "We need to go over the assignment," she told him. She tugged at the handcuff again. "Come on. Unlock me. Joke's on me. But now the joke's over. Let me go."

"Right," Faraday said. "So you can kick my ass from here to Abu Dhabi. I'll unlock you in a little while."

"I'll still kick your ass from here to Abu Dhabi," she told him matter-of-factly. "It'll just hurt more later."

He considered her in that thoughtful way again as he enjoyed another sip of his drink. Another slow, thorough, fascinating, provocative, heat-inducing sip that went straight to Lila's head. If he kept this up, she was going to be under the table soon.

"Maybe," he finally said.

It took a minute for her to realize he was talking about the ass kicking, not the under-the-tabling. No maybe about that first one. She'd totally kick his ass, she thought. But she kept it to herself.

"So tell me what you know," he said.

"Did you read my report?" she asked.

He nodded.

"Then you know everything I know."

"Reports only cover the facts," he said. "Not gut feelings. Not impressions. Not theories. So what are your gut feelings, impressions and theories on this thing?"

Faraday didn't need to identify the *thing* any more than he had. Adrian Padgett had been the focus of Lila's job for some time. Before she'd come along, *he'd* been arguably OPUS's best agent. He'd operated by his own rules, to be sure—kind of like Lila, come to think of it—but he'd still stayed within the parameters of Doing the Right Thing. OPUS itself often bent its own rules to ensure political unity and security, so no one had really bothered to rein in Sorcerer, even when he started overstepping those parameters. He always collected exceptionally good intel, always bagged the bad guys, always got the job done. So who cared how he went about it?

Eventually, though, he began to stray so far beyond the parameters that there was no coming back. Several years ago Sorcerer had decided to become a free agent of sorts, and blackmailed the organization who employed him, threatening to expose it and many of its agents if he wasn't paid millions of dollars and left alone. Had he not been such a good agent, the threat would have been laughable. OPUS was built on a framework of secrets—so many secrets that there were few in the organization who could honestly describe how it all worked.

With Sorcerer, though, as good as he was, the risk was too great to ignore the threat. Even so, before OPUS could amass the cash necessary to pay him off, Sorcerer leaked enough information to compromise dozens of assignments and agents. One assignment was so badly compromised, in fact, that the agent completing it ended up dead. Maybe the man hadn't died by Sorcerer's hand, but he'd died by Sorcerer's actions. The agent had been the father of Lila's regular partner, so there was a bit of personal vendetta involved in her desire to catch him, too.

She was surprised Faraday would want to know about her gut feelings and impressions and theories with regard to the assignment, since facts alone were the lifeblood of an archivist's existence. There were twelve OPUS archivists in all, all headquartered here in Washington, and it was their job to keep records of every assignment ever conducted by OPUS. They were the ones who completed the final analysis and wrote up the final reports for every assignment. They looked at what went right and what went wrong during an operation and figured out why. Then they filed it all away somewhere, in case there was ever a need to reference a case again.

A case like, oh, say…Sorcerer. That guy probably had more paper and megabytes assigned to him than any other agent or event in OPUS's history.

"You want to know my gut feelings about Sorcerer?" Lila asked. "My impressions? My theories?"

"I wouldn't have asked if I didn't want to know," Faraday replied.

She nodded. "Then maybe I'll have that tea after all. And you might want to refill that cognac. And make yourself a sandwich. This could take a while."

CHAPTER TWO

JOEL FARADAY ENJOYED another taste of his cognac and watched the woman handcuffed to his bed daintily sip tea from the mug in her unbound hand. He hadn't bothered with a sandwich. Something else he'd heard about Lila Moreau, code name She-Wolf, was that she minced partners, not words. Despite her assurances to the contrary, this wouldn't take long. And he was reasonably certain he should keep at least one hand free at all times.

She wasn't what he'd expected. He'd been hearing about her for years, just like everyone else who worked for OPUS, but the stories had made her sound like a larger-than-life legend. A brisk, brassy bombshell with a big mouth, bigger cojones and no moral fiber to speak of. A woman who put the job before anything and did anything to get the job done. Joel had pegged her as a tall, voluptuous siren, whiskey-voiced and two-pack-a-day redolent, with the hard eyes of a woman who was edgy and brittle and coarse.

Instead, she looked like the girl next door. Small in stature, slender in frame, pretty more than beautiful in an almost wholesome-looking way. She'd removed her knit cap, and a mass of pale blond hair now cascaded down to her shoulders, scooped back from her face with a careless hand. Although the clingy fit of her clothing revealed some *very* nice curves, she was by no means the bump-and-grind type. Her voice was a clear, euphonic tenor, and as he'd wrestled with her on the bed, he'd noted the faint scent of lavender about her. As for her eyes…

Well, now. The eyes were certainly something. A clear sapphire-blue that shoved Joel completely off balance. Her eyes were indeed the stuff of legend. With them, he could see how Lila Moreau had earned her rep as a woman who could glean just about anything she wanted from any man she wanted, be it information or something else entirely.

But he detected no edge to her, nothing bitter or coarse. She didn't even seem all that brassy, truth be told, threats to kick his ass notwithstanding. She'd spoken of that as if it were a simple statement of fact, which, he had to admit, it probably was.

Nevertheless, the realization that this woman, who was a good foot shorter than he and probably almost half his weight, had earned herself a bona fide, justified reputation as the most dangerous woman in the world certainly gave a man pause.

The jury was still out on the moral fiber thing—she had, after all, broken in to his house for the express purpose of imprisoning him and showing him who was boss—but he was willing to give her the benefit of the doubt. Besides, morality, like so many things, was relative—and fluid. His own moral history being what it was, he was the last person to make a judgment call on something like that.

He'd managed to leave her tea on the nightstand closest to her without losing a limb, so he figured they were off to a pretty good start. Still, he'd completed the action in record time and immediately retreated to the opposite side of the room when he was done. Now he leaned back in his wooden desk chair with an ominous creak, swirled his cognac in its snifter and never once took his eyes off Lila Moreau.

Instead of offering him the information he'd requested of her a little while ago, however, she asked him a question of her own. "Do you know exactly where Sorcerer is right now?"

"I haven't pinpointed his *exact* position, no," Joel admitted. "But I've gotten pretty close."

"And do you know what he's doing?"

He shook his head. "Not really. That's your job."

She nodded. "And *I've* done *my* job. *I* know exactly what Sorcerer is doing."

Her intimation being, of course, that Joel *hadn't* done his job, since he didn't know exactly where Sorcerer was. Not that he cared about impressing her. Although it might come as a shock to Lila Moreau, she wasn't the one in charge of this operation. Nor was she the most important cog in the machine. Naturally, he didn't tell her that. He only said, "You didn't include your discovery in your report."

"That's because it's a theory," she said.

Joel narrowed his eyes at her. "You just told me you know it for a fact."

"No, I said I know exactly what he's up to."

"But—"

"I just don't have any proof. Yet."

He leaned back in his chair again. "Then you don't know exactly what he's up to. Like you said, it's still a theory."

She set her tea back on the nightstand and met his gaze defiantly. "No, it isn't."

"But you just said—"

"I know exactly what he's doing," she repeated.

"You can't know for sure if you don't have proof."

"Yes, I can."

"No, you can't."

"Yes. I can."

"No. You can't."

"Can."

"Can't."

"Look, Faraday—"

"Call me Joel."

He could practically see her back go up when he said it. Obviously she didn't like addressing her coworkers by their first names. Or, more likely, she resented being told what to do. Which was too damned bad. Because Joel was going to be giving her a lot of instruction in the days ahead. And she'd sure as hell have to get used to following orders.

"Virtuoso," she amended, using his code name instead.

Which was strange to hear spoken aloud, since archivists were a pretty chummy bunch and rarely referred to each other by their code names. They were supposed to do so in professional situations, but... They were left so much to their own devices that over the years they'd splintered off into their own group within the organization, with their own practices and policies. Joel and the other archivists just weren't as formal as the rest of OPUS.

But fine, he and Lila could compromise on this one. Compromises weren't such bad things. Joel just liked being the one who offered them, not the one who agreed to go along with them. He'd be magnanimous. This time.

"Whatever," he replied, telling himself he did *not* sound ungracious when he said it.

She grinned at him, smugly, and it surprised Joel how much he wanted to walk over to the bed and do something about that smugness. What surprised him even more was that the something he wanted to do was in no way professional. He'd learned a long time ago to temper his knee-jerk reactions and not to let his emotions get the better of him. Lila, he was beginning to realize, could jerk a hell of a lot more than a man's knee. And he didn't want to think about what she could potentially do to a man's emotions.

"Between what I know about Sorcerer and his comings and goings the past couple of years," she continued, "and what I learned over the past few months, I can safely say that what the guy is trying to do is take the entire planet hostage."

Joel narrowed his eyes at her. "What are you talking about? How can he take the entire planet hostage?"

She picked up her tea, sipped it carefully, swallowed slowly, sipped it again. And never once did her eyes leave Joel's. She was baiting him. Trying to make him impatient for whatever information she might have. Trying to make him lose his cool. Trying again to show him who was in charge. Well, as she'd said earlier, the joke was on her. If there was one thing Joel Faraday had in spades, it was patience. He could wait all night if it came to that. At least he could take bathroom breaks. The way Lila was sipping her tea, she'd figure out soon enough who was really calling the shots here.

Finally she lowered her cup and said, "Sorcerer's trying

to create a massive computer virus that will infect systems around the world with enough velocity, tenacity and toxicity to cripple the entire planet's commercial, political and financial momentum. Not that he necessarily wants to unleash it," she quickly qualified. "Since taking advantage of the planet's commercial and financial arenas is one of his favorite pastimes, and watching its political machinations is his greatest source of amusement. He's greedier than he is power mad. What he'd rather do is blackmail the planet into paying him billions of dollars *not* to unleash it."

Joel thought about that for a moment, weighing her information with what he knew himself. He'd developed his own theory about what Sorcerer was doing, but hers made more sense, since, ultimately, it was infinitely more profitable. "So it's your classic Mafia neighborhood protection racket," he finally said.

"Yep," she replied. "Except that Sorcerer has brought it into the twenty-first century with global, high-tech potential. Pay up or be burned to the ground, figuratively speaking."

"I suppose it's possible that's what he plans to do," Joel said. "But frankly, something of a scope that massive doesn't seem possible to effectively execute."

"Maybe not," she agreed. "But if anyone can pull it off, it's Sorcerer."

"Unfortunately, I can't argue with you about that. And even more unfortunately, what you just described fits well with what we learned about him while we still had him in our sights in New York."

For years, Sorcerer had been popping up in various parts of the country and causing trouble, then disappearing just as quickly without OPUS getting any closer to capturing him. Six months ago he'd turned up in New York, misrepresenting himself online to lure a lonely young woman into helping him further his plans. Unfortunately, although the young woman, Avery Nesbitt, had done her best to help OPUS catch him, Sorcerer had managed to evade them yet again.

"If what you *theorize* is true," Joel said, deliberately emphasizing that word to piss Lila off—hey, two could play her power game—"then Sorcerer can't do it alone. As smart as he is, he doesn't have that specific kind of know-how. He knows computers, sure. But not sophisticated programming like that. That's why he approached Avery Nesbitt. Because he knew she did. But she's out of the picture now," he pointed out.

"Yeah, but there are other people like her in the world," Lila countered. "People who are whizzes with all things programming-related, including viruses. Hell, especially viruses. Some of those people are just kids. And a lot of them, regardless of their ages, are socially backward enough that they could easily be manipulated. Especially by someone like Sorcerer."

"He's looking for another patsy to help him do his dirty work," Joel said. "Maybe more than one patsy. Avery Nesbitt wasn't the only person he contacted when he was trawling the Net for virus builders, though she was without question his prime target. Understandable, considering her history. But when we had him under surveillance in New York, Sorcerer seemed to be shopping around a lot, contacting a number of people, as if he were trying to put together a geek squad of sorts."

"So is he still looking?" Lila asked. "Or has he found the people he needs?"

"Well, that's the big question, isn't it?" Joel replied. "He's been off our radar for a while now. What we have working in our favor is that guys like Sorcerer tend to be creatures of habit, no matter how much they might think otherwise. The fact that they're convinced their behavior is untraceable, not to mention the fact that they have staggering great egos, only helps us out, because people like that aren't always thorough in covering their tracks. At least, not as well as they should."

"How close have you gotten to finding him?"

Joel set down his cognac and rose from his chair to bend over the mahogany rolltop desk that had belonged to his great grandmother. It was overflowing with untidy heaps of files, notebooks, maps, sketches and other paper paraphernalia, but he knew exactly where to locate what he wanted. Picking carefully through the mess, he withdrew a diagram he'd sketched himself of precisely the geographic region he was talking about. Moving to the foot of the bed, he unrolled it so that it was facing upside down from himself and toward Lila.

"I've narrowed it to an area of roughly three hundred square miles," he told her as he ran his hands briskly over the paper to smooth it out. When the edges began to turn up again, he retrieved his iPod and cell phone from the desk, placing one on each side of the drawing to anchor it down again. By then, Lila had repositioned herself on one hand and both knees, her handcuffed arm extended behind her, to inspect the map.

"Three hundred square miles isn't what I'd call narrowed down," she said.

"It's not as big an area as it sounds like," he told her. "It's pretty much relegated to one city and its immediate environs. And within that area, there are two smaller ones that I think will produce Sorcerer for us."

"You know for a fact he's here?"

"Not for a fact, no," Joel admitted. "No one's registered a physical sighting of him since your sister's house."

Five months after disappearing from New York, Sorcerer had turned up again, this time in Cleveland, Ohio, because he'd mistaken Lila's twin sister, Marnie Lundy, who lived and worked there, for Lila herself. And although Marnie, too, had aided in the investigation, even posing briefly as Lila because Lila had been keeping a low profile at the time, Sorcerer had again slipped through their fingers. His disappearance then had just made Joel that much more determined to locate him now.

"Taking into account Sorcerer's past actions and appearances, his personal history and his proclivities," he said, "I'm reasonably certain he'll turn up in one of two places within this city. All *you* have to do is go into those places and flush him out."

"So what city are we talking about?" she asked, looking up at him. And Joel had to give himself a good mental shake to keep from falling into the fathomless depths of her blue, blue eyes. "You haven't labeled any streets or landmarks here."

"Haven't gotten around to it yet. But don't worry." He pointed to his temple. "I've got them all stored up here."

"Feel like sharing any of them?" she asked. Sounding impatient. Glaring at him impatiently. Giving her handcuffed wrist an impatient jerk.

Just like that, Joel felt the upper hand slip firmly back into his grip. This time he was the one to grin. And he hoped he didn't look too smug when he did.

Oh, who was he kidding? He went out of his way to look as smug as possible.

He told her, "It's a city known for showbiz mayors, tasteless pornography and dubious art exhibits."

"Oh, great," Lila groaned, looking down at the map again. "I have to go back to Vegas?"

He shook his head. "Not Las Vegas. Cincinnati."

"Cincinnati?" she echoed incredulously, sitting back on her heels. "Just how much have you had to drink tonight, guy? Cincinnati is the heartland of America. It's *Ohio,* for God's sake. Have you ever been to Ohio? Me, I just left Ohio a couple of weeks ago. Walt Disney would gag on its sweetness. How does all that stuff relate to Cincinnati?"

Joel lifted a hand and counted them off. "Jerry Springer," he said in response to item number one, extending his index finger. "Larry Flynt," he added, thrusting up another—rather significant, at that—finger. "And the Robert Mapplethorpe exhibit," he concluded, adding a third finger to the mix. "Trust me. Cincinnati has a dark side you can't begin to imagine."

She burst out laughing at that. "Dark side. Cincinnati. Right."

"Yeah, okay, maybe that's pushing it," he conceded, dropping both hands to his hips. "It's still the place where we're going to find Sorcerer. Mark my words."

"How do you figure?"

"Like I said, he was in contact with several people when

he was reeling in Avery Nesbitt. An inordinate number of them were located in the Cincinnati area. Also located in the Cincinnati area is a very small, very exclusive private college. Waverly College. Ever heard of it?"

"Yeah, it's like a small-scale MIT."

Joel nodded. "Except a degree from Waverly is more prestigious, and it's a harder school to get into. What you end up with is a streamlined student body full of big brains that are light-years ahead of the intellectual norm, all of them tech majors, the vast majority in the field of computers. The place is thick with hackers. In fact, a few years ago, a small group of underclassmen was arrested, tried and convicted on charges of treason after hacking into top secret CIA files and selling them to terrorists to pay for their pornography and gaming habits."

"I remember that," she said with a nod that nudged a stray lock of pale blond hair over one eye. She immediately shoved it back behind one ear, but not before Joel's fingers curved instinctively in preparation to do that himself.

Terrific, he thought. Barely an hour after meeting Lila, he was responding to her in a way that he really couldn't afford to be responding. Wanting to touch her, however innocently. Hell, wanting to touch her in ways that weren't innocent at all. Being mesmerized by the incredible blue eyes to the point of momentarily forgetting what he'd intended to say. Battling a very uncharacteristic—never mind completely politically incorrect—wave of arousal every time he looked up and saw her handcuffed to his bed. It had been months, maybe years, since he'd experienced such an immediate attraction to a woman. And Lila was the last woman he should be experiencing it for.

She added, "So you think Sorcerer stopped by Waverly on the way home from work to pick up a dozen eggheads with his usual gallon of milk?"

He nodded. "I think it's extremely possible. And very likely."

She thought about that for a minute. "Makes sense. Especially when you consider his recent appearance in Cleveland. It's only a few hours' drive from Cincinnati."

"Also interesting, and significant," Joel continued, "is the fact that there have been a rash of online scams and crimes committed in recent months that have been traced back to a user or users in this part of the country." He pointed at the map again. "They started off as petty mischief, like worms and viruses and hoaxes, exactly the sort of thing college students enjoy most. But whoever's been creating them and sending them out has covered his or her—or their—tracks well. We've only been able to pinpoint the city, not an actual address. Over the past several weeks, however, the crimes have escalated into some pretty major—and pretty ballsy—thefts and cons that are starting to rake in some significant money."

"You don't know who's perpetrating them?" Lila asked.

He shook his head again. "Only that it's someone in the Cincinnati area. Most likely someone at Waverly. But the activity shows signs of having started off with amateurs, becoming more sophisticated just recently."

"Like maybe someone or a handful of people who were once only in it for the fun are now also in it for the profit."

"Exactly like that."

"Like maybe someone suddenly joined up with this person

or persons and injected them with a little more ambition and organization."

"Yep."

"Like maybe Sorcerer has indeed found his band of merry hackers."

"Which means he's now stronger and smarter than he's ever been before," Joel concluded.

He traced his finger on the map in a circular motion around an area near the Ohio River. "Dormitory housing is pretty sparse at Waverly, so a good number of the students live in the city proper. And there's an area downtown around Vine Street that especially caters to students. Lots of student-type apartments, coffee shops, clubs, student-friendly retail establishments, that kind of thing. I think that's probably the best place to start looking. There and on Waverly's campus. If my calculations are correct—and it goes without saying that they are," he added, since Lila was right about modesty being overrated when it wasn't warranted, "you'll find Sorcerer in one place or another. Along with his accomplices. It's just a matter of being in the right place at the right time."

"And being uncharacteristically lucky," she added.

He smiled. "So all that good karma you've been scoring over the years will come in handy now."

She laughed at that, a deep, full-bodied, throaty laugh that made something inside Joel shimmy like mirage heat on a strip of desert highway. Only, instead of being way off in the distance like mirage heat usually was, it surrounded him and closed down hard. Once again he reminded himself that he was in no position to be feeling such things. Even under the best of circumstances, he did not need a sexual attraction to a woman whose emotions—at least the positive ones—ran about as deep as a fingerprint.

Note to self, Faraday: You're not into meaningless sex anymore. Remember?

Well, evidently not…

"Do you have a list of the people in the area Sorcerer contacted and may or may not have followed up on?" Lila asked.

Joel shook off his wayward thoughts—again—and focused on the matter at hand. Which happened to be the woman he was trying not to think about. Damn. "We do," he said. "It will be in a dossier with other information I have for you. But remember, there are almost certainly others we *don't* know about."

"Do you know if Sorcerer established any contact with any of the people you did identify?"

"You'll receive a detailed account, but yes, we intercepted a number of e-mails between him and several students at Waverly. They were mostly exchanges of inconsequential information, though. Getting-to-know-you type stuff, the same thing he initially sent to Avery Nesbitt. Sorcerer assumed several different identities, each tailored to be most attractive to whomever he was in touch with. Most often, he was a young student at another university close enough to arrange for a physical meeting, should it come to that. With women, he invariably went the romantic route. With the men, he posed as another gamer and attempted to strike up a friendship through those avenues. Online gaming is huge at places like Waverly."

"And did any such physical meetings take place?" Lila asked.

"A couple of times either Sorcerer or his mark would extend an invitation to meet up somewhere, but to the best of our knowledge, no such physical meetings ever took place."

"To the best of your knowledge," she repeated. "That means it's entirely possible that he *has* made physical contact. With any number of those people."

She was right, as much as Joel hated to admit it. Intelligence and surveillance could go only so far. And Sorcerer certainly knew how to keep himself from being tailed. He'd built a career on it. Not to mention, according to Sorcerer's past habits—which, lately, Joel had been building his own career on—Sorcerer would delight in putting one over on OPUS by completing such a meeting just for the hell of it. He'd be careful, as he'd been in New York when he lured Avery Nesbitt into such a meeting, but he'd carry through. Unfortunately, Joel had an even bigger reason to agree with Lila.

"It's more than possible," he admitted. "It's probable. Except for those few appearances in Cleveland, Sorcerer's been off our radar for a while now. That's given him ample opportunity to operate with total freedom. And there were plenty of gaps in our surveillance even when we *did* have him in our sights. Not that he can be sure he *hasn't* been under constant surveillance, so there's still some small chance he's gone into hiding and stayed there, but—"

"Oh, he's been sure he wasn't under surveillance," Lila told him with what sounded like absolute certainty. "He's known about every gap and failure. You can count on it."

"Well, I don't know if I'd *count* on it," Joel said, "but

somehow the guy always does seem to know what OPUS is doing. Sometimes it even seems like he knows it before we do."

"There's no *somehow* to it," Lila said. "And no *seems,* either."

Joel looked up from the diagram where his gaze had fallen to find Lila staring at him with a very troubling expression. As if she knew something he didn't. Which, if Sorcerer was involved, wasn't good. "What do you mean?" he asked.

"I mean the reason he manages to stay one step ahead of OPUS is because he *does* know what we're doing. Every step of the way. And he knows it, sometimes, before the field agent even gets handed the assignment."

Joel narrowed his eyes at her. "That's impossible. The only way he could know that would be if—"

He halted before finishing, not wanting to put voice to the thought that flashed into his head.

So Lila finished his statement for him. "Someone inside the organization has been helping him all along."

CHAPTER THREE

"HOW CAN YOU KNOW THAT?" Faraday asked. "And why wasn't it in your report?"

Lila tugged meaningfully on the handcuff that still connected her to his headboard. In a fantasy, she might have found the idea of being handcuffed to the bed of a sexy stranger profoundly arousing. In reality, it was damned annoying. Probably because Joel wasn't a stranger to her anymore. She was getting to know him pretty well. What was weird—and unwelcome—was that she still found him sexy. Where getting to know him should have made her dislike him, she instead found herself feeling curious about him. Even worse, the stuff she was curious about had nothing to do with the job they both had facing them.

"Uncuff me," she told him, "and I'll reveal everything."

He arched a dark eyebrow at that.

"Everything I know," she clarified with an exasperated sound.

The eyebrow dropped back down again, and for a minute he almost looked disappointed. Interestingly, though, his expression registered no fear at the prospect of releasing her, and that, Lila had to admit, was pretty admirable. Stupid, but admirable. Most guys wouldn't have had the gall to cuff her in the first place. Men who'd tried to restrain her in the past had generally ended up horizontal, usually unconscious and always bloody. And even if one of them had managed to capture her—yeah, right—no way would he have been brave enough to release her while he was still anywhere in the same ZIP code.

Of course, Joel Faraday wasn't exactly hurrying to carry out her instructions, was he? So maybe he hid his fear well. Which, to Lila, was even more admirable.

"Promise me you won't kick my ass to Abu Dhabi and back again," he finally said.

Okay. She'd just kick his ass to Aberdeen and back again. "I promise I won't kick your ass to Abu Dhabi," she vowed.

"Or back again."

"Whatever."

But he still didn't move. "Promise me you won't even kick it as far as Arlington."

She sighed heavily. Fine. She'd just kick his ass to Foggy Bottom. "I promise I won't kick your ass as far as Arlington," she repeated dutifully.

"Promise me you'll leave my ass the hell alone."

Well, now, she didn't want to be hasty. She'd already noticed that, even in baggy pajama bottoms, his ass was kind of nice. She might have plans for it later. After she'd kicked it around for a little while. "Look, I promise I won't kick your ass tonight, all right?"

"Ever," he insisted.

She bit back a growl. "All *right*. I won't kick your ass ever. Or any of your other body parts, either," she added when he opened his mouth to say more.

"Promise?"

This time she growled quite distinctly. "You want me to sign something in blood?"

He actually seemed to consider it for a moment.

"All *right*." She finally ground out the words. "I promise."

He must have believed her, because he made his way cautiously to the nightstand where he'd placed the key. And watching him move, all fluid and stealth and leisure, Lila realized she had no desire to kick his ass anyway. It really was a nice ass. And it was attached to a very nice torso. Which had extremely nice shoulders. Fastened to lusciously nice arms. In fact, she decided as she watched him palm the small key and turn toward her, it would be a shame if anything happened to *any* of Joel Faraday's body parts. Unless, of course, his body parts happened to be naked at the time, and Lila happened to be the one doing anything—and everything—to them.

Yeah, it was definitely going to be an interesting assignment.

He hesitated a moment at the side of the bed, still just beyond her reach. Then, even more cautious than he'd been before, he extended his empty hand outward, palm up, presumably in a silent request for her to give him her hand that was uncuffed. Not sure why he would want it, Lila nevertheless started to do so without hesitation. Then, for some reason, her hand stopped when her fingertips were just shy of his. She glanced up to find him gazing at her face, a silent question in his eyes. But he didn't move his hand forward to take hers, only waited without speaking for her to touch him first.

Still not sure why he didn't just unlock her, and never once removing her gaze from his, she gingerly pushed her hand the remaining distance necessary to meet his. But the moment their fingers finally connected, she instinctively wanted to pull back.

It was the strangest thing. Lila never retreated from anyone without a damned good reason. As in, without a life-threatening reason. Joel Faraday was in no way a threat to her life. He wasn't even a threat to her wrist at this point. But there was something about the way her bare palm skimmed over his—a perfectly innocent touch—that made her want to jerk back again.

She fought the sensation by dropping her gaze and focusing it on the fingers that folded gently over her hand. But for some reason, that only compounded her confusion. Because not only did Joel's fingers nearly swallow her hand whole, he touched her in a way that made goose bumps pebble her flesh. His hand was warm, the skin duskier than hers, dusted with black hair that made it appear darker still. His fingers were long and blunt compared to her small, slender ones, unadorned save the heavy Georgetown University ring he wore on his ring finger. His was a no-nonsense hand. A working hand. A manly hand. But it held hers so gently.

Maybe that was what put her off-kilter. She'd never thought of a man's hands in terms of gentleness before. On the contrary, men's hands were not to be trusted.

Joel continued to hold her free hand as he bent forward to reach for her cuffed one. He had to lean over her body to get to it, and when he did, the V-neck of his T-shirt fell away from his body at eye level. That gave Lila a view of a long, muscular torso and trim waist, all of it naked, and all of it dusted by dark hair. She sucked in an involuntary breath at the sight of such masculine beauty, filling her nose with the scent of him, a scintillating mix of Dial soap, expensive cognac and raw, unmitigated male. Her heartbeat quickened in response, and in an effort to slow it, she turned her gaze to her left hand, which had pulled taut the short chain imprisoning it to the bed. But seeing Joel insert the key into the lock and give it an uneasy twitch only made her pulse skyrocket again.

Looking away once more, she found herself gazing at his throat, mere inches from her face. And she saw that she wasn't the only one suffering from a fast, irregular pulse. Joel's was hammering hard near his collarbone, and she could hear his breathing now, too, coming in short, ragged bursts. Heat pooled in her belly and spread, filling her breasts to bursting and making her damp between her legs.

My God, she thought, closing her eyes. It was as if they were indulging in some kind of incredibly erotic foreplay. Yet neither had said or done anything to generate this kind of heat. Just the simple act of touching hands and being in close proximity was turning both of them on. What the hell was going on?

After loosing the cuffs from Lila's hand and the bedpost, Joel straightened and dropped both cuffs and key back on the nightstand, then retreated to the far side of the room. And if he seemed to make the trip in record time, Lila wasn't going to mention it. She was just happy to be able to breathe normally again. If one could consider quick, shallow, dizzying gasps to be normal.

She dropped her recently freed wrist into her other hand and rubbed idly, not so much because she needed to soothe it as she simply needed something to do with her hands that didn't involve reaching for Joel. But when she looked at him again, he seemed to be watching what she was doing with an inordinate amount of interest. For a second time, something exploded in her belly and seeped into parts of her that were better left alone.

She did her best to ignore the sensation and return to the topic of their assignment. "Okay, here's what I know," she began. But her voice sounded husky and aroused, so she cleared her throat and tried again. "With that bogus attempted-murder charge floating around, I had to stay on the lam for five fuh—uh…for five freaking months," she quickly amended.

Her language had appalled her sister, Marnie, that single evening the two of them had spent together getting caught up after being separated for virtually their entire lives. Only then had Lila realized just how rough her vocabulary was, compared to that of polite—i.e., non-OPUS—society. But she'd spent her childhood in a trailer park among neighbors who were, at best, bikers and, at worst, junkies, her adolescence on the streets of Las Vegas and her adult life in the company of spies and thugs. Language was a weapon in such environments, and Lila had simply adopted the behavior she saw practiced around her. Once she'd realized how uncomfortable it made Marnie, however, she'd done her best to gentle her vocabulary and deep-six the profanity. Even outside Marnie's presence, Lila still tried to watch what she said and how brazenly she said it. Such was the good influence her sister had already brought to her life.

"During the five months I was lying low," she began again, "I learned a lot of stuff about Sorcerer on my own. Stuff that I couldn't report back to OPUS, because they'd forced me into hiding. And whattaya know, in that five months Sorcerer dropped off the face of the earth. He went into hiding, too, because he couldn't know what OPUS was doing or where they'd be next, since I hadn't given them any intel to go on. Without me sending in reports, his contact couldn't send them back out again. He couldn't know where he stood with us, so he disappeared."

Joel studied her hard in silence for a moment, then said, "That sounds like speculation on your part."

"It was at first," she admitted. "So I started to dig a little deeper where I could at my end. And I had my partner do a little discreet checking around at OPUS. Between the two of us, we found evidence that there could definitely be a leak somewhere within the ranks of the organization."

"*Could* be a leak," Joel repeated. "Not that there definitely *is* a leak."

"Which is why it's not in my report," Lila told him. "Neither of us has proof yet, but my gut tells me there's someone inside who's helping Sorcerer. Who's been helping him for a long time now."

"You think it's someone who knew him when he was still working for OPUS? Or someone who's come to work for us since? Is it possible it could even be someone he placed himself? Hell, how do you know it's not me?"

"I don't know that," she replied honestly. "But I don't have any reason to suspect you. Yet," she added pointedly because… Well, just because. "I've thought a lot about all the possibilities, and at this point I just don't know. It would make more sense if the leak were someone Sorcerer worked with years ago, but it could be someone he recruited, too. The guy is a charmer," Lila said frankly. "Very charismatic. Very attractive. Very sexy."

"Why, Miss Moreau," Joel said in an affected, golly-gee-whiz kind of voice, "you sound like you're the president of the Adrian Padgett aka Sorcerer Fan Club."

"No," she immediately denied. She hesitated before saying the rest, then figured, what the hell. Even if Joel was only her temporary partner, he was still her partner. And she was reasonably sure he wasn't the leak in the organization, since he wasn't a part of the information-gathering arm. Anyway, what she was about to tell him wasn't anything Sorcerer didn't already know. So she added, "But I'd be lying if I said I'm immune to him. There's something about him that is undeniably seductive."

Her remark seemed to surprise Joel, though whether it was what she'd admitted or the fact that she'd admitted it that caused the reaction, Lila couldn't have said. Frankly, she'd surprised herself when she'd had a one-night stand with Sorcerer shortly after being assigned to the undercover team looking for him. But she'd found herself in a position where she could get close enough to him physically to potentially bring him down. She supposed she'd just taken a page from Adrian's own notebook and overstepped the usual parameters of the job. Not that that had been the first time she'd stepped over the line. But to get as close to him as she could, she had done something she'd never done on an assignment before—or done since. She'd had a sexual liaison with the suspect.

At the time, she honestly hadn't thought much about it. Mostly because it hadn't been any hardship to have sex with Adrian Padgett. He was a gorgeous, sexy guy, and as such, Lila had been powerfully attracted to him on a physical level. At that time, too, she'd been going through some things in her personal life that had allowed her to disengage herself from her feelings, even more so than usual. He'd turned her on, and he'd wanted her. She'd taken advantage of both facts. Unfortunately, he'd figured out she was part of the OPUS machine before she could make use of her new position in his life.

"And were you seduced?" Faraday asked her point-blank.

"No," she replied honestly. "When I had sex with Sorcerer, I was an active and willing participant."

His mouth flattened into a tight line at that, and a muscle twitched in his jaw. "So you really did sleep with him?"

"I won't apologize for what I did that night," she told him. "It wasn't exactly protocol, but neither was it against the rules. Plenty of agents before me—male and female—have used sex to garner information from someone they were investigating."

"And did you?" Joel asked. "Garner information from Sorcerer?"

"Some. I could have gotten more if I'd had an opportunity to extend our…liaison. As it was, he figured out who I worked for before I had the chance."

"And was the desire for information the only reason you slept with him?" Joel asked.

Honesty, she reminded herself. She had to be honest. So she told him, "No. It was the desire for something else. And I found Adrian Padgett to be genuinely attractive."

"Even knowing what he is?"

"I didn't think about what he is," she said. "I thought about how he made me feel. How he made my body feel," she corrected herself. Since that was the only place she'd felt anything while she was with him.

"And would you have slept with him knowing what he is if you *hadn't* needed information?" Joel asked.

Why he was belaboring this she couldn't begin to imagine. It wasn't as if he had a stake in it. Again, being honest, she replied, "No. Not knowing he was Sorcerer. Had he just been some guy I met, yeah. I might have. But I don't sleep with the enemy just because the enemy turns me on. The enemy needs to have something else I want more than physical gratification."

"Information."

She nodded. "Information."

Her encounter with Adrian Padgett had come at a time when Lila wasn't much concerned with moral or ethical repercussions. Hell, that was one of the reasons OPUS had recruited her in the first place. She was the perfect candidate for the job they wanted her to do. Estranged from what little family she had—not even knowing about half of it when they recruited her—and coming from a background that had prevented her from forming emotional attachments to other people, she was a vessel waiting to be filled by OPUS policy and procedure. The fact that she wasn't bad to look at and was used to being kicked around hadn't hurt, either. Nor did the fact that she was accustomed to hard work. Add it all up, and OPUS found in Lila Moreau the quintessential femme fatale. And boy, did they exploit it.

And her. Why shouldn't she exploit herself, too? At least she was the one in control then.

"I won't apologize for what I did," she said again. "Because circumstances being what they were at the time, I wasn't out of line to do it. And it did lull Sorcerer into a false security that allowed us to extend the life of the investigation in Indianapolis long enough that we almost caught him."

"But you didn't catch him," Joel reminded her.

"No," she agreed. "Unfortunately, we didn't." She met his gaze levelly. "But this time, I promise you, I'm taking that son of a bitch *down*." She hesitated for a moment, then added, "And I'm going to do it in less than two weeks."

Faraday arched his dark eyebrows again. "We don't even know exactly where he is. How can you set a timetable at this point?"

She grinned, mostly because she couldn't help herself. Lila always grinned when she thought of what would be happening in two weeks. "'Cause I have someplace I need to be in two weeks, that's why."

Now he narrowed his eyes at her. "I haven't heard anything about another assignment for you. In fact, they made clear to me that this is the only thing on your agenda right now and to take all the time we needed."

Lila studied her manicure. "Yeah, well, just shows how much they know."

Faraday straightened and hooked his hands on his hips. "Where do you have to be in two weeks?" he demanded.

She sat back on her haunches and mimicked his challenging posture, settling her hands on her hips, too. "That's none of your damned business."

Up went the eyebrows again. "Excuse me?"

Enunciating more carefully, she repeated, "It's. None. Of. Your. Damned. Business."

His gaze never once leaving hers, he glared at her harder, shifted his weight to one foot, crossed his arms over his chest, expelled a soft sound and said quietly, "Don't push me, Lila."

It spoke volumes about his effect on her that she actually found herself relenting. Then again, it wasn't as if her whereabouts in two weeks would be top secret. "Fine," she muttered, relaxing her stance. "If you must know, I have a wedding to go to in two weeks."

His mouth dropped open a fraction, and he eyed her blandly. "A wedding."

She nodded. "Yeah, a wedding. I'm gonna be the best man. So I need to wrap this thing up before then. I need to bring down the son of a bitch one way or another before the Saturday after next."

Faraday didn't reply right away, only looked at Lila in a way she found a little disconcerting. It kind of made her feel the way a bug must feel when it was pinned under a microscope, while some guy in a white lab coat loomed over it holding a big ol' pair of tweezers in one hand and a specimen slide in the other.

Finally he said, "We."

Confused, Lila asked, "What?"

"We," he said again. "*We* are going to bring the son of a bitch down."

She narrowed her eyes at him. "What are you talking about?"

"You and I," he clarified. "We'll be bringing in Sorcerer together."

She shook her head. Oh, she didn't *think* so. Aloud, she told him, "No, we won't. I'll be going to Cincinnati, and you'll be staying here with all your gizmos and files. The wonders of technology and all that. Even hundreds of miles away, I can report in daily. That's the way it always works. Me in the field sending intelligence where I find it, my partner manning home base collecting and dissecting that information. Yeah, we're usually no more than a few miles apart at most, but it shouldn't be a problem, you staying here in D.C."

Now Faraday smiled in a way that Lila found *really* disconcerting. Like maybe the guy in the lab coat just lit the flame on a Bunsen burner. He pointed behind himself at the overflowing desk, where, at the bottom of a pile of papers, sat a laptop, now folded closed. "The wonders of technology," he echoed. "As long as I have a wireless connection, I can be hundreds of miles away from all my gizmos and files and still have everything I need at my fingertips. Meaning I'll never have to be more than a few miles at most away from my partner."

Oh, no, Lila thought. No, no, no, no, no. He was *not* saying what he seemed to be saying.

He continued, "See, Lila, you may *officially* be back to tabula rasa with the big guys, but they're not *quite* ready to cut you loose to your own devices again."

She studied him morosely, a nervous knot forming in her stomach, and wondered why she hadn't seen this coming from a hundred miles away. Man, she really had been out of the game too long. She'd forgotten the most rudimentary rule of OPUS. They didn't trust anyone anytime anywhere anyhow anyway.

"I'm going to have to be on a leash for a while," she guessed.

Faraday nodded.

"And you're going to be the one holding it."

He nodded again.

She sighed, much more softly than before. Even though it wasn't necessary for him to spell it out any further, he did. Probably just his little way of showing Lila who was going to be in charge.

"I'll be going to Cincinnati with you," he told her. "And you'll be reporting to me pretty much every day. If you don't, I'll be obliged to tell your superiors that you've gone missing again, something I doubt either of us would like to see happen. In other words, Lila, I'll be the one running this operation. And you'll be the one doing whatever I tell you to do. And maybe, *maybe,* if you're a very good girl, and do exactly as you're told, we'll get you to your wedding on time."

CHAPTER FOUR

A LITTLE MORE than twenty-four hours after leaving Joel Faraday's Georgetown town house, Lila was back again—this time arriving at his front door, and with more than just the clothes on her back. This time she had some clothes packed in a carry-on bag, as well. Along with some assorted toiletries. And some official files. And some lethal weaponry. And a good book to read on the plane. Normally, carrying weaponry, lethal or otherwise, onto a plane, even with a good book, might pose a bit of a problem. But not when one was flying chartered. Government charter. Top secret government charter at that. In fact, Lila wasn't sure, but she and Joel Faraday might just be flying to Cincinnati in Wonder Woman's invisible jet. Which she had to admit, even to her jaded self, might be very cool.

When she'd left his house yesterday, the sun had just been staining the eastern sky with the pinks and oranges of early dawn. Now the sun had fully crested the horizon, but the western sky was still a bit smudged with remnants of blue and purple left over from the fleeing night. Lila wished she could retreat with it and stay in the darkness, where she felt infinitely more comfortable.

There was something about the light of day that made everything scarier. More threatening. Less comforting. At least in the dark she knew where she stood. Daytime exposed too much ugliness, revealed too many sights to consume and digest and make sense of, released too many people who assumed too many roles. At night, everything was pretty cut-and-dried. People who populated the nighttime never worried much about making a good impression or keeping up an appearance. At night, not many people bothered with artifice. Daytime dwellers often had people to impress. Schedules to keep. Jobs to protect. So they often had much to hide. It was harder to trust those people.

Joel Faraday was just such a daytime dweller. But that wasn't why Lila had trouble trusting him. It wasn't even because she couldn't be positive he wasn't the leak. No, with him, it was the same as it was with everyone else. She didn't trust him because… Well. Because he was human. And, she supposed, because she was human, too.

Before moving her hand to the doorbell, she first ran it briskly over the front of her white linen shirt and beige linen trousers—and immediately chided herself for taking even that small effort with her appearance. Flat beige skimmers completed the outfit. She'd pinned her hair atop her head when she showered and hadn't bothered to take it down once she was dressed, nor had she bothered with jewelry or cosmetics. Not her typical attire or appearance by a long shot, but she liked to dress for comfort when she traveled. She'd slip into character once they arrived in Cincinnati. For now, she didn't have to be She-Wolf. For now, she could still be Lila Moreau if she wanted. So for now, she would dress and act and talk however she wanted.

She adjusted her carry-on over her shoulder, pressed her finger to the doorbell and waited for Joel to answer. And waited. And waited. And waited. And waited. She was bent over with her bag open and was wrapping the fingers of one hand around her lock pick and the fingers of the other around her .32 when he finally opened the door. Her gaze lit first on his bare feet, then moved up long legs clad in faded jeans, then up more, over a pin-striped white oxford button-down in the decidedly *un*buttoned—and untucked—position. Again she was assailed by the elegance and power of that half-naked torso dusted with dark hair, and again she was hit by the splash of heat in her belly that immediately spread outward. It only burned more fiercely when her gaze finally landed on his face and she was reminded yet again what a beautiful, beautiful man he was.

The adjective should have diminished his masculinity. Using it twice should have doubly diminished it. But the potency of the man's virility was nearly overwhelming. His features were too ruggedly carved, his dark eyes too turbulent, his muscles too finely sculpted for anyone to ignore the sheer maleness of him. At the same time, the way he was put together was nothing short of a work of art.

What was strange was that Lila's regular partner, Oliver Sheridan—at whose wedding she would appear as best man, by God, she vowed again—was also a *very* attractive man. His fiancée, Avery Nesbitt, obviously agreed, because even when Oliver, using the name Dixon at the time, had dragged her kicking and screaming—literally—out of her safe life and into a potentially dangerous undercover role with OPUS, she'd fallen head over heels in love with the guy. Of course, that had been due to more than his looks, but still. He was a great-looking guy. Yet not once, not even for a second, had Lila ever felt even a flicker of sexual attraction toward—or even a sexual awareness of—him. So why such an immediate captivation with Joel? Hell, she and Oliver even got along well, whereas a definite spark of tension had sputtered between her and Joel from the very beginning. There was no reason she should be reacting this way to him. But she was. Really badly, too.

And, dammit, since when had she started thinking about him as Joel?

"Hi," he greeted her now in a voice that was more than a little brusque.

A strand of wet hair fell over his forehead, indicating he'd been in the shower when she rang the bell. This in spite of the fact that they were scheduled to be leaving for the airfield in—she glanced down at her watch—less than fifteen minutes. And they still had a few things to go over before their car arrived, things they couldn't discuss in the presence of anyone else, even a driver or pilot for OPUS.

"Oversleep?" she said by way of a greeting as she zipped shut her bag and stood to face him.

"A little," he confessed with clear embarrassment.

She nodded. "You sure you're up for a field assignment?" she asked. Not just because it was a good question, but also because she knew it would bug the hell out of him.

Okay, okay. So maybe part of that spark of tension was her fault, she admitted. She couldn't help herself when she was around Joel. Something about him begged to be bugged. She'd provide the same service for anyone who had usurped her power. It was the least she could do.

"I'm sorry I overslept," he said with barely a trace of apology. "It won't happen again." He took a step backward and pulled the door open in a silent invitation for her to enter. As she did, he continued, "Look, I just need to shave and finish dressing. And, okay, maybe pack a few more things. Help me with that last, and I can be ready to leave in ten minutes. Fifteen max."

"Good," she said. "Because the car will be here in twelve. And we still have a couple of things to go over."

"Come upstairs," he said as he closed the door behind her. "We can talk while I shave and finish dressing."

They did both in ten minutes, Lila leaning in the doorway of first Joel's bathroom, then his bedroom as he completed his morning ritual. She'd never done that before—watched a man go about his morning routine—and something about sharing the experience with Joel now, even though she didn't know him well, made her feel as if the two of them were sharing some strange kind of intimacy. She especially enjoyed watching him shave, and not just because he removed his shirt to do it to keep from messing it up.

Still, the way the muscles in his left arm bunched and relaxed with every stroke of the razor across his face was rather intriguing, she had to admit. And the spicy scent of the sandalwood shaving soap he used was more than a little sexy. But it was the act of standing there talking business in such a personal setting that really seeped into her awareness. In all the times she'd opened her eyes in the morning after a sexual encounter, she'd never hung around any longer than it took to get dressed and bolt. There had been times—rather a lot of them, actually—when she hadn't even woken her partner to say goodbye. Sex and intimacy had nothing to do with each other as far as Lila was concerned. But she hadn't realized that something as simple and nonsexual as this could be intimate, either.

When Joel finally emerged from the bathroom capping his toothbrush holder, Lila was tossing the last of his things into his bag and getting ready to close it. She paused long enough for him to toss the toothbrush into the bag, then finished with a soft *zzzzip* that punctuated their race for time quite nicely. They both seemed to realize it, chuckling as one at the sound.

"Nicely done," she told him.

"Couldn't have managed it without you," he conceded.

She didn't say what should have been the obvious next remark. So Joel took it upon himself to say it.

"We make a good team."

Lila said nothing in response to that, either. The team thing remained to be seen. So she drove her gaze around the room, looking for something that might change the subject. Ultimately, her gaze fell on the collection of childishly executed artwork. There were primitive sketches of stick people and stick animals, a few more progressive ones of houses and trees and suns, and a handful of portraits that actually weren't half-bad. Provided they'd been drawn by someone under the age of fifteen. Which, judging by the rest of the exhibit, they most likely had been.

"Who drew all the pictures?" she asked, jutting her chin up toward the one nearest them.

Joel's features softened at the question in a way that made his entire face seem as if it was smiling. That should have diminished his masculinity, too, she thought. But somehow it just made him even more potent.

"My sister's kids," he said. "She sends me a lot of their work. Since she became a mom, she thinks everyone needs the influence of children in their lives. Makes them more human, she says. The grown-ups, I mean," he hastily qualified. "Kids, any kids, she thinks are already pretty much perfect."

"Well, except for the part about them being odious little miscreants," Lila said.

He laughed at that, as if she'd made a joke. Funny thing was, she hadn't been. She didn't much care for children. She supposed they had their purposes—mostly to serve as warnings to always use birth control—but she didn't want any in her own life. She studied Joel more closely, trying to discern if he was being sarcastic or maudlin when he talked about the alleged perfection of his nieces and/or nephews. Neither, she finally decided. Weird as it seemed, he was just being matter-of-fact. He actually agreed with his sister.

Huh. How about that.

She asked, "So are you one of those people who doesn't think life can be complete without the Dutch Colonial in the suburbs, the two-point-five kids and the dog named Sparky?"

He smiled in that should-have-diminished-his-potency-but-didn't way again. "Well, the house could be a Tudor and the dog could be named Pal and life would still be complete, but…" He left the sentence unfinished, but the gist of his feelings came through just fine.

Lila was surprised by the little stab of disappointment that jabbed her chest when she heard him voice the sentiment.

So what if Joel Faraday had bought into that suburban myth of home, hearth and riding mower? she asked herself. So what if he was the settling-down kind? So what if he wanted a traditional life with a traditional partner in a traditional community? What did she care? If that was the sort of thing he wanted, it just hammered home how ill suited the two of them were. Because that kind of life would strangle her.

And why the hell was she even thinking in terms of the two of them suiting each other in the first place? That was beyond nuts. Nobody suited Lila. And she sure as hell wasn't looking to suit anyone herself.

He started to speak again, even got as far as saying, "But the thing is—" when the doorbell chimed, heralding the arrival of their driver. By the time they were seated in the back of the big black Town Car, however, Joel must have forgotten what he'd intended to tell her, because he never revisited the topic. Instead, he started a new one.

"So since you and I are going to be working together so closely for this assignment—"

"You mean living together?" Lila interjected, already knowing that the plan OPUS had outlined would involve their sharing living space. She'd read the entire dossier through last night and knew all the particulars of their undercover operation—at least, the particulars to which OPUS had decided she would be privy for now. There was no telling what Joel knew that she didn't. He was, after all, the one in charge.

Talk about your odious little miscreants.

"Yeah, that," he said. And if she hadn't known better, she would almost have sworn he sounded a little flustered about the prospect of shacking up, even as a job requirement. "So maybe we should know a little more about each other's habits ahead of time."

"Like what?" she asked.

He looked at her in a way that indicated he didn't like her asking him the question he'd intended her to answer first. But he replied anyway, "Like the fact that I'm the early-to-bed and early-to-rise type, but I suspect you're not."

"Oh, really?" she asked. "So what happened to Mr. Early-to-Rise this morning?"

Joel expelled an exasperated sound. "Okay, so today Mr. Early-to-Rise overslept a little."

"Actually, he overslept quite a bit."

"He hasn't been getting as much sleep as usual," Joel continued as if she hadn't spoken. "People keep breaking in to his house in the middle of the night and trying to cuff him."

Lila smiled. "Some people are so rude."

"Aren't they, though?"

"If I were you, I'd want a piece of someone's hide."

He arched his eyebrows at her suggestively, opened his mouth to say something in retort, then seemed to think better of it. Which was a shame, because Lila found herself looking forward to that retort. Among other things.

Ultimately, he only said, "I think I'll just settle for alerting the authorities."

"Oh, good idea," she said. "The authorities *always* know the right thing to do."

"Anyway," he said, circling back to the original topic, "as I said, something tells me you're not the early-to-rise type."

She grinned. "Wow, you're really good at this fieldwork.

I can see why they gave you this assignment. That was a brilliant deduction."

"Hey, I work for an information-gathering arm of the U.S. government," he told her with clearly affected self-importance. "It's my job to make brilliant deductions."

She waved off his concern quite literally. "Don't worry about it. I'm highly adaptable. I can match my hours of operation to yours with no problem."

He eyed her thoughtfully. "Something about the way you said that indicates you'd rather not."

This time Lila shrugged off his concern literally. "I prefer to work at night—big surprise—but when the assignment calls for daytime activity, I don't have a problem with it."

"You're just not as happy working during the day."

"Happiness isn't a word that appears in my job description," she told him.

"But you'd still be happier if this was one of those nighttime infiltration things, wouldn't you?"

There was no reason to deny it, so Lila relented. "Yeah. I'd be happier if it were. But—"

"Why?" he interrupted before she could finish.

She hesitated before replying, just long enough to let him know she resented his interruption. Finally, though, she said, "Because I work better at night."

"I beg to differ," he contradicted.

Lila gaped at him. She wasn't used to people contradicting her, especially as immediately and absolutely as Joel just had.

He obviously understood the reason for her silence, because he told her, "I've studied the particulars of every assignment you've carried out for OPUS, Lila, and statistically speaking, you're always *very* effective regardless of what you're doing or when you're doing it."

A thrill of something warm and fluid purled through her when he addressed her by her first name. She told herself she should be offended at the familiarity and his lack of protocol. Then again, she'd only a short time ago been giving herself permission to drop protocol until they arrived in Cincinnati, and she herself had been thinking of him not as Virtuoso, but as Joel. Besides, she kind of liked the way her name sounded when it was spoken in that deep, velvety baritone.

Then the essence of what he'd told her finally gelled. "You've read over *every* one of my assignments?" she asked incredulously. She hadn't kept track, but considering the years she'd put in with OPUS, the total number must be staggering. And God knew how many pages were devoted to each.

"Once I knew we'd be working together, I needed to familiarize myself with you," he said. Immediately he corrected himself, "I mean…with your methods. How else was I going to do that if not by reading about your standard M.O. when you work?"

"You could have learned about my standard M.O. by looking at a handful of my most high-profile assignments. Then you could have looked at my personnel file for anything else you wanted to know."

He schooled his features into what Lila supposed was meant to be a bland expression. But it was in no way convincing. Her sarcasm of a moment ago had been warranted— he really wasn't equipped to be working out in the field. What the hell was OPUS thinking, letting him tag along?

"Your personnel file," he said, "is off-limits to everyone except a few people who are a hell of a lot higher up the ladder than me."

Lila couldn't help the derisive chuckle that escaped her at that. "Right. And God knows they never leak any information about me to anyone else in the organization. I mean that whole rumor about me having tried to murder the Big Guy must have started with the lunchroom ladies in the OPUS cafeteria." She sighed and lifted a hand to rub her forehead in an effort to relieve a fast-approaching headache. "Look, um, Virtuoso, don't talk to me like I'm an idiot."

"I'm not doing—"

"Virtuoso," she said again.

"Joel," he corrected her. "Please call me Joel. I know it's not protocol, but we're not in Cincinnati yet, and *I* feel like an idiot whenever someone uses my code name. It just seems like such a Hollywood affectation."

"Is that why you don't call me by my code name?" she asked, trying to change the subject. And also wanting to know why he called her Lila when, professionally speaking, he shouldn't.

He grinned. "Don't try to change the subject."

Although she noticed he didn't answer her question, she let it go. "Then don't talk to me like I'm an idiot," she repeated.

"I'm not."

She met his gaze levelly. "Don't pretend you didn't read over my personnel file, too. It makes perfect sense that they would give it to you. Even if they didn't give me yours."

She told herself she did *not* sound petulant when she

uttered that last comment. The reason she hadn't been given any more information about Joel than the essentials of name, rank and serial number—at least, technically speaking—was that she already knew the most important thing about him: That he'd never been out in the field. And also because— dammit—he was the one who would be in charge of the operation, feeding her whatever information she needed as she needed to know it. Clearly, anything personal about him was nothing she needed to know. At least, the higher-ups at OPUS didn't think so. Nor did Joel, evidently, because he certainly wasn't talking.

And why that bothered her so much, Lila would just as soon not ask herself.

She continued, "I'm sure you know every intimate detail of my background and personal life. At least, the parts that OPUS knows." Which, granted, was pretty much everything, she had to concede. But there was no reason Joel couldn't think she had one or two secrets she was keeping to herself.

He studied her in silence for a moment longer, as if he were going to continue the charade. Finally, though, he admitted, "Okay, I know everything OPUS knows about you. But you don't strike me as the sort of woman who would worry about other people discovering all the skeletons in her closet."

She chuckled at that, too, though with genuine good humor this time. "Ah, no," she admitted freely. "The skeletons in my closet got tired of the crowded conditions and made their break a long time ago. There's not much left in there to discover." Quickly, before he had a chance to comment on that, she added, "Still, you get to know everything about me, and I know almost nothing about you. So much for our *partner*ship."

She emphasized the first half of the word deliberately, hoping to goad him. Goading people had always helped Lila keep them at a distance, which, she told herself, was the only reason she was trying to goad Joel. To drive the wedge between them a little deeper. It wasn't because she was hoping it would present a challenge that made him offer up some snippets about himself, too.

He eyed her in silence for a moment, long enough to let her know he understood exactly what she was doing. Then he asked, "What do you want to know about me?"

She arched her eyebrows in genuine surprise. If OPUS hadn't given her information about Joel, then she wasn't supposed to have it. Anything he might tell her about himself that she wasn't already privy to would be in violation of the organization's rules. Not a huge violation, especially if he only told her things like how he'd come in third in the fifth-grade spelling bee or how his favorite food was Mallomars. It was still a violation. And it surprised Lila that he would overstep the rules by even that much. Maybe archivists played by their own rules, but their rules weren't generally in violation of OPUS's. Joel especially seemed like the type of guy who would abide by regulation.

In spite of that, she said, "Where did you grow up?"

"Falls Church, Virginia," he told her readily.

"You've lived your whole life in the D.C. area?"

He nodded. "My father was a Virginia senator until he retired a few years ago."

Lila's mouth dropped open at that, but she said nothing.

"He still does a little advising for the current administration," Joel continued matter-of-factly, "but mostly he and my mother enjoy their respective retirements, usually on another continent."

"Respective retirements?" Lila echoed. "What did your mother do for a living?"

"She edited the *Washington Sentinel*. Her family owns it. Among other things. They're big in the publishing world." Before Lila had time to digest that, Joel was adding, "My grandparents lived in D.C., too. My grandfather worked for Eisenhower, and then Kennedy. The house I live in now belonged to him and my grandmother. She left it to me when she died, since my sister and her husband already had a place in Tysons Corner and she knew I wanted to stay close to home after I graduated from Georgetown."

Lila's head was spinning by now, thanks to the rarefied atmosphere she'd just entered. Senators, presidents and newspaper families were the sorts of creatures she never had much chance to meet, but to Joel, they were a part of everyday life. Falls Church, Georgetown and Tysons Corner were all very refined, very affluent areas. Certainly Lila was no stranger to the lifestyles of the rich and powerful. But she'd been a part of them only as an outsider looking in. And only when she was working on assignment. Never in her life had she been a part of that environment for social reasons. To Joel, there was no other life.

"You come from money, then," she said, stating the obvious.

"I do," he admitted. Again without hesitation, but also without apology or vanity. It had been Lila's experience that rich people usually copped to their wealth in either one way or the other. To Joel, however, it seemed to be a part of his makeup, the same way his lungs were.

"Must be nice," she couldn't quite keep herself from saying.

"It was," he told her. But once more, he spoke without any kind of inflection. "Still is."

"And you have a sister. Anyone else?"

He shook his head.

"She's older?"

He nodded.

Well, goodness, this conversation was offering Lila all kinds of insights into Joel's background and character. If this kept up, she might even find out what his favorite color was, and that would *really* violate regulation.

She grinned. "If you could be any vegetable in the world, what would you be and why?"

That, finally, got a reaction out of him that *wasn't* matter-of-fact. Not a big reaction. Mostly just the squinching up of his eyes so that he was looking at her as if the sun had gone into total eclipse and thrown the planet into complete darkness, but hey, it was something.

Even so, his voice remained unchanged from its usual straightforward delivery when he replied, "One of those bags of salad that's already washed and ready to serve."

Lila's smile broadened. "Really?"

"Yeah."

"But that's not actually a vegetable, is it?"

"Of course it is," he insisted. "And it's a damned interesting one, too."

"Okay, so why would you be that?"

He gazed at her blankly. "Are you kidding? Salad already washed and ready to serve? That's like a party just waiting to happen."

After that, the remainder of the ride to their jet passed in a surprisingly swift and tension-free manner, with Lila learning all kinds of things about Joel. Like, for instance, if he could be any fruit in the world, it would be a coconut, because they never took themselves too seriously. Any animal, he would be a jellyfish, because, hey, no pressure there. Any musical instrument? An electric guitar, because it was so soulful. Supermarket product? A TV dinner, because they were bad for you but, oh, so good. Mode of transportation? A bullet train. Because, well, for obvious reasons.

Of course, she thought when he uttered that last. What guy wouldn't be a bullet train for obvious reasons? Still, it did make her wonder. About a lot of things. Things that had nothing to do with transportation. Well, not conventional transportation, anyway. A guy who was a bullet train could doubtless transport a woman to a lot of places. Hence the wondering about a lot of things. Until the wondering became visualizing and started threatening to make Lila lose track of what her and Joel's actual goal was, which was…

Well, hell. She'd known a little while ago. Before Joel became so charming and approachable and bullet-trainy and made her start wondering about and visualizing things she had no business wondering about and visualizing when she should instead be focused on…

An assignment, she finally recalled. An assignment to capture a man who was a threat to national—even international—security. A man who had eluded OPUS—who had eluded *her*—for years. A man whose presence roaming free in the world was a smack in the face to Lila's skill and determination as an agent. A man she was tired of chasing.

It was time to catch Adrian Padgett, she told herself, refocusing her attention on the man it really needed to be on. Past time. She *would* catch him this time. And she would see him tossed into the most fail-safe prison in the country, if she had to slam the door shut and lock it behind him herself. Then maybe she could get on with other more pleasant pursuits. Like, oh…she didn't know. Her *life,* maybe.

For some reason, her gaze fell on Joel as that last thought formed in her head. Even though she told herself he was *not* going to be one of her pursuits, never mind have anything to do with her life. He wasn't her type, he wasn't her goal, he wasn't her match. Hell, he wasn't even her partner, not really. Providing Oliver survived his upcoming wedding to Avery Nesbitt, he and Lila would return to being a team. She hoped.

Joel Faraday would just be a blip on the time line of Lila's life. One man of many, and by no means the most important. That man was hiding somewhere in Cincinnati. And she was *this close* to bringing him down. For good.

CHAPTER FIVE

LOUNGING WITH A SNIFTER of an exceedingly good Armagnac in the living area of his exceedingly luxurious suite at the Four Seasons Cincinnati, Adrian Padgett was exceedingly bored. But then, that was hardly anything new, was it? He couldn't remember the last time he'd been intrigued/fascinated/captivated/even remotely preoccupied by anything intriguing/fascinating/captivating/even remotely worthy of preoccupation. Life could be so boring when one was corrupt. Where was the challenge in anything? Where was the mischief? Where was the sneaky underhandedness? When a man was amoral to begin with, there were no lines to cross, no rules to break, no crosses to double. If one had no allegiances to begin with, one couldn't exactly betray them, could one?

Truly, dammit, where was the fun? Taking the entire planet hostage wasn't turning out to be nearly as diverting as Adrian had thought it would be.

Of course, he thought as he contemplated his companions, it would have helped if he'd been able to amass some proper henchmen instead of the ragtag group of college students he'd collected over the past few months. The three young men draped over the furniture in his suite weren't exactly Adolf

Hitler and Genghis Khan when it came to villainy. More like Boris and Natasha. Only, without the elegant wardrobe and charming accents.

Oh, sure, they *said* they wanted to take over the world with Adrian. And if they'd put forth half the effort to take over this world as they had taking over the worlds in their godforsaken video games, Adrian would be master of time, space and dimension by now. But that was just it. Unless something was a graphic on a game screen, they didn't view it as a challenge. And it wasn't as if Adrian hadn't given them plenty of incentive. He'd promised them that once they had the world in their possession, the boys could have Daytona Beach, all incarnations of MTV, the Playboy mansion, Nintendo *and* Jessica Alba to divvy up however they wanted.

He blew out an exasperated breath. Where were tomorrow's despots supposed to come from, if not from today's universities? Where were the future Slobodan Milosevics and Saddam Husseins? It was criminal how college campuses weren't producing tyrants anymore. Well, except for the Young Republicans. But even they were more interested these days in making sound business investments than they were in global domination. At this rate, by the time today's youth grew to maturity, the world wasn't going to be worth taking over. Which was all the more reason why Adrian had to do it *now*.

Unfortunately, the timetable wasn't up to him, since it wasn't he who knew the secret code that would finally put the world in his grasp. No, that was up to Moe, Larry and Curly over there. The ones currently focused on the big-screen television, playing a game that seemed to involve a hedgehog who was dressed in large red sneakers and big white gloves, having evidently eschewed any other clothing.

Typical cartoon character, Adrian thought. All accessories. No pants.

"I wanna be Sonic now," Chuck Miller said suddenly, tossing down the game controls he'd held in both hands and seizing—without asking permission—the controls from his companion to the left.

Neither of his playmates took offense, however, since they were all old pals. In fact, Adrian knew the trio's friendship went all the way back to their freshman year in college, three whole years ago. Donny Grawemeyer, who was seated on Chuck's left, only swatted Chuck's hat and sent it flying, and Hobie Jurgens, on the right, only laughed and called him Buttwad.

It warmed the cockles of Adrian's heart to see the boys getting along so well. And such charming, articulate creatures they were, too.

The three young men went to great pains to make clear their nonconformity from the campus cattle who did their academic grazing en masse, but each was dressed in some kind of iconic costume of his generation that indicated a desperation on his part to belong *some*where. Chuck was the typical suburban faux gangsta in his ropey gold chains and oversize pants and T-shirts—today's color scheme was blue on brown. Donny was the self-proclaimed metalhead, his wavy red hair streaming past his shoulders over a black System of a Down T-shirt—whoever the hell they were—and blue jeans. And Hobie, with his cropped blond locks and baggy Jams and red Billabong T-shirt—whatever the hell that was—was the surfer dude. This despite the fact that the only surf one might find on the Ohio River occurred when a passing coal barge increased its speed to more than one knot.

Adrian supposed that, to the three students, he was something of an icon, too—albeit from their parents' generation. To them, he was The Suit. A suit who went by the name of Nick Darian, since there was no way on God's green earth he would ever give any of them his real name.

Now that his work day had ended, however—though his work day these days didn't much involve any work—he had shed his espresso-colored jacket and tie and unfastened the buttons of his mustard-colored dress shirt at his throat and cuffs, rolling the latter back to his elbows. Adrian clung to his Fortune 500 wardrobe selections, even though his job these days consisted of little more than watching his back and trying to figure out where to strike next with his band of half-assed men. And also making sure that his half-assed men didn't stray from the path of world domination any further than obtaining the next level in Fire Emblem. Whatever the hell that was.

Adrian identified with none of the boys. He admired none of them. He respected none of them. He liked none of them. He did, in fact, resent all of them, since they were all essential to a plan he couldn't execute without them. Because they knew things about computers and code and other such things that Adrian simply could not grasp himself. Unfortunately, the little bastards couldn't focus their brains on anything besides gaming for longer than fifteen minutes at a stretch.

When they did focus, though… Good God, they were magic. There was potential for them as a group that Adrian had barely tapped, and if they would just think about something besides half-naked hedgehogs, it would be they, not he, who ruled the planet.

"Dude, you're always Sonic," Donny said now, his carrot-colored hair falling forward as he reached for the controls Chuck had taken from him. "Gimme back the controls."

But Chuck only nudged with his foot the controls he'd abandoned, scooting them closer to Donny. "You can be Tails," he said. "Live a little."

"Tails sucks, man," Donny said. "He don't do jack." But instead of reaching for the controls that Chuck held firm, he leaned over his friend and snatched the controls Hobie held.

"Hey!" Hobie objected eloquently.

"I'm Knuckles now," Donny announced. He tossed the controls formerly known as Chuck's to Hobie. "You be Tails."

"Tails sucks, man," Hobie said. "He don't do Jack."

Adrian closed his eyes in a silent plea for patience. Oh, what he wouldn't give for a good, solid two-by-four at the moment. How could people who claimed the IQs of NASA engineers have the maturity of eggplants?

"Boys, don't make me separate you," he said as he pinched the bridge of his nose with his thumb and forefinger. "You know how much you hate being put in time-out."

They, of course, ignored him. Worse than ignored him, actually. They didn't even hear him. And if there was one thing Adrian hated more than anything in the world, it was going unnoticed.

He opened his mouth to say something that would, he hoped, wrest their attention from the colorful graphics zipping by on the TV screen for even a moment, when the door to the hotel suite beeped at the use of a key card, then opened to reveal the final member of the group. She, too, barely acknowledged Adrian as she strode by him, tossing a halfhearted "Hey, Nick" over her shoulder at him as she approached the boys instead.

Ah, Iris, he thought as he watched her take a seat on the sofa, thrusting one long leg over the arm to swing her foot anxiously above the floor. She was always doing something anxiously. The antithesis to the boys, who could sit idly for hours in front of their games, Iris Daugherty could never be still for more than a few minutes at a time. She was an icon of her generation, too, though she took greater pains to establish her own identity of Goth Girl. She was dressed today as she always was, completely in black, from the cropped T-shirt to the baggy, zipper-ridden cargo pants to the studded belt and high-top sneakers. Her ears were pierced probably a dozen times, as was her eyebrow, her nose and her navel. Scores of black rubber bracelets encircled one wrist, and a black studded wristwatch was wrapped around the other. She carried with her, as she always did, an enormous black bag, chunky with its contents, slung diagonally over her shoulder and torso. As he always did, Adrian wondered what she could possibly have it filled with, as it was indeed always completely stuffed. She dyed her straight, chin-length hair and eyebrows black to match her clothes, even painted her bitten-down nails black. Heavy black liner encircled pale blue eyes, and black lipstick stained her mouth.

Whenever Adrian saw her, he couldn't help wondering what she'd looked like before the transformation. Especially since she was an aging Goth Girl who couldn't hang on to this persona much longer without looking ridiculous. At twenty-six, she was older than the boys by half a dozen years, having started college a bit later than the others and taking her time to complete her degree. Adrian didn't know a lot about her, but from what he'd heard and observed of her, he'd formed an impression of a rich kid who was even more bored by life than he was. He'd been around wealth often enough as an adult that he was reasonably adept at recognizing those who were born to it. Perhaps because his own background was so completely opposite to theirs.

Although Iris was certainly as comfortable around computers as the boys were, Adrian had come to the conclusion that the main reason she hung out with them was that she was a geek groupie. He'd overheard enough conversations between the young men when she wasn't around to know that she'd slept with all three of them at some point—and more than once with all of them at the same time, something that intrigued Adrian rather a lot.

Ah, well then, he thought as the realization formed. He stood corrected. There was something—or rather, someone—he found intriguing after all. In fact, he found Iris rather fascinating. Rather captivating. And more than worthy of his preoccupation.

"Hello, Iris," he greeted her as she slumped back on the sofa and watched the boys play.

She had the courtesy to turn around then and reply, "What's up, Nick?" But she promptly returned her attention to the game and gamers, indicating she hadn't expected a reply to the question. And when she realized what the boys were still arguing over, she uttered a loud sound of obvious disgust. "You're playing Sonic *again?*" she said disdainfully. "What are you, a bunch of fifth graders? I thought we were going to break out the new Resident Evil this afternoon."

"We *men*," Chuck said manfully, emphasizing his gender, "are playing Sonic. You do what you want, Iris."

What Iris did was roll her eyes dramatically and leap up from the sofa to make her way to the minibar, from which she withdrew, without asking permission, a soft drink. Not that Adrian minded. Much. It wasn't as if he'd be drinking it himself. The beverage was, to his way of thinking, about as appealing as a big glass of bile. Not to mention that any expenses racked up during his stay here in the suite were more than covered by the money the group had appropriated over the past few months. Mostly by raiding other people's computers and appropriating their financial information—and then their finances themselves. And Iris was no slouch herself when it came to hacking and designing viruses. Plus, there was the small matter of, when it came time to check out of the suite, Adrian would be gone before the bill was tucked under the door, leaving behind absolutely no traceable evidence of himself or the others.

He was currently on week three at the Four Seasons. One more, and he'd be moving to the Omni, just up the road. Although he alone stayed at the suite around the clock, he'd given the others key cards and indicated they were welcome whenever they wanted to drop by. That, of course, wasn't true—Adrian didn't welcome them at all, ever—but he needed them to think he was one of them, or at the very least striving to be one of them. They were valuable tools, the way he saw it. And he wanted to have them close by for whenever he might need them.

Like tonight.

He watched Iris as she screwed the top off the soda and enjoyed a healthy swallow before lowering it again. And for some reason he found the sight of her black-stained mouth covering the rim of the bottle to be more than a little arousing. He hadn't really thought about giving Iris a go himself, since the last time he'd mixed business with pleasure, he'd regretted it. What he'd thought was simply an alluring sex kitten named Tiffannee, someone who didn't have the brains of a sponge mop, had turned out to be one of the most dangerous— and cunning—women in the world. And she'd come *this close* to returning Adrian to the not-so-loving bosom of OPUS, who would have then locked him up and thrown away the key.

He would not make the same mistake twice. His information pipeline at OPUS might not be running quite as freely and quickly as it once had, but he'd been able to learn enough about each of the boys to be reasonably certain they were precisely who they claimed to be. Iris remained a big question mark, but since she wasn't really a player in their game, Adrian wasn't too concerned about her background anyway.

What mattered was that bits and pieces of information had begun to flow from his source again, and a background check of each of his, ah, colleagues was at the top of his list of needs. It shouldn't be long before he knew more about them than they knew themselves. In the meantime, they'd more than proved their worth by breaking every law he'd asked them to, without question or compunction. There was almost no chance any of them were working for anyone other than him. Would that they just worked a little better. Then Adrian would be a very happy man.

"So what's on the agenda tonight?" Iris asked.

The question dispelled his troubled thoughts and replaced them with much nicer ideas. He was rather looking forward to this evening. He had his eye on a certain Swiss bank account he was hoping the boys could bleed dry.

Iris moved to the desk in the corner where Adrian's laptop was folded closed and opened it. Again without asking permission. Again without Adrian minding. Much.

"It's been a while since we did anything fun," she added as she seated herself and tapped the mouse pad with her middle finger to bring the computer out of sleep mode.

As she began to type, Adrian set his snifter on a side table and strode across the room to stand behind her. Looking over her shoulder, he saw that she'd gone to the iTunes music store and pulled up information on a band he'd never heard of before. He had to remind himself he was only forty-six and in no way ready for the retirement home. But having spent the past few months with this group, he'd been forced to accept the fact that pop culture no longer catered to his generation. Actors, singers, dissidents, serial killers—they were all younger than Adrian these days. College students were making millions selling Web sites they designed on a lark, and the teenage offspring of bestselling novelists were hitting the lists even higher than some of their parents. Society was now geared to those who were younger, hipper, faster. The ones who required less sleep and more distraction, thereby ensuring that the entertainment industries made money around the clock.

Maybe he wasn't old, Adrian thought, but he was older. And he was no longer a part of that demographic that *every*one wanted to attract. All the more reason to take as much as he could as quickly as he could. So that he could disappear on his own terms, instead of on theirs.

"We haven't had fun for a while, have we?" he told Iris over the din of the still-arguing boys on the other side of the room.

He completed another step, an action that placed him immediately behind her, close enough that he could have settled both hands on her shoulders had he wanted to. Funnily, he realized he did want to. But he didn't. Yet. Instead, he only gazed down at the crown of her head, scrutinizing the part in her hair that zigzagged across her scalp. He smiled when he found what he was looking for. There, very faint, he saw that her roots were blond. Very blond. Nearly white-blond. His grin broadened. He'd always had a predilection for blondes.

"You're right—we should do something fun this evening," he agreed as Iris began to download music from that band Adrian had never heard of onto his laptop. Without asking his permission. Not that he minded. Much. And although he himself had one or two additional ideas as to what that "fun" might involve, he decided to focus instead on his original plan.

For now.

IRIS DAUGHERTY WAS MORE than a little aware of Nick Darian's nearness as he stood behind her and watched every move she made on his computer. Good. 'Bout damned time he started noticing every move she made, since she'd been watching his every move since the day Chuck had introduced the two of them. Even if he did have probably twenty years on her and dressed like a corporate drone. And even if he was interested in any of them only because they knew 'puters and didn't mind overstepping the law. Kind of hard not to watch a guy who looked as good as Nick did, with that thick auburn hair and those amber eyes and those cheekbones sharp enough to slice tomatoes. And those shoulders that were broad enough to strain the seams of his shirt. And that waist just narrow enough for a woman to wrap her arms around. And a chest just perfect for that same woman to settle her head against.

Not that Iris had done any of those things to Nick. Not that she was likely to in the near future. But a girl could dream, couldn't she? Hell, yeah.

She wondered—not for the first time—just what his story really was. He'd told them nothing about his past, and she'd known better than to ask. You didn't have to have an IQ to rival Mozart's—even though Iris did—to see the Do Not Enter signs Nick had posted all over himself. She only knew he carried a chip on his shoulder that was even bigger than hers—no easy feat, since hers was roughly the size of Rhode Island—and that he craved wealth and power (hey, who didn't?) and that there was a ruthless quality about him that sometimes gave her pause.

Not that he scared her. She'd been spawned by a man far more ruthless than Nick could ever hope to be. Which, she hated to admit, might be the very thing that drew her to him. She would have sworn she was too smart to be attracted to men like her father. But since escaping—that was a much more appropriate word than *leaving*—home when she was eighteen, Iris had discovered that the world was full of grasping, possessive losers. And, unfortunately, she'd encountered more than her fair share.

Nick, though, wasn't a loser. He was by far the most successful man she'd ever been attracted to. Hell, her father would probably even like him. Of course, since Iris hadn't seen or spoken to that son of a bitch for eight years, it might be a little awkward when it came to introductions…

She pushed the unpleasant thought out of her head. There were infinitely better things to think about than her genetic family. Especially since the one she'd adopted on her own was so much better.

"I'm Sonic!" Chuck shouted.

"No, I am!" Donny countered.

"Nuh-uh! Me! I'm Sonic!" Hobie insisted.

Iris sighed and rolled her eyes. All right. So maybe she felt like the big sister to a bunch of snot-nosed, bratty little brothers. They were still better than the pack of wolves who had raised her.

"Stop being such a bunch of assholes!" she called out to the guys. To distract them, she scrolled through the songs she'd just downloaded, cranked up the sound on Nick's computer and blasted them with the Offspring's "Self-Esteem." 'Cause, you know, they *were* a bunch of suckers with no self-esteem. Whoa, yeah.

Their reaction to the music was swift and powerful. All three guys jumped up from the Xbox and began to play air guitar. Iris blew out an exasperated sound that was almost identical to the one Nick emitted at the same time. When she looked over her shoulder at him, he smiled at her, and something in his expression made a river of hot, gooey deliciousness run through her, starting in her belly, seeping simultaneously up into her breasts and down between her legs. Her face went hot, her fingers curled closed over the keyboard and her lips parted slightly, because she suddenly needed more air.

She started to stand, halting when Nick dropped his hands to her shoulders and gently prevented her from rising. She noticed his cheeks were stained with red, too, and that his pupils had expanded to nearly eclipse the amber of his irises. Whatever she was suddenly feeling—and she was suddenly feeling *a lot*—he was feeling it, too. But he didn't want the others to notice what was happening. So Iris stayed where she was, returned her attention to Nick's laptop and tried to control her breathing.

Surprisingly, once Chuck and Donny and Hobie finished their concert, they didn't go back to their game and instead strode over to the computer to see what Iris was doing. By then she'd managed to pull herself back together enough that she could pretend nothing had happened between her and Nick, even though she knew it would be a long time before she stopped trying to figure out what had happened between her and Nick. All she knew was that one minute the two of them had been sharing their frustration with the guys, and the next they'd been looking at each other as if they wanted to make a meal out of each other.

Oh, great. Now she was feeling that hot, gooey deliciousness between her legs again….

"So what are we doin' tonight?" Chuck asked. Then he leaned over Iris and brushed her hand away from the mouse pad so that he could trace his own finger over it. "See if the new Brotha Lynch Hung download is available yet."

Iris was about to slap his hand out of the way and go back to what she'd been doing, but Nick's words stopped her.

"Now, Chuck," he said in a contrived fatherly voice, "that's very rude. I believe Iris was using the laptop for something else. Either ask her if it's all right for you to intrude, or wait your turn."

It was a small thing, Nick's interceding, but Iris felt as if he'd just given her a diamond as big as the Ritz. No one had ever done anything like that for her before—acted as her champion. Even for so small a thing. A soft ripple of delight wound through her now that felt even better than the warm, gooey deliciousness of a moment ago. She sat up straighter in the chair, squared her shoulders and felt, for the first time in a long time—perhaps the first time in her life—like someone who deserved a little respect.

"Yeah, Chuck," she said, preening like Gwen Stefani. "Wait your turn. Don't be such a prick."

Chuck's mouth turned up at one corner as he emitted a small sound of disbelief. "Who the hell crowned you queen?" he demanded.

"I did," Nick said. "And you'd be wise to pledge your fealty to her now."

Chuck's eyebrows shot up to nearly the plastic strap of his backward-facing cap. "My what?" he said, his voice tinted with unmistakable challenge. "I might want to do what with my what?"

Iris turned fully around in her chair now to look at Nick, only to find him staring back at Chuck with an expression that was a hundred times more intimidating than Chuck's tone of voice had been. Chuck seemed to recognize it, too, because he immediately dropped his hand from the mouse pad and took two steps backward, away from Iris.

"Pledge your fealty," Nick repeated. "It's what intelligent men in far more violent times than these used to do to ensure their survival."

"Uh, okay," Chuck said. He looked at Iris. "Iris, whatever the hell fealty is, I pledge it to you." Then he turned back to Nick. "Satisfied?"

Nick smiled a very dangerous-looking smile. "Not by a long shot," he said. "But you're learning, Chuck. Something I find rather amazing."

Before Chuck could reply—not that he seemed to have any idea what to say—Nick effortlessly switched gears, as if they'd never been off topic to begin with.

"Tonight we're going to try something new," he told the others. "Because I have it on good authority that we may be having company soon. Evidently our activities have raised some flags at that government organization I told you all about, and they may be sending someone in to check us out. So over the next week or two, perhaps even the next few days, if you encounter anyone who seems in any way suspicious, or anyone who asks a lot of questions, I want to hear about it, all right?"

Everyone nodded their assurance that they would, Iris included. Not that she for a moment believed they had anything to worry about. She'd decided a long time ago that Nick's certainty that their little group was being watched was, at worst, paranoia and, at best, a manufactured threat to keep them all in line. Chuck and Donny and Hobie were of the same opinion, though none of them would ever say so to Nick's face. Nick didn't realize how good they all were when it came to hiding their tracks. The four of them had been wreaking havoc on the Net a long time before Nick showed up. The guys might be a bunch of slackers in a lot of ways, but not when it came to gaming or computers. And Iris was better even than they were.

But it seemed to make Nick less antsy when they went along with him, so they did. The Cold War had still been in full swing when he was born, and he was old enough to remember things like Vietnam and the Berlin Wall and all that Communist crap. To the rest of them, that was the stuff of spy novels. It just didn't ring true in this day and age. Not that Iris and the guys doubted for a minute that there was a boatload of conspiracy and government corruption across the board. It was why Nick's plan to take the planet hostage didn't bother any of them much. Well, that and the fact that taking the entire planet hostage felt like one big computer game.

"Sure, Nick," Chuck said. "We'll keep our eyes wide open."

When the other guys murmured similar sentiments, Nick turned to look at Iris. "And you, Iris?" he asked. "Can I count on you to keep me informed?"

"Sure," she said. "You know me, Nick. I always do what you tell me to."

This time he was the one to nod. Then he smiled the smile of hot, gooey deliciousness again. "Yes, you do," he murmured softly. Sweetly. Seductively. "It's just one of the many, *many* things about you, Iris, that I like."

CHAPTER SIX

WAVERLY COLLEGE, LILA discovered the moment the campus came into view, was nothing short of a picture postcard, nestled on the banks of the Ohio just outside Cincinnati. With the rolling green hills of Kentucky behind it and the limitless blue sky above, it was a collection of short, redbrick buildings scattered under towering oaks and maples that were just beginning to go green. It looked little like a cutting-edge technology school, reminded her instead of movies about English professors who taught their young students lessons about life that lurked in the subtext of classic literature. Surely she would run into Mr. Chips and Mr. Keating if she spent any length of time on campus.

Of course, the point was to spend as little time as possible on campus, she reminded herself as she and Joel cruised the college grounds in a car that was small enough, old enough and battered enough to pass for credible student wheels—and was nondescript enough to simply pass. The sooner they brought in Sorcerer—and whoever he'd found to help him do his dirty work—the better. Not just to ensure the domestic tranquillity of the planet, but to ensure her own peace of mind by parting ways with Joel Faraday quickly and efficiently and completely.

The past thirty-six hours had been a jumble of new and unusual—and not especially wanted—feelings for Lila. The small measure of camaraderie she and Joel had achieved during their ride to catch their flight had evaporated almost immediately after the jet left the ground. Because that was when he started briefing her on more of the assignment, and she'd been forced to remember that it was he who was in charge of the operation, making him her superior, even if only temporarily. And she knew better than to get involved with someone in his position. Even temporarily.

She knew that from experience, in fact. Once, years ago, Lila had succumbed to an attraction she had for her immediate superior in OPUS. They'd been working together on a very dangerous assignment, had survived—barely—a very perilous situation, and they'd allowed their overwhelming relief at their survival to manifest itself sexually. They'd both realized immediately that they'd made a colossal mistake, and neither had made any effort to repeat it. They'd even gone out of their way to avoid each other for a long time afterward. It had taken years for the two of them to be comfortable in the same room again, but they'd finally managed to reach a point where they were genuinely friends again.

Good thing, too, since the man in question, Noah Tennant, was now engaged to Lila's sister, Marnie. Sorcerer hadn't been the only one to mistake Marnie for Lila in Cleveland. All of OPUS had, until Marnie had convinced them otherwise. Then, in the same way Lila's partner Oliver had tapped Avery Nesbitt to aid their investigation of Sorcerer, Noah had recruited Marnie. She'd been trained by OPUS to pose as Lila in an effort to lure Sorcerer out of hiding. Had Lila not finally come in out of the cold, it would be Marnie, not Lila, working with Joel right now.

That was what had brought Lila in out of the cold, in fact. She hadn't wanted her sister to be placed in danger any more than she already had been. All Marnie should have to think about was starting a new life with Noah, and her only worry should be planning the wedding. Catching Sorcerer was Lila's job, Lila's responsibility. And Lila would do it by the book, at least where her position and Joel's were concerned.

Joel had evidently arrived at the same conclusion, because ever since they'd climbed aboard the plane in D.C., he'd adopted a more professional, more distant demeanor. Gone was the lighthearted banter they'd shared. Gone were the playful, speculative looks. Now they were back to a wary tolerance of each other, which, Lila told herself, was exactly where the two of them needed to be.

Gone, too, in effect, were Lila and Joel, since both had dropped into their undercover personas since their arrival in Cincinnati. Because it was easy for her to pass for a woman a decade younger, Lila would be posing as a graduate student named Jenny Sturgis who was working on a master's degree in computer engineering. She'd colored her blond hair dark brown and trimmed the front to give herself long bangs. Brown contacts hid the normal blue of her eyes. To further conceal her appearance, she'd added extra-dark Avril Lavigne–type eye shadow, and she'd used cosmetics to fill in her usually high cheekbones and round out her normally aquiline nose. Jenny bore very little resemblance to Lila, but she still managed to be smokin' hot, something that should be advantageous in attracting not just Sorcerer, but anyone he might have recruited to aid him in his quest for—cue the over-the-top villain music—global domination.

Joel would be posing as Jenny's live-in boyfriend, Ned Collins, with whom she was having a rocky on-again, off-again relationship—currently in the *off* position. Lila had thought up the on-again, off-again, currently *off* thing all by herself and was pretty pleased with it. Joel not so much. Nevertheless, he'd seen her point that college guys flocked around girls who were in floundering romances, hoping they might recoup the spoils. Of course, that wasn't why Lila had suggested the addition to the script. She'd suggested it because it would give her more opportunity to snipe at Joel.

OPUS had secured living quarters for them in downtown Cincinnati, in an apartment building that catered to older married Waverly students. It was only two blocks away from a coffee shop that also deserved a closer look, thanks to its ties to some intercepted Sorcerer e-mails. OPUS had arranged for Lila to work there in a very part-time position so that she might observe both the patrons and the employees. She would investigate the computer lab in the Waverly library for the same reason.

She had a ratty backpack laden with enough textbooks and products beginning with a lowercase *i* to make Jenny totally credible, and was as good to go as she would ever be. The sooner they found Sorcerer, the better. She had a wedding to go to, after all. As the song said—sort of—for God's sake, get her to the church on time. Or at least to the majestic Nesbitt estate in the Hamptons, since that was where Oliver and Avery would actually be tying the knot. In less than two weeks. So the clock was ticking. Not that Lila needed to be reminded of that.

"It's too bad we couldn't coordinate this at the beginning of a semester," Joel said from the driver's seat as he wheeled the car into a parking space near the university bookstore.

He was dressed appropriately for Ned, in battered khakis and a rumpled, untucked white shirt that complemented nicely Lila's snug ripped jeans and even snugger long-sleeved, olive-drab T-shirt. That was as far as he'd needed to alter his appearance—not that that altered his appearance in any way—since his face wasn't one that was recognized outside OPUS. His long dark hair was swept back from his forehead the same way it had been that first night Lila met him, and his dark eyes, though hidden at the moment by sun-glasses, still reminded her of bittersweet chocolate.

"What difference does it make when we start?" she asked, pushing memories of that first night out of her head, because thinking about it made her want to think of little else. "As long as we finish as soon as we can?"

"Several of Sorcerer's e-mails went to sorority houses," he told her. Behind the sunglasses, Lila knew, he was surrep-titiously scanning the parking lot as he spoke. She was, too, but she was good enough at doing it that she didn't need sun-glasses to hide what she was doing. "There's one in particu-lar we'd like to check out," he added. "There's a fraternity we're interested in, too, but I think you'd have better luck in-filtrating the former."

She chuckled at that. Not the part about her being unable to infiltrate a fraternity—for her that would actually be easier—but she could definitely see Sorcerer targeting a sorority. Mostly for the scantily-clad-pillow-fighting-coeds potential.

"It's just as well," she told Joel. "My talents as an actress only go so far, and sorority girl isn't a role I could pull off." She grinned as she added, "Even if it would have, like, *totally* filled the empty place I've always had inside me because I, like, *totally* missed out on Greek life in college. I could have, like, *totally* used a bunch of friends named Muffy and Bitsy and Pepper."

He pulled down his sunglasses far enough to meet her gaze eye to eye. "You're right," he said. "You suck. I never met any sorority girls who talked like that."

"Hey!" she objected. Even though she had, like, *totally* asked for it.

"Don't knock Greek life till you've tried it," Joel said, returning his sunglasses to the bridge of his nose. "Some of us have very fond memories."

Lila told herself she shouldn't be surprised by his revelation, but she was. He didn't seem like the wild fraternity animal. Unless…

She smiled. Still adopting her best Muffy/Bitsy/Pepper voice, she said, "Shut *up*. You were, like, a frat boy? A smart guy like you? You must have been, like, one of the *geek* Greeks, weren't you? Ohmigod, that is, like, *so stinkin' cute.*"

He said nothing in response at first, but even in the windshield-tinted sunlight filtering through the windows, Lila could see his cheeks turn ruddy. Good God, he could blush. She didn't think she'd ever met a man who even had the capacity to do that, never mind the propensity. Then she realized it was because she'd embarrassed him with what she'd said.

"Eta Kappa Nu," he said in a voice that revealed nothing

of what he might be thinking or feeling. "Alpha iota chapter. Georgetown."

Oh, not embarrassed, she realized then. Angry. He thought she was making fun of him. Which, she supposed, she was. But OPUS agents always did that to each other. Teasing and making fun were one of the best ways to alleviate the tension that went along with undercover work. Of course, having never worked undercover, Joel wouldn't know that, she reminded herself. Nor would he be used to it.

Before she had a chance to apologize, however, he continued, "It was the fraternity for electrical and computer engineering students, the most intelligent guys on campus. They never would have rushed you, even if you *did* have the balls you seem to think you have."

Oh, so the archivist could give as good as he got, could he? Lila thought, surprised. Fine. She just wished she could tell if he'd been joking or serious with the balls comment. Deciding to give him the benefit of the doubt and go for joking, she replied, "So then I guess you guys didn't have a lot of raging keggers where you slipped roofies to the freshmen girls, huh? Your idea of a swingin' Saturday night was probably a couple of twenty-sided dice, downloading pictures of Teri Hatcher from the Internet and putting on Spock ears."

"As opposed to those of you at UNLV who spent the weekends doing…what?" he quickly retorted, not sounding particularly jovial—alas. "As far as I can tell from your file, the only thing you did in college besides attend class was work your ass off at three jobs. Hell, at least I had friends and fun when I was in school."

Okay, that crossed the line, Lila thought. Maybe her college years hadn't been filled with enriching extracurricular activities, but she hadn't viewed college as an opportunity to make friends and create memories. College had been her escape from ending up like her mother—poorly educated, lacking in self-esteem, the constant victim of one scummy son of a bitch after another. For Joel to call Lila friendless and joyless during that time wasn't teasing and making fun. It was hitting way too close to home.

It was also falling out of his Ned persona, she thought further, which, all right, they'd both kind of been forgetting to maintain ever since they started talking. But it was for *that* reason and no other that she immediately put them back on course.

"I didn't attend UNLV, I attended Ball State," she said quietly, since that was how Jenny Sturgis's phony transcripts read. "I've never been to Las Vegas in my life. I grew up in Indiana and my parents, Phil and Doreen Sturgis, still live there. You obviously have me mistaken for someone else, Ned Collins. Strange, since you and I have been living together for two years now."

As she'd spoken, Joel's features had gone slack and his cheeks had grown ruddier. He was obviously as chagrined as she to have forgotten the role they were both supposed to be playing. At least he had an excuse, Lila thought. He wasn't accustomed to being someone else. She'd been playing parts all her life—even before she started working for OPUS. Normally, once she was in character for an assignment, she stayed there without even having to think about it. Why, suddenly, was she forgetting to do the most basic part of her job?

"Besides," she added, still striving to be Jenny but unable to keep herself from saying what she had to say, "some people have to work three jobs to pay tuition and living expenses, since scholarships only go so far. Of course, other people, people like, say, the son of a senator and a newspaper heiress, probably wouldn't know much about scrimping and saving and working his ass off to survive."

Joel said nothing in reply, only studied her in silence for a long, taut moment. Then he started to lean toward her. For one insane moment Lila thought he was going to hit her, and she reacted instinctively, jerking her head backward and throwing her arm up to shield herself. At the same time Joel reached behind the passenger seat where she was crouching to retrieve a clipboard he'd placed there when they first entered the car.

He halted just shy of reaching it when he must have realized why she'd reacted the way she had. He didn't retreat, but he removed his sunglasses, his mouth falling open in disbelief. She immediately dropped her hand and relaxed, but there was no way to explain her reaction as anything other than what it was. So she only turned her head to look through the windshield and said nothing.

"You honestly thought I was going to hit you?" he asked, his voice as incredulous as his expression had been.

In an effort to make light of the situation, she smiled and said, "Well, you could *try.*" But the smile felt forced and the comment was in no way funny.

He said nothing for a moment, but when Lila braved a glance back at him, she saw a sad sort of resolution mixed with his disbelief.

"You really think I'm capable of something like that?" he asked.

She sighed and glanced away again. "Look, it's nothing personal. All you guys are capable of it, and too many of you are prone to it."

"Meaning you've encountered more than your fair share," he concluded.

"Hey, at least I know how to handle them," she said evenly, looking at him again. "A lot of women aren't so lucky."

He started to say something else, evidently decided against it, and only nodded. Then he grabbed the clipboard, the top sheet of which looked like notes for a chemistry assignment, and dropped it into his lap. Lila relaxed a little more as she watched him flip idly through the pages beneath it, each containing notes of a different kind, all encoded. But somehow she suspected he wasn't looking at any of them as closely as he should.

"Have a good day at school, Jenny," he said, emphasizing her name as if needing to remind them both who she was and why they were here. Then, doing a better job of being Ned Collins now, he continued, "I hope you don't get lost wandering around campus or forget your schedule."

Meaning, Lila translated, he wanted her to familiarize herself with the campus layout and the schedules of their primary suspects.

"Figure out where the cool kids hang out," he added, "and try to make some new friends."

In other words, Lila thought, find out which buildings and establishments were most popular with the type of student they'd pegged as Sorcerer's most likely contacts and try to put faces to the few names OPUS had managed to cull from the handful of e-mails they'd intercepted.

"Don't worry about your library books," he told her, "since they aren't due until tomorrow."

Meaning she could wait until tomorrow to check out the computer lab at the library.

He continued, "Get as much studying done as you can over the next few days, because once you start work at the coffee shop later this week, you're going to have less time for homework."

Translation, hurry up and get this thing done.

He didn't need to tell her twice. Lila was finding more reasons every moment to finish this job as soon as she could.

"When you get home tonight, Jenny," he concluded, "we'll have lots to talk about. Lots of plans to make."

Lila nodded. She understood that tonight he'd expect a full report on everything she saw and heard today so they could decide what their next step in the investigation would be. Dealing with Sorcerer, OPUS had learned, was best done in small steps. Too much planning, and the guy slipped through their fingers. One day at a time was the best way to go about dealing with a guy like Sorcerer.

And maybe for other guys, too, Lila was beginning to realize.

"I'll do my best," she said as she opened the car door and stepped out. And then, just because it seemed like the sort of thing a young woman having problems with her boyfriend would say in farewell, she told him, "Tonight, Ned, you and I can figure out how we're supposed to make this thing work."

YOU AND I CAN FIGURE out how we're supposed to make this thing work.

Lila's words echoed in Joel's brain as he watched her cross the parking lot toward the student center. She had some way of walking, he'd grant her that. It wasn't so much a sexy walk as it was one of supreme confidence. She held her head high, took long strides, moved along at a quick enough clip that her now-dark hair blew away from her face. Her backpack dangled off one shoulder comfortably, as if she carried one every day, and she offered no indication that she was making a thorough survey of her surroundings, even though he was sure she'd be familiar with every brick on campus by day's end. Had he not known better, he would have thought she was just another college-age kid laughing in the face of both menace and mortality because she was too innocent of the world and too arrogant with youth not to be.

But she wasn't young. And she wasn't innocent. He remembered the quickness with which she'd reacted when she thought he was going to hit her and wondered how many men in her past had tried to hurt her. How many had succeeded? How many hands had connected with that beautiful face before she'd learned—or become strong enough—to deflect them? How often had she started to care for someone who had then turned on her? Hell, it was no wonder she threw up as many barriers as she did. No wonder she closed herself off emotionally from the rest of the world.

He sighed as he watched her figure grow smaller, and only when she was completely out of sight did he finally turn the key in the ignition and back out of his parking space. Lila wasn't the only one with a job to do today. Or, rather, Jenny wasn't the only one with a job to do today. Joel was having a tough time seeing her as anything other than what he knew her to be, which was obvious by the way he'd fallen so completely out of character while talking to her. Hell, he'd never even been in character.

But then, Lila hadn't, either, he reflected. He, at least, had an excuse for his lapse—he wasn't used to working this way. For her, though, there was no other way. Yet she'd crossed the line from professional to personal while they were talking, too. Why?

He immediately pushed the question away. There were millions of reasons. He wasn't her usual partner, so of course she wouldn't be as comfortable playing a role as she normally would. They'd just started being Jenny and Ned— maybe it took her time to get into character and stay there. Infiltrating a college campus wasn't quite as dangerous as infiltrating a foreign government or domestic crime situation, so maybe she didn't think it was as necessary to maintain a veneer when it was just the two of them seated in a closed-up car.

Whatever.

Whoever he was, Joel had some things to unpack and set up in their apartment, and he wanted to familiarize himself with the area around Vine Street. Not that he'd be out in the field much, since that was Lila's job, but a guy liked to have at least some idea of what was going on around him.

He expelled a derisive chuckle at the thought. As if any man could know what was going on around him when he was anywhere near Lila Moreau. And now Joel would be living with her. Separate rooms and separate beds, to be sure. Separate jobs and separate timetables. But not separate lives.

It had been a long time since Joel had allowed anyone of the feminine persuasion to get as close to him—emotionally *or* physically—as Lila had in only a few days. Already he'd wrestled with her under covers long enough to appreciate the luscious curves of her body, and already she'd pushed enough of his buttons to get out of him reactions he hadn't had for a very long time.

He'd sworn almost five years ago that the next time he shared a roof with a woman, it would be because she'd agreed to share her life and herself with him, too. Now he'd be sharing a roof with a woman who went out of her way to keep her life and herself distant from others. And already he was thinking about what it would be like to wrestle with her under covers again. Worse, he was thinking about what it would take to get her to respond to him with the same sort of passion she'd roused in him. Good and bad. Hot and cold. Better and worse.

You and I can figure out how we're supposed to make this thing work.

Only two days into their assignment, Joel thought, and he was already beginning to fear that both it and he were doomed.

HER SECOND DAY ON CAMPUS, Lila struck pay dirt. Or, at least, some kind of dirt. And she found it in the Waverly library.

It was newer than the other buildings, made of cement instead of brick, and where libraries generally connoted great works of literature, the Waverly library was filled to capacity with tech journals and textbooks and all kinds of technological wonders. Lila had no trouble finding the computer lab when she went specifically in search of it, because the rest of the library seemed to have been built around it.

According to her information, a computer engineering student named Chuck Miller was supposed to be working his shift in the lab from two until four, meaning he was right in the middle of it when Lila entered the building. He was one of less than a dozen Waverly students OPUS had been able to positively identify as some of Sorcerer's contacts, and the first on Lila's list of people to investigate, since he was easiest to find, thanks to his having a job. He was twenty-one years old, had an IQ that made da Vinci look like a drive-through worker, and was scraping by with barely passing grades because he spent most of his free time—and most of his school time and meal time and sleeping time, too—on gaming.

Sure enough, when Lila stumbled into the computer lab— literally, because she was trying to look stupid, since she suspected Chuck was the kind of guy for whom that would be a turn-on—he wasn't working behind the information desk, but had plugged game controls into one of the school computers and was blowing the heads off virtual zombies. So he wasn't even noticing that Lila was being stupid to lull him into a false sense of security.

Man, she hated it when that happened.

"Uh, excuse me?" she said.

No response from Mr. Miller.

"Um, hello?"

This time his response was, "Die, you alien zombie scum, die!" But Lila was pretty sure he wasn't talking to her.

"*Excu-u-u-u-se* me?" She tried again. "Could you help me out? I'm kinda new here."

Her voice must have finally cut through the video-induced daze, because he turned his head far enough to mutter, "Hang on—lemme finish this level" before going back to his game.

While he was finishing up, Lila took a moment to compare what she saw of him now to what she'd learned in his file. Sandy hair poked out from beneath the backward-turned ball cap embroidered with the words "Ghetto Mafia"—yeah, play that urban hip-hop, white boy. Although he still had his back to her, she knew from his photo that he sported a goatee of a slightly darker shade than his hair, that he had gray eyes and that he wasn't a bad-looking kid. Although broad shoulders strained at the sleeves of his gray T-shirt, he had a lanky build, standing six-two and weighing only 170 pounds. And he'd just broken up with a steady girlfriend, due to his habit of hooking up with any woman who came on to him in a drunken stupor at parties.

Squeezing info from him ought to be a piece of cake for someone like Lila. Hell, squeezing info from him would be a piece of cake for anything that claimed two marginally human X chromosomes.

Thankfully, Lila did *not* have to maim him to get his attention again, because he finished the level he was trying to complete right when she was cracking her knuckles and looking around for a blunt object. Kind of a shame, too, she thought as he tossed down the game controls and stood to hitch up the baggy black cargo pants that dipped below the waistband of his tie-dyed boxer shorts. She'd never smacked anyone upside the head with a book trolley before. She wouldn't have minded seeing how effective it was. Could come in handy someday.

Ah, well. Maybe another time.

"Yeah?" Chuck said eloquently as he turned around. Still hitching up the baggy cargo pants that still dipped below the waistband of his tie-dyed boxers.

Miraculously, Lila was able to refrain from saying, "Hey, moron, if you'd buy your pants the right size, you wouldn't have that problem," and instead asked—again— "Can you help me out? I'm looking for the computer lab. Could you point me in the right direction?"

She threw him her most vapid smile, then tucked her hands into her extra-low-riding jeans to push them even farther down, thereby revealing an even wider strip of naked torso beneath her cropped black sweater. She didn't have the exposed underwear problem that Chuck did. Mostly because she wasn't wearing any underwear, something else she hoped he noticed.

She was fairly certain he did by the way he dropped his gaze to her torso and licked his lips. Honestly. This was going to be way too easy. College guys were no challenge at all. At this rate, Lila would have Sorcerer tucked into her back pocket in no time. Except for the fact that the pockets on these damned extra-low-riding jeans were pretty much nonexistent. Obviously, guys weren't the only ones who wore pants in moronic sizes.

"Um, hello?" she said when Chuck remained silent and only continued to stare at her midsection. She took a few steps forward and waved a hand in front of his face to get his attention, until he finally pulled his gaze up from her torso.

But it halted again at her breasts, the generous tops of which were revealed by the low-cut sweater. Oh, yeah. Chuck wasn't going to be any problem at all.

"My name's Chuck. Chuck Miller. Nice to meet you," he told her breasts.

"You, too," Lila replied on their behalf. "I'm Jenny Sturgis. And I could really use your help."

Finally, finally, he drove his gaze up to her face. Then he smiled, clearly liking that part of her, too. Whew. That was *such* a relief. She'd sleep *so* much better tonight, knowing Chuck Miller approved of her physical appearance.

"What can I do for you?" he asked, clearly having heard not a word of what she'd said so far.

"I'm looking for the computer lab," she said again, donning the most empty-brained expression she had in her arsenal. Though Chuck's brain was certainly giving her a run for her money on that score. "This is my first semester at Waverly," she added, "and I'm not all that familiar with the library."

He grinned, one of those grins guys used when they were vastly amused by something. "You're standing in the computer lab," he said.

Lila uttered a single, embarrassed chuckle and rolled her eyes. "Oh, duh," she said. "I've never had to use it before, so I didn't know."

"Don't worry about it," Chuck told her magnanimously. "It's a big library. Easy to get confused."

Yeah, if you were a carpet remnant, Lila thought. Tiny Waverly library was about as difficult to navigate as the inside of a sock. "So then could you help me?" she asked. "I have this huge paper due in a week, and I need to find a lot of stuff on the Internet. I could use some tips."

"No problem," he assured her. "Just tell me your needs. I'm sure I can satisfy *all* of them." He threw her what she guessed was supposed to be a sexy, suggestive smile, but mostly he ended up looking like some creepy guy who was leering at her.

"Cool," she said, battling a major wiggins. "Thanks." She turned toward the computer he'd just vacated and upon which still danced the graphics of his abandoned game. She lifted her chin toward it and asked, "What were you playing? Looked interesting."

"Alien Annihilation," he told her. "Just came out. It's awesome. You into gaming?"

She lifted a shoulder and let it drop in a way that made the scoop-necked sweater fall onto her arm, then didn't bother to fix it. Chuck, she noticed, noticed. "Some," she said. She wrinkled her nose becomingly. "Not the bloody ones, though. I like RPGs. Golden Sun. Final Fantasy. Stuff like that."

Now Chuck was the one to roll his eyes. "Fairies and magic. Bullshit crap that doesn't even exist."

Instead of calling him on the excremental redundancy, Lila retorted, "Oh, yeah, like alien zombies are *so* much more realistic."

They talked games more than they did research for the better part of the hour that ensued, long enough for Lila to impart nearly everything she'd learned about gaming…and to charm Chuck into inviting her to a party the following night at the very fraternity Joel had said OPUS was interested in further investigating.

After writing down directions for her, Chuck hooked his hands on his hips—then immediately had to hitch up his pants again—and added, "Bring a date, if you want." But he said it in the way guys do when they really don't want a woman to bring a date—unless her date is another woman.

"Yeah, well, I guess I could, but maybe I'll come by myself," Lila replied in a way that indicated she was indeed dating someone but was currently really pissed off at the SOB.

Chuck smiled. "Sounds good."

Lila smiled back as she tucked the paper he'd given her into her back pocket, deliberately shoving her jeans even lower on her hips. Chuck, she noticed again, noticed again. "Yeah," she told him as she watched him lick his lips once more, "it does sound good."

CHAPTER SEVEN

"HI, HONEY! I'M HO-OME!"

Only when Joel heard Lila's voice in the living room—followed by the slamming of the door behind her, which he was absolutely certain must have been accidental—did he realize how late it was. He'd been in his bedroom working at his laptop with only minimal breaks ever since he'd heard her leave for school that morning—following the slamming of the door behind her, which he was absolutely certain must have been accidental—and now it was...

He turned his wrist to glance at his watch. Wow. After six. She was supposed to have been home two hours ago. He launched himself into a full-body stretch, scrubbing his hands through his dark hair and removing his glasses to rub his eyes. His stomach grumbled hungrily its neglect, and he absently dropped a hand over the untucked navy blue T-shirt he wore with his jeans. He stretched some more and stood, donning his glasses again before padding barefoot toward the living room to greet her.

They had been in Cincinnati for three days now, and each evening had been more difficult than the one preceding it. In spite of how they'd parted ways on campus the day before, assuring each other they would talk when they regrouped, by the time evening had arrived and they'd sat across from each other at the table, they'd barely been able to share information. Not because they had nothing to say. Not even because they weren't getting along. Yes, their relationship had been strained since leaving D.C., but save for the occasional exchange like the one yesterday about college life, they'd managed to be civil to each other and behave in a reasonably professional manner.

Until nightfall.

Something just…happened…when the sun went down. Things between them just…changed. Joel didn't know why, but whenever he and Lila were sharing the same air in the evenings, that air seemed to become heavy and stifling and dense. Not exactly noxious—well, not quite—but not sustainable for life, either. It was hard to breathe around Lila once the sun went down. Which made it hard to communicate. Hard to think. Except about things he shouldn't be thinking about. Like what two people living together often did once the sun went down.

During the day he was alone, with plenty of work to keep him occupied, just as Lila was. But in the evenings—and at night—she was home, too, shattering not only his solitude, but his peace of mind. And she seemed no less immune to the tension, because she was no more communicative, no more cooperative than he was. She seemed to have as much trouble articulating her thoughts as Joel did. And she seemed to find it as difficult to analyze their individual discoveries as he. As a result, three days into the investigation they weren't much further along than they'd been when they arrived, something that only added to their frustration.

Which, consequently, made the tension in the air multiply. Which started the cycle all over again.

Not that there had really been much information for them to share yesterday that was a revelation, anyway, since most of what Lila learned on campus the day before had only served to back up what OPUS already knew. Joel was hoping that today, however, by approaching Chuck Miller, the first of their suspects, she might have learned something that would provide them with a breakthrough of some kind. Or, at the very least, something to focus on other than the awkwardness that descended on them whenever they were alone together.

"So…Jenny," he began as he made his way out of his bedroom, stumbling over her assigned name, just as he always stumbled over it when he had to call her that. "How was school today?"

He halted in his tracks when he saw her, his gaze falling on the creamy band—none too narrow—of bare back that was revealed between her jeans and her brief black sweater as she bent to place her backpack on the floor. Had the waistband of those jeans been any lower, he was certain they would have revealed more of her backside than she'd be comfortable having him see. As it was, he was treated to the sight of two *very* alluring dimples on each side of her spine at its base. He knew her attire was part of her cover and nothing more than a deliberate ploy to wreak havoc with the college boys she was investigating, but Joel was no less immune than some randy kid would be.

That was made all the more obvious when she spun around quickly enough to send her sweater flying off one shoulder, even though she immediately tugged it back into place again. Because thanks to even that quick wardrobe malfunction, he now knew she wasn't wearing a bra under her sweater, just as he was reasonably certain there were no panties on earth minuscule enough to hide beneath jeans as low as hers. And having the knowledge ricocheting around in his head that she wore so little made other parts of his body react in ways he'd just as soon not have them reacting. He was just thankful his shirttail was long enough that he didn't have to worry about Lila being able to witness his quickly rising, ah, mood.

Although the apartment claimed two bedrooms, it was uncomfortably small, as suited a couple of struggling college students. The tiny galley kitchen in whose entrance Lila stood was barely a dozen steps from where Joel leaned in his bedroom doorway. Between the two of them was the living/dining area, a near-perfect square of scuffed hardwood floor and beige walls, furnished, as furnished apartments usually were, with really ugly furniture in varying shades of brown. The kitchen cabinets were also brown, as was the aged linoleum on the floor in there. The bathroom was the only room in the place that boasted anything remotely resembling color. If one could consider yellow as pale as a stick of butter a color. The tiles, it went without saying, were tan.

"What's for dinner?" she asked by way of a greeting, turning back around again before Joel had a chance to reply. She punctuated the question by stepping into the kitchen to investigate the cabinet contents, with the slamming of several doors that he was absolutely certain must be accidental.

"Whatever you want to have delivered is fine with me,"

he said without moving from his position. "Or we could go out and get something."

"You didn't cook?" she asked, turning to look at him again. But this time it was slowly enough that none of her clothing went missing. Alas.

"*You* didn't cook?" he immediately replied.

"I *don't* cook," she told him.

"I don't cook, either."

She shifted her weight to one foot and crossed her arms over her midsection, hiding that expanse of naked flesh. Alas. "This could get problematic," she said.

"How so?"

"One of us needs to be able to cook."

"Why?"

"Because if we order in all the time, we'll draw attention to ourselves."

"No, we won't. We're college students who are either too lazy or disinclined or lacking in knowledge to cook."

She wanted to argue, he could tell. Not that that was surprising, because Lila had wanted to argue about everything since discovering that the two of them would be working together. That was the one method of communication they *had* managed to master. She knew as well as Joel did that it made no difference what their eating habits were. She just wanted to pick a fight with him. And he wasn't going to rise to the bait. Which, he knew, would make her that much more determined to fight about something else.

Ah, well. Looked as if it was going to be business as usual this evening, after all.

"Aren't you going to ask me why I'm late getting home?"

she asked. "I mean, I *am* late. I told you I'd be back by four. You've probably been worrying for hours."

To be deliberately obtuse, he replied blandly, "Are you? I hadn't noticed. What time is it, anyway?" He turned his wrist to look at his watch again. "Wow, you are late," he added dispassionately. But he said nothing more.

Okay, so maybe Lila wasn't the only one who'd been finding opportunities to pick fights, he conceded. There was just something about her that always made him feel horny. *Ornery,* he immediately corrected himself. Irritable, he further amended. Just a shot in the dark, but that probably had something to do with the fact that, simply by looking at her, he felt himself reacting in ways he didn't want to react. In ways he'd sworn he *wouldn't* react. Not until he met the woman with whom he intended to spend, if not the rest of his life, then certainly the next big chunk of it. Lila Moreau wasn't one for relationships. She wasn't one for companionship, either. Or even friendship. No, the only -ship that woman could be counted on to board would be one that passed him in the night. Before slamming into a giant iceberg.

For a long moment neither of them spoke, only glared at each other from opposite sides of the apartment as if each was daring the other to look away first. And although Lila didn't look away, she did finally say, "How about if I order a pizza?"

So Joel figured he could concede the next point by being the one to break eye contact first. "Fine," he said as he removed his glasses to rub his eyes again. By the time he put them back on, Lila had already retrieved the Yellow Pages from atop the fridge and was hastily flipping through them.

"But I only want veggies on my half," he added. "Whatever they've got."

"I'll have the meat lover's version on my half," she decided. Doubtless just to be contrary. Or maybe to remind him what a predator she was.

"So what did you learn at school today?" he asked when she hung up the phone.

She sauntered with great self-importance into the living room and collapsed onto the ugly brown sofa. "Well, it was a helluva lot more than that the capital of Nevada is Carson City, lemme tell ya."

Joel covered the half dozen steps necessary to fold himself into the ugly brown chair next to the ugly brown sofa. Leaning back, he propped his feet on the rickety—and ugly brown—coffee table and wove his fingers together in his lap. "Such as?"

"Not only did I make a new friend named Chuck Miller, but I was invited to a frat party this weekend. At the very house where you wanted to be rushed, but you didn't on account of you're such a big geek and joined that other one instead."

He narrowed his eyes at her, stifling the disgusted growl he felt threatening. He hated sharing information this way, as if they really were Jenny Sturgis and Ned Collins, struggling college students and quarrelsome lovers. He knew OPUS protocol dictated they stay in character at all times during the investigation, and they could certainly make their points through double entendres and carefully phrased remarks. But he didn't see why they should. There was no way Sorcerer could know they were here, and even if he suspected they were, there was no chance he knew where they were living. That information had been carefully guarded, so he was confident they weren't under surveillance and were perfectly safe to speak frankly.

Nevertheless, hoping he didn't sound too uncaring for a guy whose girlfriend had just been hit on, he replied, "Terrific. I can't wait. When are we expected?"

"*I'm* expected tomorrow at seven," she said. "Your name wasn't included in the invitation."

He threw her an oh-I-don't-*think*-so glare and said in a phony, chirpy voice, "Gosh, Jenny, but I'm your boyfriend Ned. I go everywhere with you, remember?"

She, too, poured on the syrup when she replied brightly, "Golly willikers, Ned, I don't want you to come with me. I want to meet some new boys. Besides, you're a terrible, um, dancer. You wouldn't know the first thing about getting down."

Oh, he knew more than she thought. But he kept it to himself. "I'm a better, um, dancer than you think. You're not going to this party alone."

She sobered and met his eyes levelly as she told him, "You're not coming with me. Those frat boys can be dangerous."

He laughed in earnest at that, dropping the pretense. "Oh, come on. It's a frat party, not Kim Jong-il's summer retreat. How dangerous could it be?"

"I'll have more fun without you," she said. Then she, too, abandoned the ruse. "Look, Joel, I'll be able to learn a lot more if you're not there."

He told himself to correct her for slipping out of character, since he was the one in charge and was responsible for maintaining protocol. But he really didn't care. They were safe, and there was no chance anyone was listening in. And quite frankly, he felt silly. Hey, James Bond never assumed alternative identities.

So he only asked, "How do you know you'll learn more without me there? I could be valuable backup."

She settled herself more comfortably on the sofa—which was suddenly much less ugly than it had been a little while ago—then propped her feet up on the coffee table within inches of Joel's. She'd kicked off her shoes, so her feet, like his, were bare, but that's where any similarity ended. Lila's feet were half the size of his, and her toenails were painted bloodred. Her toes were crooked, he noticed, the big ones of each foot bending slightly inward, the third of each rising slightly above the rest. Strangely, Joel found the imperfections sexy as hell.

"If you tag along," she said wearily, "it will have to be as my date. A woman with a date in an environment like that is generally left alone. A woman *alone* in an environment like that is generally surrounded. Especially if she's had too much to drink."

"You don't drink," Joel reminded her.

"They don't know that. And I fake inebriation supremely well." She grinned. "As a drunk chick, I'll be led immediately to parts of the house you'll never see, plagued as you are by the equipment you're carrying around. I'll have access to the guys' private quarters." She smiled as she added, "And to their bedrooms, too."

Joel clamped his teeth together tight at her mention of his

equipment, since that equipment was in no way plaguing him. In fact, at the moment it was functioning way better than it generally did, thanks to her inadvertently having flashed him the way she had in the kitchen. Though if she kept sniping at him, that probably wasn't going to be the case for long.

What bugged him even more, though, he was irritated to realize, was how much it bothered him that she was thinking about other guys', ah, private quarters, even if she was only thinking of them in terms of doing the job.

This was Not Good, he thought. He was once again feeling as randy as a teenager. Hell, randier, because as a teenager he hadn't known what he was missing when it came to sex. As a man of thirty-eight, he'd been around the block more than a few times, and he could imagine too well what sex with Lila would be like. Incredible. Mind scrambling. Life altering. And possibly illegal in at least seventeen states.

He pushed the thought away. Hell, it would be back soon enough. "And if you find yourself in a part of that house outnumbered by a bunch of drunken college boys," he said, "which is entirely possible the way these parties often play out, it might be good for you to have a little backup."

"Oh, please," she said. "I can handle a bunch of drunken college boys."

"Maybe," Joel conceded. "But I'd feel better if I went to the party with you."

She raised her arms over her head and folded her elbows, cradling the back of her head in her hands, an action that caused her sweater to rise over her midsection again. Her abs were flat and well-defined, faintly sculpted musculature covered by silky, flawless flesh. Just like that, Joel's equipment was up and running again. At maximum throttle. With a full tank of gas. And an all-night drive ahead of it. Damn.

"If you tag along," she said, "it'll just make it more difficult for me to connect with Chuck and the boys."

He blew out an exasperated breath. Mostly because he knew she was right. If she went to the party alone, dressed even half as provocatively as she was right now, she'd have those guys eating out of her hand. But booze and college boys could be a toxic libation, and Lila was used to dealing with men much older and not so ruled by their hormones. Joel remembered—too well at the moment, in fact—what unbridled young testosterone could do to a guy. And he wasn't sure Lila really appreciated that after being away from it for so many years.

"Compromise," he finally said. "I'll go with you to the party as your boyfriend." He held up a hand when she opened her mouth to object. "Let me finish. We can show up looking like we're obviously on rocky terms. Maybe we just had an argument before we left, maybe we can stage an argument while we're there. Then you can go look for a little revenge by cozying up with Chuck. At least I'll still be around if you need me."

"I won't need you," she said with absolute conviction.

Joel didn't doubt it for a moment. But he was pretty sure the two of them were thinking in completely different terms about what she wouldn't need him for. Lila thought she wouldn't need him for anything, ever. And, okay, maybe she *didn't* need him outside the job. But until he could convince himself that she didn't need him inside it either, he was going to stick close. What bothered him was that he was beginning to suspect he would always want to do that, regardless of how things were with Lila.

Great, he thought. Just great. He hadn't been this attracted to a woman in ages. Maybe never. That was the reason he'd been able to keep his promise to himself for as long as he had and had abstained from having sex for almost five years. His decision hadn't come about because he'd awoken one morning and suddenly become morally righteous. It was because, after spending nearly a decade moving from one woman to another—monthly, weekly, even nightly sometimes—sex, for Joel, had become no more meaningful a bodily function than perspiring or digesting food.

He'd been a late bloomer sexually, so had worked hard to make up for lost time. But instead of being exciting and erotic, the frequency and variety and abundance of women had made sex seem almost routine. He'd finally realized that for sex to mean something to him, the woman with whom he was having sex would have to mean something, too. So he'd decided to wait until he met someone special who would make sex special, too. He just hadn't expected his celibacy would last as long as it had.

Just his luck that when he finally met a woman who was special, she'd be so special that she was one of a kind. Joel hadn't known Lila for even a week, and once the assignment was over, he'd never see her again. Even so, he knew without question that she would be with him forever.

Pushing that thought away, too, since he was sure it would also come back later to haunt him, he folded his arms over his midsection and met her gaze again. And then he said, "So tell me what else happened at school today."

CHAPTER EIGHT

IN HIS SUITE AT THE Four Seasons, Adrian Padgett sat in midnight-blue silk pajama bottoms and matching robe—appropriate, since it was just after midnight—and cradled his usual snifter of Armagnac in his left hand. He ignored three now-closed file folders that were stacked neatly on the desk before him, because he was much too interested in a fourth that lay open with its contents fanned out before him. Where Chuck and Donny and Hobie had turned out to be precisely who they claimed to be, and were therefore in no way remarkable, Iris Daugherty was, as of this moment, even more fascinating/intriguing/worthy of preoccupation than Adrian had initially thought. She, like he, was pretending to be someone she wasn't.

She'd been born Trisha Harrington. Of the Philadelphia Harringtons. A family that wielded rather a lot of power in that city and others, thanks to generations-old wealth, generations-old power and a generations-old reputation. To put it politely, the Harringtons of Philadelphia were a family who had achieved their social status through less than ethical means. To put it truthfully, the Harringtons of Philadelphia were a bunch of thugs.

Such thugs that every other crime family in the north-east—and in the South and on the West Coast and in the Midwest, too—gave them a wide berth. The Harringtons weren't trustworthy criminals, the other families said. They were loose cannons who didn't abide by any code of honor, even the bendable one generally adhered to by thieves and pushers and pimps and murderers. The Harringtons would just as soon shoot you—or stab you or poison you or pound you with a brick—as they would look at you. And then they would chop you up into little pieces. And then they would bake part of you into a cake. A birthday cake. For your child's birthday. And then they would wrap up the rest of you in brightly colored paper as a gift for the same child.

Iris, née Trisha, was the granddaughter of the Big Man himself, Nathaniel Harrington. Her father, Benjamin, was currently being groomed by Nathaniel to take over that grand vizier of crime position himself, because the old man was looking to retire and move to Florida, where he could play shuffleboard and bet on the ponies at Hialeah and chop up a new crop of people into little pieces for dessert. And since Benjamin had no other children besides Trisha, she had been raised and expected—and groomed—to move into the number two position her father currently occupied and would be soon vacating.

There was just one small problem. Trisha Harrington had disappeared only days after turning eighteen, and even after a years-long exhaustive search, none of the Harringtons had been able to find her. Ultimately, they'd had no choice but to conclude she was dead, probably killed by a rival family. Or even someone within the Harrington gang, looking to end the direct Harrington line and move leadership into a new direction. Or perhaps even by one of Nathaniel's trusted confidantes, who just couldn't stomach the idea of a woman rising to the upper echelons of power. So the Harringtons had officially called off the search for Trisha years ago, had done whatever passed for grieving among those who had no hearts and Benjamin had taken a new protégé under his wing.

They hadn't, however, canceled a reward they'd been offering since day one of Trisha's disappearance, for any information leading to her whereabouts. To the tune of one point five million dollars.

It was only because OPUS was OPUS and had ways of finding out things others could not—even the Philadelphia Harringtons—that Adrian's source in the organization had managed to discover that Iris was really Trisha. All Adrian had to do was pick up the phone this very moment, dial a number his source within OPUS had also provided, and he would be in touch with the very person who was in a position to award him seven figures for the return of the missing Harrington dame. It was no small change, even to a man bent on world domination. And it would be the easiest money he'd ever made. He would even be making it legitimately, which was virtually unheard of for him.

Or, better still, if he returned Iris to her father and grandfather, the two most powerful criminals in the country—perhaps even the world—Adrian would win their gratitude. He might even be able to manipulate the opportunity into winning the men as allies. And with allies like that in his corner, he wouldn't need amateurs like Chuck, Donny and Hobie. The Harringtons surely had a more effective network of hackers and thieves at their disposal, just waiting for the guidance and creativity of someone like Adrian.

He looked at the phone as he enjoyed another sip of his Armagnac, even went so far as to stroke the receiver as he gave the matter more thought.

One point five million dollars and a potential seat at the right hand of Nathaniel Harrington and his second, soon-to-be first, in command, in exchange for Iris Daugherty. Who had, Adrian gathered, muscled her way out from beneath the bosom of her psychotic family under her own steam nearly a decade ago and had been in hiding ever since. He settled his hand comfortably on the receiver, but something made him hesitate to pick it up. Something that felt vaguely like…

What? he asked himself. He was having trouble identifying what the feeling was. Probably because it was something he couldn't recall ever feeling before. It was somewhat familiar—he just couldn't put his finger on quite how. But there was a definite feeling there of…

Protection, he was astonished to finally realize. A desire to protect Iris. How bizarre. The only person Adrian had ever worried about protecting was himself. Yet here he sat, thinking that if Iris was hiding from her family, it meant she had no desire to be reunited with them, even if they were still looking for her. And strangely, where Adrian would normally look to capitalize on such a situation, he instead found himself leaning toward keeping Iris's secret.

He didn't have much time to think about his epiphany, however, because a beep at the door signaled the key card was being inserted to open it. It wasn't unusual for one of the boys to use the suite from time to time, especially on the weekends with a date in tow. More than once, Adrian had returned to his room after a late evening looking for love, or something, in all the wrong places—and usually finding it, thankfully—only to discover that some other love had occurred in his own bed while he was out. And college boys weren't known for their tidiness when it came to sex. On those nights, Adrian had been forced to sleep on the sofa bed in the adjoining room. But he needed the little bastards on his side, so he never rebuked them. He'd be damned, however, if he would vacate the premises for them. Besides, the weekend was still a day away. It was a school night, for God's sake.

He was about to call out something along the lines of "Beat it, you thoughtless little bastard, it's a school night" when the door was pushed open from the other side and Iris's head poked through the opening. When she saw him seated at the desk, she entered, closing the door behind her and leaning against it. She was dressed in her usual black garb and makeup and was carrying her usual enormous black bag, and Adrian found himself wondering if she owned anything that claimed even a splash of color. He also wondered what she was doing here at this hour. Not that he couldn't think of one or two reasons to go visiting after midnight. He just doubted hers mirrored his. Unless she was as big a fan of naked Twister and Crisco as he was.

"I'm glad you're still up," she said. "I didn't want to wake you."

He began gathering up the contents of her file, feigning a casualness he didn't feel, but not wanting her to become suspicious. "What are you doing here, Iris?" he asked cautiously.

She took a few steps into the room, but halted suddenly, as if she were uncertain of her reception. "Is it okay if I crash here tonight? I'll sleep out here in the living room."

He was about to ask her why she would do something like that when the two of them could have so much more fun together in the bedroom—even without the Crisco and Twister board—but for some reason kept his mouth shut. Again he was surprised by his behavior, because he normally would have taken complete advantage of the situation—and Iris. Again he decided to think about it later.

"Of course you can stay," he told her. Then, deliberately, he added, "Problems at home?"

She uttered a small, helpless sound and muttered, "You have no idea."

He arched an eyebrow. "You could enlighten me."

She crossed her arms restlessly over her midsection, then uncrossed them and settled her hands on her hips. But that must not have been comfortable either, because she then cupped both hands nervously behind her neck. Finally she said, "My roommate's scumbag boyfriend is spending the night again, and the two of them are so drunk, they're trying to get me to go along with a threesome."

Adrian's other eyebrow joined the first. "Really," he said. "And you object to this because…?"

Iris gaped at him. "Because the guy is totally heinous, that's why. He's like Napoleon Dynamite. Only without the dancing."

Whoever the hell that was, Adrian thought, feeling himself starting to age again.

Oh, well, he tried to console himself. As long as Iris's reluctance was due only to the third member of the party being unpalatable. Adrian started to ask her why she hadn't brought her roommate with her to the hotel then, so that he could be the additional member of the party—to put it a bit crassly—but again stopped himself. There was plenty of time for fun and sex games later. Right now he had another sort of game in mind. Besides the naked Twister and Crisco, he meant.

"Drink?" he asked Iris as he lifted the snifter to his mouth again.

She shook her head. "No. Thanks. Just a place to crash."

"Do you have everything you need?" he asked further. "Should I call down to the concierge for anything? Shampoo? Toothpaste?" *Crisco? Twister board?*

She shook her head again. "No, I have everything I need in here." She slung her enormous bag over her head. "I always keep it ready, because I never know when I have to jam."

Adrian narrowed his eyes at that last comment. Wait a minute. He recognized that line. Wasn't that what Ally Sheedy's character had said in *The Breakfast Club?* And no one had taken her seriously either. Then again, Ally's dad hadn't been all mobbed up, had he? If he had, maybe Judd Nelson and Emilio Estevez might have been more apt to listen to her. In any case, what a remarkable event. Adrian and Iris had just connected on a level he could appreciate. She'd cited a pop culture reference he actually understood. Of course, it was probably a coincidence and Iris doubtless had no idea who Ally Sheedy was, but Adrian was going to celebrate his and Iris's union anyway by enjoying another sip of his drink. Which he did, draining it.

"Are you hungry?" he asked when he lowered the empty snifter. "I could order you something from room service." He dipped his head toward her bag. "Just a shot in the dark, but

I'm betting you don't have a nice succulent filet in there." Not that the filet he'd had for dinner had been especially succulent, he recalled. "Or even a club sandwich." Not that the club sandwich he'd had for lunch had been especially succulent, either.

She thrust her chin up indignantly at his suggestions that she did not, in fact, have everything she needed in her disreputable-looking bag. "I'm a vegetarian," she told him. Then, as if to illustrate that fact, she unzipped the bag and reached into it, withdrawing a pear from which she enjoyed a big, crunchy bite.

Adrian sighed and reached for the phone. "Fine," he said as he pushed the number for room service, which, by now, he knew by heart. "I'll ask them to send up a salad." As he waited for an answer at the other end of the line, he added, "And a nice pinot noir. And another Armagnac for myself." And maybe he'd see if they had a Twister board, just in case. In lieu of Crisco, which he was reasonably certain hotels didn't stock for their guests, they could just use the butter pat from the bread that came with the salad.

"Thanks," Iris said.

Adrian waved off her gratitude quite literally as someone at the other end of the line picked up.

"Mind if I use your shower?" she asked once he'd concluded the order and hung up. She shifted her weight from one foot to the other, as if she felt awkward about voicing the question.

"Not at all," he said, extending his hand in that direction. "By the time you're finished in there, your food should be here."

She opened her mouth as if she intended to say something else, but closed it again before any words emerged. With a single quick nod, she retreated to the bathroom, and a moment later Adrian heard the water running. He indulged in a quick fantasy about slipping out of his robe and pajamas and joining her, then decided against it. For some reason, he rather liked the idea of Iris approaching him first. Which was a startling thing to realize. Usually he liked to be the initiator of any sexual contact. And he liked to be the one who concluded it. In fact, he liked being the one in control of anything sexual at all times.

With Iris, however, he found the idea of her coming to him first intriguing. Maybe because she worked so hard to keep herself to herself and went out of her way to illustrate her indifference to everything. Not that Adrian thought for a moment that she *was* indifferent about everything. But she certainly worked hard to make others think she was. If she emerged from her seemingly impenetrable shell far enough to take the initiative in a sexual liaison, it would mean she was exceptionally interested and, therefore, exceptionally eager.

He was still pondering that when she emerged from the bathroom after a lengthy soak in the tub, still dressed in black. This time in baggy black pajama bottoms decorated with tiny white skulls and a black tank top. She'd removed all her hardware and washed off the heavy eyeliner and lipstick, and Adrian was stunned to realize just how beautiful she really was. But it was a healthy, wholesome kind of beauty that evoked images of prairies and picnics and Sundays in the park, the sort of beauty to which he'd never, ever been attracted.

He told himself he liked her better with the black eyeliner and lipstick. Then he pictured her with the pale blond hair he knew was her natural color, and the cheerleader-in-the-heartland imagery returned. This time Adrian found himself liking what he saw in his mind's eye. The picture he had of Iris then was…fresh. Innocent. Full of possibility and potential. Empty of anger and artifice. The way life, he imagined, must be for other people. The way it should have been for him. And Iris, too.

"So. Iris," he began as she approached the desk where the attendant had left her dinner. "You and I have never really had a chance to chat."

She folded herself into the chair, but reached past the salad for the glass of wine first. "Yeah, well, you and the guys always seem to have something else going on," she said, the words tinged with just a hint of resentment. "You're all such busy little planners. Busy, busy, busy."

"No one ever said you couldn't be part of the planning," Adrian pointed out.

"No one ever said I could be, either," she replied.

His mouth dropped open. Was that petulance he heard in her voice now? And if so, what had caused it? Could Iris's feelings have been hurt? She, the woman who worked so hard to make them all think she didn't care about anything?

Well, color him shocked.

Before he could say anything, she was talking again. "I know what you guys think. You think because I don't have a pair, I don't know as much about computers and gaming and scamming as you guys do."

Oh, Adrian wouldn't say she didn't have a pair. She just

had a pair of something different, that was all. And quite a nice pair it was, too.

"But you might be surprised by some of the things I know," she told him. "You might be surprised by some of the things I've done."

"I don't think I'd be surprised," Adrian said. And then, before he realized he intended to do it, he added, "Trisha."

He had no idea what made him say her name aloud like that. He honestly hadn't made a conscious decision to out her. He'd still been toying with the idea of the reward, had still been thinking he might call that number and reveal her whereabouts to a family that still wanted her back very much. He told himself he must have made the decision subconsciously, to see if he could squeeze even more money out of Iris by agreeing *not* to report her location to her family. But there was nothing avaricious about his thoughts at the moment. There was only…curiosity. About Iris. As a person, not a price.

Her face paled at the sound of her name spoken aloud, and her blue eyes went dark as her pupils expanded in her terror. The wine glass slipped out of her fingers and onto the desk, splitting in two to spill a river of ruby-red across it and onto the carpet. Neither Adrian nor Iris moved to clean up the mess. They only looked at each other in silence—her eyes filled with fear, his, he imagined, filled with speculation.

She recovered quickly, however, leaping up and grabbing the linen napkin from her tray to mop ineffectively at the quickly spreading puddle. "Why did you call me Trisha?" she asked. And he had to give her credit, because there was nary a tremor in her voice when she spoke.

"Because that's your name," he replied. She continued to blot at the wine on the desktop, but mostly all she did was push more of it onto the floor. That was the problem with panic. The more you tried to contain it, the bigger the mess became. "Trisha Harrington," he continued when she neither confirmed nor denied his assertion. He steepled his fingers and leaned back comfortably in his chair as he went on. "Daughter of Benjamin Harrington. Granddaughter of Nathaniel Harrington. Last known address in the heart of Philadelphia's Chestnut Hill area—a quite lovely community, if I do say so myself. I never would have suspected such an ugly, ruthless crime element was thriving there," he added parenthetically. "Anyway, Trisha is currently missing and presumed dead, but she's quite valuable to anyone who could return her to her grieving family."

Iris continued to swipe fruitlessly at the spill, but her movements had slowed and become more mechanical. "A million five last time I heard," she finally said. "Though it's been a while since I checked."

"It hasn't gone up," Adrian told her. "It's still a million five."

She nodded, still wiping, still not looking at him. "I guess they've given up on finding me alive, then. But don't worry, Nick, they're not grieving. That would be impossible for them."

"Why is that?" he asked.

Her motions slowed some more, but she was still trying to clean up the mess—without much result. "Because you can't grieve when you don't have a heart."

Instead of commenting on that, he said, "I wouldn't say

they've given up on your being found alive. They've not re-scinded the reward. If they didn't think there was a chance of locating you, they would have taken that off the table a long time ago, wouldn't they?"

She lifted a shoulder and let it drop. "They're a pretty te-nacious lot. They don't like losing. Anything."

Interesting she would refer to herself as an any*thing* instead of an any*one,* Adrian thought.

Finally she looked up at him and met his gaze levelly. "So…have they located me?" she asked softly.

"Not yet," he replied honestly.

She straightened and squared her shoulders a little, look-ing like someone who was trying to decide whether or not there was any point in doing battle. "How long before some-one tells them where I am?"

Now Adrian folded his arms behind his head and leaned back even more in his chair. "I guess that depends on who else finds out where you are."

"You haven't told anyone?"

"No."

"Are you going to tell anyone?"

He started to reply with an honest *I don't know,* but instead heard himself reply with an honest, "No."

And he realized then, for the first time, that he genuinely had no intention of turning her over to her family. Not for profit. Not for gain. Not for anything.

"It could be worth a lot of money to you," she reminded him.

"Yes, it could."

"My family would be in your debt."

"They would indeed."

"They're very powerful."

"Yes, I know."

"They could do a lot for a guy like you."

"I know that, too."

She studied him in silence for another moment. "You're really not going to tell them where I am?"

He shook his head.

"Why not?"

He opened his mouth to reply honestly again, then closed it. Because he didn't want to reveal that just yet. He didn't want Iris to know that the reason he wouldn't reveal her whereabouts to her family was that she was worth so much more than her reward, and that he would rather have her in his debt than her family. As powerful as the Harringtons were, Iris was infinitely more so. Because she had made—and was making—Adrian feel and think things he hadn't thought himself capable of thinking or feeling. And until he had a handle on why that was, he would just as soon Iris not know how potent she was.

So he said dismissively, "Well, it's only a million five."

She expelled a single, humorless chuckle. "*Only* a million five. Nick, I have family members who would blow up a kindergarten for a fraction of that, then torch a nursing home to celebrate."

"Then they are exceedingly lacking in ambition," he said. "Because you and I, Iris, we could make a lot more than that together." Strangely, he realized he was talking about something other than money when he said that. He just wasn't sure he wanted to think about what.

Her dyed-black eyebrows arrowed downward. "How do I know I can trust you?"

Nick met her gaze unflinchingly. "I don't suppose you can know that," he said. "I suppose you'll just have to trust me."

"I've never trusted anyone before."

"Well, then. We have something in common. Neither have I."

"You could still call my family," she pointed out.

"I could."

"You could do it tonight, after I go to sleep."

He didn't bother to deny it. "I could indeed."

"I could wake up tomorrow surrounded by some of my father's favorite thugs."

"That's entirely possible."

"They could drag me back to Philadelphia, kicking and screaming, and you could just stand there counting your money."

"Right again."

"So how do I know you won't?"

His gaze never left hers. "You don't."

She inhaled a deep breath and released it on a long, shaky sigh.

"You're going to have to trust me, Iris. Or you're going to have to… How did you put it? Jam."

To illustrate that, Adrian rose and strode across the room to where she had dumped her big, ugly black bag. He picked it up and walked back over to where she stood, extending it toward her. Iris took it from him and clutched it tightly to herself.

"Everything you'll ever need is in there," he reminded her.

She shook her head slowly, her eyes never leaving his. "No," she said. "Not quite everything."

Adrian nodded, smiled and marveled at the warmth that suddenly seemed to radiate from somewhere deep inside his chest. But all he said was, "Sleep well, Iris."

CHAPTER NINE

THE DELTA UPSILON CHI house was one of a half dozen fraternity houses dotting a dead-end side street within walking distance of the Waverly campus. It fringed a neighborhood of tidy middle-class homes built shortly after the Second World War, Dutch colonials and bungalows interwoven with looming two- or three-story Federals. Most of the frat houses, including DUC house, were of that last persuasion. The fraternity's Greek letters hung above the expansive front porch of the square gray frame building, all but one of them looking fairly straight, and the yard wasn't *too* awfully unkempt.

Chuck Miller had two friends, Hobie Jurgens and Donny Grawemeyer, who were also on the short list of suspects and who also lived at DUC house, so their three computers would be the focus of Lila and Joel's search this evening. Joel, however, was going to try to hit every computer in the house before night's end.

She'd once again opted for the less-is-more approach when dressing for the party. Her low-slung khaki pants ended just below her knee, revealing a nice length of calf in addition to a swath of torso between them and the cropped, wine-colored tank top boasting the Waverly College logo. The black hoodie she'd thrown on in deference to the cool evening wasn't much longer than her top. Her dark hair tumbled loose past her shoulders, and she was starting to get used to the bangs hanging nearly in her eyes. Joel wore charcoal cargo pants and a baggy black sweater, which, coupled with his little black glasses and long dark hair—not to mention his own youthful looks—made convincing his role of bookish postgrad student.

What didn't fit the scenario was that Lila found the bookish postgrad-student look really, really sexy. She normally didn't go for the quiet type. Every man to whom she'd ever been drawn had been edgy, rough and not a little dangerous. So how come she kept having to battle the urge to slip those glasses from his nose, tug off the sweater and let nature take its course?

"Do you want to go over everything one more time before we go in?" he asked quietly as they turned up the walkway to the frat house.

"It's not necessary," she assured him. "Once is always enough for me." Before she could stop herself, she added with deliberate suggestiveness, "When it comes to the job, I mean."

She immediately regretted the comment. Joel might not realize it was a joke, the way her regular partner would have. She just hadn't been thinking. She'd already switched into undercover mode, which meant she had her flirtation device on, so she would be replying suggestively for the rest of the evening to anything said by anyone who claimed a Y chromosome. It was nothing personal when it came to Joel. It wasn't. She was just doing her job.

When she turned to him to explain, however, it was

obvious he *hadn't* taken the joke the way her partner Oliver would have. Oliver would have laughed and retorted with something like "So I hear from the boys in the OPUS mail room" and moved on. But Joel's dark eyes had somehow grown even darker, and his cheeks were ruddy with…something. Lila wasn't sure what. Embarrassment maybe. Anger perhaps. Because it surely couldn't be arousal. Not over such a lame comment. And not when the two of them were about to embark on an undercover penetration.

Oh, dammit, she thought as those final two words formed in her brain. Maybe Joel wasn't feeling aroused, but now Lila was. It had just been too long since she'd been in a position to—

Well, that was just the point. It had been a while since she'd been in a position. Any position. Preferably doggy-style, or maybe sitting astride him in a chair, or, wow, on the stairs—that was always fun—but it had been so long since Lila had been with a man that even the missionary position was sounding pretty damned hot.

Um, what was the question?

"What did you say?" he asked as he came to a halt beside her.

No, that wasn't the question. The question had had something to do with sex—she was sure of it.

Joel looked so flummoxed and flabbergasted and all those other old-fashioned terms for embarrassed that Lila finally remembered there hadn't been a question at all, and that what had actually happened was that she'd said something inappropriate. Well, inappropriate to a guy like Joel, anyway, who, in this day and age could still manage to be flummoxed and flabbergasted and all those other old-fashioned terms for embarrassed.

"Uh...that came out wrong," she said, doing her best to tamp down all thoughts of positions and undercover penetrations. "I'm sorry. Once I get into character for an undercover penetra—uh, I mean undercover operation, I just stop being me and start being whoever I'm supposed to be."

Except for the fact that, by saying what she just had, she'd dropped completely out of character and started being herself. Why was she having so much trouble maintaining her role? That was the easiest part of an assignment. Then she realized she hadn't really been playing the part of Jenny Sturgis since she'd arrived home from school at the apartment earlier in the day. But then, she thought further, if that was true, wouldn't it mean that when she made her suggestive comment to Joel just now, she'd done it as Lila, not Jenny?

Before she could ponder that, Joel said quietly, "Sounds to me like you're doing just the opposite now."

She bit her lip anxiously. He was right. In spite of that, she told him, "It was nothing personal."

But somehow that came out sounding wrong, too. Because it made it sound as if she didn't think Joel was worthy of a flirtation. And that wasn't true, either. At all.

"And I don't need to go over the plan again," she added, still out of character. And not much caring. Which should probably concern her. But she wasn't much concerned, either.

The plan was simple. Immediately upon arrival, Lila and Joel would make clear that Jenny and Ned weren't getting along, and their tension would grow as the night progressed. When the timing was right they would argue, and he would threaten her, so that Chuck could step in and be a hero. That would give Lila an excuse to remain close to him and his friends for the remainder of the evening. Joel, the boyfriend scorned, would storm off in a huff, then return unnoticed later, when the party became rowdier, and investigate the guys' computers. He and Lila planned to meet at their car at 3:00 a.m.

"Then it's showtime," he told her.

As they turned back toward the house, Joel surprised her by taking her hand in his. She couldn't remember the last time she'd held hands with a man. Maybe she never had. She'd become sexually active at an early age, and when teen-agers coupled, they got right to the main event. Her adult sexual unions hadn't been a whole lot different. Not to mention the guys she'd always dated hadn't been big on romantic gestures. Their idea of romance had been saying "please" before "take off your clothes" or asking if they could keep her panties as a souvenir.

Then again, Lila had never exactly been Ms. Romance herself. To her, sex had never been more than a vehicle for satisfying a basic physical need, the way food was for eating and air was for breathing. Things like holding hands and murmuring sweet words and playing footsie under a table had always seemed silly. Romance had always seemed silly. It didn't serve a purpose. What was the point?

But holding hands with Joel didn't feel silly at all, she thought as she felt her skin grow warmer against his. In fact, holding hands with Joel felt kind of…

Before she could identify the strange feeling coursing through her, she remembered that they were supposed to be a feuding couple, and she told herself they shouldn't be holding hands. Then the warmth in her hand spread to her arm, and then into her chest, and then it settled nicely in the cradle of her belly. And, as seemed to be becoming her habit, she didn't care if she and Joel were acting out of character.

Inside the house, the party was a little livelier, enough that no one seemed to pay much attention to their arrival beyond a few polite smiles and hellos. Lila scanned the room in an effort to identify faces from the OPUS dossier, but none was familiar.

In spite of that, "See anyone you know?" she asked Joel as they approached an entertainment unit in the corner of the room that had been turned into a bar. Not far from it there was a pool table that had also been turned into a bar. Along with an aquarium turned into a bar. And a BarcaLounger. And what looked like a freshman. Maybe a sophomore. Lila would have to get closer to know for sure, and frankly, she'd just as soon not.

"Yeah," he said as he turned a bottle of cognac to inspect the label, flinched at the brand and began to pick through the assortment of beers instead. "I'm pretty sure I went to school with all these guys." He finally made a selection, pulled the tab on the can with an errant hiss, then turned to survey the crowd again. "No matter when or where you go to college, you'll always have your jocks, your stoners, your over-achievers, your wannabes, your Greeks…."

Lila, too, plucked a beer out of the assortment, opened it and pretended to sip it. "Your geek Greeks," she added help-fully, smiling up at him. This time she hadn't said it to needle him, however, she realized. No, this time she'd said it to flirt with him. *She'd* said it. Not Jenny.

She was about to say something else flirtatious—not that she had any idea why she would do something like that, since flirting for any other reason than to lure some poor sap into a false sense of security was even sillier and more pointless than romance—but Joel prevented her from saying a word. Because in one swift, fluid gesture, he moved to stand in front of her, arced an arm over her head, braced it against the wall behind her and leaned in *very* close.

Then he murmured near her ear, "Like I said, don't knock it till you've tried it. You might be surprised how much a guy like me could have taught a girl like you in college. You might be surprised how much I could teach you now."

Something hot and impulsive exploded in her belly unlike anything she had ever felt before, something completely out of character—for both Lila and Jenny. No way would Jenny feel the way Lila suddenly did about a man she was supposed to fighting with. And no way should Lila be feeling it about any man at all. Because in that moment, towering over her as he did, his silky hair falling over his forehead, his dark eyes turbulent, his mouth hooked into a grin, Joel Faraday took her breath away. Literally.

She tried to stifle the gasp that escaped her as he loomed over her, but the way his eyes darkened and his lips turned up in a knowing smile, she realized he'd heard it just the same. She inhaled a slower, deeper breath in an effort to steady her racing pulse, but when she detected the clean masculine scent of him and felt the warmth of his body mingling with hers, she was filled with something else instead. Something hot. Something hungry. Something needy. Something that made her want to forget who she was. Who she was supposed to be. And never go back to being either of those women again.

Ignoring the way her heart was pounding in her chest with enough force to make her hot and dizzy, Lila bluffed. "Yeah, I could've learned a lot from a geek, couldn't I? Things like chemistry and physics and calculus. Hoo, boy. Who wouldn't want to know more about those?"

Instead of leaning back again, Joel dipped his head even closer, his lips skimming her sensitive flesh, her neck growing damp with the warmth of his breath. Even more quietly than before, he assured her, "I was thinking about a different kind of chemistry and physics. And a different word that starts with *c* and ends with *u-s*. Take all the time you need to think about that one."

Lila didn't need any time at all. Before he even finished speaking, one heated image after another began to tumble through her brain, each more graphic than the previous one. But before she could say a word—not that she had any idea what to say—he was pulling back again, removing his arm from the wall above her head and turning to lean his back against it instead. From there, he sipped his beer and surveyed the room dispassionately, as if the past few minutes had never happened.

Her mouth dry, and without thinking, Lila lifted the beer for a healthy swig. Then she nearly choked on it, so unfamiliar and unpleasant was the taste. Lifting the back of her hand to her mouth, she looked over at Joel, but he continued to gaze indifferently out at the crowd, as if he didn't even know she was there.

Some geek, she thought, her body still humming with the

heat and hunger he'd stirred up. Just what the hell had that been about?

"Just what the hell was that about?" she demanded.

When Joel turned to look at her, his expression was vacant, save—and she might have just been imagining it—a little smugness. "What was what about?"

She expelled an incredulous little sound. "Oh, don't even try to pretend."

He grinned, and there was something smug about that, too. "Just trying to be authentic," he said quietly, cryptically.

But authentic as who? she wondered. Joel or Ned? And why did the answer to that question suddenly seem so important?

He glanced beyond her and frowned a little. "We're starting to draw some curious eyes," he said softly.

Oh, there was a shocker. Considering their exchange of body heat over the past few minutes, the two of them probably looked as if they were about to give everyone a free preview of *Lila Does Waverly.*

"People are dancing in the other room," he added. "Let's go in there."

She followed him into the dining room, which contained not a stick of dining room furniture, all the better to convert it into a makeshift dance floor. Plenty of people had done just that, making it easy for Lila and Joel to thread their way to its center and blend in with the crowd. He pulled her close as they halted, draping his arms casually over her shoulders and linking his hands loosely at her nape. Then he leaned in again—though not quite as close as he had before—and whispered, "We should start setting the stage. Pretend you're getting uncomfortable with me."

Lila didn't have to pretend. Their exchange of a few minutes ago still had her reeling. Her uneasiness only compounded when he looped his arms around her waist and urged her closer, because the brush of his bare forearms over the bare flesh of her back sent even more heat zinging through her. Instead of circling her arms around his neck, the way she normally would when dancing with a guy, she folded them against his chest in an effort to keep some distance between them. She figured that was what Jenny Sturgis would do if she were miffed at her boyfriend. But Lila wasn't acting as Jenny when she did it. She needed to keep some distance between herself and Joel. Not because being this close to him felt awkward. But because it felt so good.

Then she felt Joel's warm fingers splay open over her naked back, and without even realizing she was doing it, she opened her own hands over his chest. The heat of him seeped through the soft fabric of his shirt and into her palm, and as she pushed her hand up toward his shoulder, she noted the bump and ridge of muscle and sinew beneath her fingertips. He muttered a soft sound of satisfaction as her fingers ventured over his shoulder and up along his neck, and she answered with one of her own when his silky hair sifted over the back of the hand she curled around his nape. And then thought became more difficult, because he began to skim his fingers lightly over the sensitive skin of her back, as if he were looking for a good place to put them.

Right there, she thought as they tripped down her spine and swept along her waist. *Yeah, that's good. Oh, no, wait,* she thought further as he opened his hands wider and moved them away from each other to cup his palms over her hips.

That's even better. Oh, yeah. Right there. That feels really, really good.

But no sooner had that thought formed than Joel's hands began to move again. He really couldn't seem to figure out what to do with them, first palming her back and hips and then moving them to the sides of her rib cage, lighting little fires everywhere he touched her. Unable to help herself—well, okay, maybe she was able, but she wasn't willing—Lila began moving her hands, too, dragging them back over his shoulders to his chest, spreading her fingers open this time over his heart. As she did, Joel seemed to finally find a place that he liked, curving his fingers possessively over her rib cage and hooking his thumbs just beneath the lower curves of her breasts.

Oh, yes, she thought as a soft little sigh rippled through her. *Right there.*

But their satisfaction at having found the perfect position was shattered by the sound of a familiar voice calling out boisterously, "We're here! We got beer! Get used to it!"

Then Lila snapped her eyes open and saw Chuck Miller's unmistakable backside—his pants this time falling down over paisley boxers—waddling backward through the front door, doing his part to balance a dolly to which was strapped an enormous keg of beer. Two other guys flanked the big silver barrel, looking ready to throw themselves over anything that might endanger it. Lila recognized them immediately from photos in her dossier as potential contacts of Sorcerer. The redhead was Donny Grawemeyer, the blonde Hobie Jurgens.

Seeing them was the cold water in the face she needed to

remind her she had a job to do. What was the matter with her, melting into Joel the way she'd been doing, completely forgetting about why they were here? Using her anger at herself to fuel the staged scenario they'd discussed earlier, she pushed Joel as hard as she could, enough to send him stumbling backward. Judging by his expression, he'd been as preoccupied by other thoughts while they were dancing as she had, but he, too, quickly seemed to remember what they were supposed to be doing.

"You bastard!" she shouted loud enough to capture the attention of everyone in the room. "I can't believe you just said that to me!"

"Yeah, well, what am I supposed to say after what you did?" Joel shouted back.

"You started it," she said, fisting her hands on her hips.

"Yeah, and I'll finish it, too," he added menacingly. He grabbed her wrist hard and jerked her toward him. "We're leaving."

Lila gave her hand a none-too-gentle tug, but deliberately didn't free herself. "You mean *you're* leaving," she spat at him. "I'm not going anywhere with a guy who treats me like you do. I deserve better." She feigned another struggle, twisting her arm first one way, then the other. "Let me go, Ned!" she yelled.

"We're leaving *now*," Joel repeated.

He started to give her arm another yank, but a big hand clamped down on his shoulder. The gesture was punctuated by Chuck Miller's admonition, "Let go of her, man. Then get your ass outta here before I kick the shit out of it. This party's by invitation only."

Joel spun around as if he were going to put up a fight, but when he saw Chuck flanked by Hobie and Donny, he did what any guy in his right mind would do, even an abusive boyfriend. He grudgingly released Lila's wrist, threw her a killing look and muttered, "We'll talk about this when you get home."

Lila rubbed her wrist as if he'd hurt her and glared at him. "Maybe I won't come home," she snapped.

He opened his mouth to say something else, glanced at the three men gazing ominously back at him, then set his jaw and turned to leave. Lila stared daggers at him until he was out the front door.

"You okay?" Chuck asked her.

She nodded, but said nothing and tried to look as wounded as she could.

"Girl like you deserves better than a dick like that," he said.

"Maybe," she said, meeting his eyes cautiously, putting just enough wounded fawn into the act to give Chuck a hard-on.

"Definitely," he assured her.

She smiled tentatively. "Maybe a guy like you could show me what better is like."

He smiled back—with manful pride. The sap. "Maybe I could. And I could start by getting you something to drink."

She nodded and brightened her smile. "That'd be nice."

The expression to which he treated her then told Lila that the night ahead was going to be a piece of cake. And everything did indeed go swimmingly for most of the night. Until the moment a drunken Chuck decided to make Lila his woman. And share her with some of his frat brothers.

Whether she liked it or not.

CHAPTER TEN

JOEL HAD JUST FILLED his third flash drive with the contents of Chuck Miller's hard drive—the last computer he had to search tonight—when he heard voices outside in the hall. He recognized Lila's first, then Miller's, then those of two additional males he couldn't place. The subject of the conversation, however—such as it was—was crystal clear. Chuck was trying to lure Jenny/Lila to his room, the two guys with him were egging him on and Lila was doing a reasonably convincing job of an inebriated young coed who couldn't quite make up her mind whether or not she wanted to accompany them.

A quick glance around the room revealed nowhere to hide. It was decorated in Traditional Frat Guy, with only the bare necessities. The closet door was open, revealing enough clothes and crap to prevent its being closed again without a backhoe coming in first, so that was out. The bed was a mattress atop box springs on the floor, so there would be no scuttling under there.

He had just scrambled over the windowsill to crouch on a section of roof that was barely big enough—and sturdy enough—to hold him when the bedroom door flew open with enough force to send it banging into the wall behind it.

The crash was punctuated by raucous male laughter and a girlie-sounding squeal. Joel braved a quick look into the room to see a convincingly tipsy-looking Lila and a genuinely drunken Chuck stumbling into the room. Immediately behind them were two men Joel didn't recall seeing earlier, also visibly inebriated. They had the markings of varsity athletes—probably football, judging by the size and weight of them.

Huge *and* smart, Joel thought. And drunk. Not a great combination. And Chuck was by no means petite or stupid himself. Never had Lila looked tinier than she did in that moment, surrounded by those three men. And never had Joel seen three men look more lecherous or rapacious. Ducking back down so he wouldn't be seen, Joel sent a silent plea to Lila that he hoped like hell she knew what she was doing.

"I really, really, really, really, really shouldn't be in your room, Chuck," he heard her slur drunkenly. "I'm totally, totally, totally, totally, totally not that kind of girl." Then she giggled in a way that completely negated the statement.

"Aw, come on, Jenny," Chuck cajoled. "The party downstairs is too loud. Dylan and Corey and I just figured it'd be easier for the three of us to talk up here."

Oh, sure, Joel thought. 'Cause everyone knew that frat guys threw parties only so they'd have an opportunity to discuss the finer points of Plato's *Republic* and the mysteries of black holes.

"I'm glad you got rid of your dick boyfriend," he heard Chuck say, his voice softer now.

"He is so lame," Lila concurred. "And he treats me like crap."

"I know a way you can get even with him," Chuck told her.

"Oh, yeah?" Lila asked with what sounded like heartfelt interest. "You gonna let me in on it?"

"Oh, yeah, baby," he told her. "You bet."

All Joel heard after that was the two guys who weren't Chuck laughing in a way that told him too well what was going on. And although he didn't need his mental picture of Chuck kissing Lila to be made any more vivid, it was made so anyway when he heard her say after another moment, in a veritable purr, "I like that revenge. But I think you and I need to be alone when we get it."

"Oh, don't worry, Jenny," Chuck cooed. "You won't even know Dylan and Corey are here. They just wanna watch."

To her credit, Lila didn't sound in any way worried or surprised when she replied, "But I'd rather it just be the two of us, sweetie. Let these guys get their own."

"Oh, they will, baby. As soon as I've had mine."

That remark was punctuated by more male laughter, along with a sound that made Joel's flesh crawl—the sound of fabric tearing.

He spent all of a nanosecond thinking about his response. Going back in through the window would let Chuck know that Joel had been in the room beforehand, and he still needed to protect the investigation as well as he could. So he scooted to the edge of the roofline and used the gutter to swing himself down into the backyard. He hit the ground running and headed straight for the back door, shoving aside anyone who got in his way. He had to shove harder once he got inside, then took the stairs two or three at a time until he reached the second floor. By the time he reached Chuck's door, adrenaline—or something—was surging through him so forcefully that he kicked it in with enough force to pull the door off its hinges and the hinges off the jamb.

All three men looked over their shoulders at his arrival, since they'd all been looking at Lila when he entered. *Down* at Lila. Lila, who was bucking against the four big hands that were holding her on the bed, two on one side, two on the other, one at each elbow and over each thigh. Chuck's hands were busy, too, tugging down the zipper of Lila's pants, having already unfastened her belt and having dropped his own pants and boxers down around his ankles. The tearing Joel had heard had been Lila's shirt, which was rent halfway down the middle and gaping open over her breasts enough to nearly reveal them.

For a single, angry moment no one moved except Lila, who continued to flail her entire body upward with enough force to make the two guys holding her grunt with their effort to keep her down. And in that moment Joel thought of at least a dozen ways to kill all three men. For now, he only doubled both hands into fists and dropped his gaze to Chuck's groin.

And then he said, "Wow, I never would have guessed such a big asshole would have such a little dick." Then, looking at Lila, who had ceased her struggle when she heard his voice, he added, "Though it explains a lot, doesn't it?"

Something crossed her face then, something that was a mix of relief, laughter and still-simmering fury. But she said, "Why do you think I'm fighting so hard? A shriveled little thing like that? Why waste my time?" Amazingly, she grinned at him before adding, "I'm used to having something *a lot* more substantial."

God help him, Joel actually felt himself stir at her words. Not that he'd call himself *a lot* more substantial, but...

He considered Chuck again. Okay, yeah, he would call himself *a lot* more substantial.

Chuck's shriveled little thing shrank even more at Lila's words, but his face reddened with his anger. "Nobody invited you to this party, you dick. So beat it."

Joel shook his head derisively. "Oh, I think you're going to be the one who's beating it tonight, Chuck. Provided there's anything left of it when she's finished with you. Which is doubtful. Something that tiny and all."

And with that, and no further warning, Joel went in swinging. The two guys holding Lila immediately released her so they could fight back, and once she was up, all hell broke loose in the room. When it was finished, Big Guy One was out the window on the roof where Joel had been crouching only moments ago, covered with shattered glass, his lip split open and at least two teeth gone. Big Guy Two was sprawled half on and half off what was left of Chuck's dresser, his nose bleeding and his arm at a funny enough angle that he wouldn't be throwing any balls anytime soon. And speaking of balls, Joel was reasonably sure Big Guy Two would never have full use of his again. And Chuck...

Well, Lila had seen to Chuck herself once she'd dispatched Big Guy One through the window. After ensuring that Chuck's ear, nose and throat doctor would have plenty to keep him busy, she shoved him out of the room—leaving his pants and boxers behind—and half shoved, half carried him down the stairs, dumping him into the middle of the party with his shriveled little thing on display for everyone. Everyone who promptly voiced their surprise that Chuck had such a shriveled little thing.

Then Lila zipped up her jacket over her torn shirt and said a few more things to Chuck that he—and anyone else within hearing distance—would never forget. And then she and Joel left the party.

Neither said a word as they strode back to the car. Joel's body was still reacting to what had happened. His skin was hot, his head was pounding, his chest was heaving and his ears were filled with the sound of rushing wind. His legs were weak and his arms hurt like hell, and he couldn't seem to stop shaking. Never in his life had he been reduced to physical violence. He'd just never experienced anything, even as a kid, that made him want to lash out. But he hadn't even hesitated back there. Hadn't questioned his reaction at all. He'd been motivated by one thing, and one thing alone.

How Lila had looked when he'd burst into that room.

If he lived to be 180, Joel would never, ever forget the image of her held down and struggling against two men twice her size. And every time the scene replayed in his head, he would feel all over again his rage, his terror and his calm but absolute certainty that he would tear all three men apart and feel not one iota of remorse for doing it.

It wasn't an easy realization to arrive at, how quickly and easily and completely the veneer of civilization could be stripped away to expose the Neanderthal lurking beneath. But that was precisely what had happened back there. Joel had abandoned quite willingly all polite behavior he'd ever learned, and he'd reverted to the most primitive version of humankind that had ever existed. What was most revealing, though, was that he knew he'd do it all over in a heartbeat. If anyone ever, *ever* threatened Lila again.

They strode side by side in silence until they were safely inside the car. Then Lila turned to face Joel and said, "Evidently, whoever gave you my dossier neglected to include some very important information."

He started the car and pulled away from the curb before asking, "What's that?"

Her voice was steely cold as she said, "No one rescues me. Ever. I take care of myself. Always."

Joel kept his attention on the road, but replied, "Looked to me like you were having a little trouble with that this time."

"Then you weren't watching very closely," she said evenly. "Didn't it occur to you that I had a plan? Did you think I was so stupid that I would have allowed myself to be led to Chuck's room with two other guys without knowing how I would get back out again?"

He expelled a long, disgruntled breath. Finally he admitted, "I guess I didn't really think at all."

"No, I guess you didn't," she said tersely. "But I did. I thought it through a lot, and I knew exactly what I was doing. I would have been fine. I've been outnumbered by way more dangerous guys than those losers, and I kicked their ass."

Now Joel did spare her a glance, long enough to see how angry she was. Her body was rigid with it, her features stark, her eyes cold.

He returned his gaze to the road and tried to inject a carelessness into his voice that he was nowhere close to feeling. "Lila, what's the big deal? You looked like you were in trouble, and I was in a position to help you out. So I did. We got what we came for, and we didn't compromise the investigation."

"Only because those guys were too drunk to be suspicious," she pointed out.

Joel said nothing. She was right. He turned again to look at her, but only long enough to see that she was still glaring at him.

"No one rescues me," she repeated emphatically. "I'm not some damsel in distress who needs to be taken care of. I take care of myself."

Quietly he said, "You know, I think you're bothered more by the fact that I helped you out back there than you are by the possibility that the investigation could have been compromised."

"Yeah. So?"

"You act like being in a position of needing help is the most heinous crime a person can commit."

"And your point is?"

He expelled a soft sound. Right. He should already have realized she'd feel that way. A little more gently this time, he said, "It's not a crime, Lila. Everybody gets in a jam at some point. Everybody needs a little help sometimes."

"Yeah, yeah, yeah. And people who need people are the luckiest people in the world," she muttered. "I get that. *Other* people," she then clarified. "Not me. I don't need help. I don't need anybody."

Meaning him, Joel translated. Not that she hadn't already made that clear dozens of times.

They made the remainder of the drive to the apartment in silence. But by the time they arrived, Joel had managed to get a handle on his reaction, and Lila's anger seemed to have cooled. She went straight to the bathroom and turned on the shower, so, as a peace offering, he brewed her a cup of decaf green tea and had it waiting for her when she emerged. Although he pretended to be more engrossed in a file and the brandy he'd poured for himself, he instead watched Lila closely from beneath his lowered lids, trying to detect any sign that she wasn't, as she insisted, fine.

She'd changed into the sort of clothes she always slept in, a pair of baggy drawstring pajama bottoms—these patterned with wide vertical stripes in varying shades of green—and a dark green cotton T-shirt that stopped just short of meeting the drawstring. She hesitated outside the bathroom door at first, seeming uncertain which way she wanted to go, then turned toward the living room. Then she turned toward her bedroom. Then the living room. Then the bedroom again. Finally she made her way toward Joel, padding barefoot into the room. She still seemed a little edgy, though whether it lingered from the altercation with Chuck or her anger at Joel, he couldn't have said. When she noticed the cup of tea, however, her face softened and her body relaxed. Her hand was steady as she reached for it, he saw, and her smile seemed genuinely unbothered.

Evidently she was indeed fine, and doubtless would have been, even without him. Joel told himself he should be reassured by that. Instead, he felt kind of defeated.

"Thank you," she said softly before enjoying a sip.

"You're welcome," he replied.

To his surprise, when she sat down she didn't fold herself into the chair, but onto the sofa beside him, near enough for him to touch her if he wanted to. Which, of course, he did. Which, of course, he wouldn't. But she *was* near enough for him to touch if he wanted to. For a moment they only sat in more silence, Lila sipping her tea, Joel watching her—but openly this time. She didn't seem to mind his attention, however, any more than she seemed to mind the silence. He didn't mind the silence either, and wasn't sure what to say anyway that hadn't already been said.

"Thank you for helping me out tonight, Joel."

Except that.

The remark surprised him, and not just because he could tell the words didn't come easily for her, something that only made them nicer to hear. As was the sound of his name spoken in her voice. She rarely addressed him by name. Technically, shouldn't be doing so now—not that he cared. And never with the…affection? Oh, surely not. Never with…whatever it was she used just then. A ribbon of pleasure unwound inside him, chasing away what was left of the acid from the episode with Chuck.

"You're welcome," he said for the second time.

She hadn't looked at him since coming out of the bathroom, but she turned to him now and gazed at his face unflinchingly. He'd gotten so used to seeing her in the dark eye makeup she wore for Jenny that seeing her without it now was almost jarring. Once again he was overcome by how little she resembled the Lila Moreau legend. She looked so fresh, so innocent, so easygoing. He supposed he was going to have to amend his idea of the Lila Moreau legend.

"I had a good time tonight," she said, smiling.

She couldn't have surprised him more if she'd just announced that his hair was on fire.

His expression must have made that obvious, because she laughed and added, "Well, I did. I never got to go to parties in college. Had I realized what I was missing out on, I would have taken a couple of nights off from work here and there. I just didn't think I was missing out on anything." She sighed. "Then again, why should college be any different? I missed out on a lot of stuff growing up."

Her voice was matter-of-fact when she voiced the sentiment, not whiny or hurt or angry or pathetic or a host of other things it could have been—justifiably, at that. She was simply stating what was what. That her life had been the sort that hadn't planted particularly happy memories in her brain.

She sipped her tea again, and as she lifted her head a strand of damp hair fell forward to lodge against her cheek. Before he realized he was doing it—and before Lila had a chance to do it herself—Joel lifted his hand to brush it away and tuck it behind her ear. She flinched at first, jerking her head away from him so quickly that his hand stayed where it was, unmoving. For a second she looked at him as if he'd done something to hurt her. But only for a second. Then her features softened the way they had when she saw the tea. But her eyebrows knitted downward, almost in confusion. And then, incredibly, she leaned back in again, until her cheek was pressed lightly against his palm.

Joel's heart rate doubled at the contact, heat exploded in his belly and he suddenly felt a little light-headed. It was the most innocent sort of touch in the world, but his entire body responded as if she'd tucked her hand between his legs and stroked him. Her skin was warm and silky against his palm, and she smelled of Ivory soap. Clean. Uncorrupted. Pure. He was afraid to move, afraid she might move, too, if he did. So he only left his hand where it was, cupping her cheek gently, his fingertips skimming the damp hair near her ears, and... touched her.

"You should have had some frat parties in college," he said softly. "You should have had a lot of things you didn't get, Lila. You should have had a boyfriend named Skip and evening curfews and homecoming mums. You should have had foam solar systems in the school science fair and pool parties at vacation Bible school. You should have had trips to Yosemite in a station wagon with fake wood paneling on the side, and walks to the ice cream store with your best friend Patsy. You should have lived out every Norman Rockwell painting you've ever seen. And I'm really sorry you didn't."

The sap level in that speech, he thought, was off the charts. But he couldn't help it. Lila *should* have had those things. She shouldn't have had to grow up the way she did. No one should. And he really was sorry she'd missed out on so much, while people like him, who'd had more than their fair share of such experiences, had taken them all for granted.

Her eyebrows had arrowed downward even more as he spoke, and he told himself whatever he saw in her eyes was simply a trick of the bad light in the living room. There was no way she could look as sad as she did just then. No way she could be gazing at him the way she was. As if she were looking to him to provide her with some of the experiences he'd just spoken of. As if she wanted to make some new memories, some better ones, with him. So there was no reason for Joel to want to kiss her the way a boyfriend named Skip might have, all nervous and uncertain and innocent. Except for the fact that suddenly, sitting here with Lila, nervous and uncertain and innocent was how he felt.

But then, somehow, he was kissing her, or maybe she was kissing him, their mouths barely touching as their lips danced over each other's, once, twice, three times, four. And then their noses were nuzzling, and he felt her warm breath against his cheek, ragged and thready, just like his own. And then they were kissing again, but still not touching anywhere else, their mouths gently grazing as their breathing grew more ragged. Joel pulled away once, pressing his forehead to hers, then Lila pushed her body closer and kissed him again.

This time she looped a tentative arm around his neck, and he settled his hand loosely at her waist. She was soft and warm and fragrant from the shower, her skin like silk where his fingers landed. His heart rate quickened until his blood was pulsing through his body with dizzying speed. After that, he couldn't register much of anything. He was too busy kissing Lila and touching Lila and holding Lila and wanting Lila.

Her scent surrounded him, a mixture of damp and heat and need and woman. He felt her fingers creeping into his hair, her breasts pressing into his chest, her thigh pushing against his. And then, when she crowded herself even closer, and he turned his body into hers, her leg pressed into his swelling cock. She must have recognized his condition, because the kiss became less innocent then. She opened her mouth wide over his, and Joel responded automatically, their tongues tangling as each warred for possession. Lila murmured something against his mouth that sounded needy and demanding, then dropped her hand into his lap, opening her fingers over his fast ripening erection, pushing them down and up and down again.

Oh, God…

It had been so long since a woman had touched him that way, and it was almost more than Joel could bear. He'd promised himself he would do this again only when the woman in question was a big part of his life. And although Lila was certainly that at the moment, she would be gone too soon.

Stop now, he ordered himself. *Before it's too late. Before things get out of hand.*

But before he could even get a handle on the thoughts tumbling through his brain, Lila had things firmly *in* hand, curving her palm deeper between his legs, cupping him possessively before dragging her fingers along his hard length again. In response, Joel pushed his hand higher, cradling the lower swell of her breast in the valley of his thumb and forefinger before moving higher still, completely covering the soft mound of flesh. When she murmured another soft sound in reply, he closed his fingers gently over her, palming her through the fabric of her shirt, feeling the push of her nipple against the center of his palm. Unable to help himself, he released her only long enough to tuck his hand under her shirt, capturing her again, this time with no fabric to hinder his touch.

Soft. God, she was so soft. He raked his fingers gently over her breast, then caught her taut nipple beneath the pad of his middle finger to draw a slow circle around it. He wanted his mouth there, wanted to taste her tender flesh and flick it with his tongue, wanted to know what kind of sounds she would utter with each new level of her arousal. He wanted her naked and writhing in his bed as he spread her legs wide and licked the musky flesh of her sex. He wanted to watch as she knelt before him and drew his cock into her mouth, pulling him deeper every time she lowered her head. He wanted her beneath him, wanted her astride him, wanted her bent over while he buried himself in her from behind. He wanted to do things with Lila, wanted to do things *to* Lila, that he'd done so many times with so many other women and hadn't enjoyed for so long. He wanted—

Oh, God, he just *wanted*. So much. Too much. And he wanted it more than he'd ever wanted anything before. Which was the very reason, he knew, that he had to make sure it stopped now.

As Lila flicked the button of his blue jeans open, Joel dropped his hand from her breast and cupped it over hers. Then he pulled his head back, met her gaze levelly and said very softly, "Don't."

She gazed back at him in silence, clearly surprised by his request, but she didn't move her hand. She was close enough now that he could feel her heart pounding against his own. Her heat, her scent, her breath mixed with his, and if he closed his eyes, he honestly wasn't sure if he'd be able to tell where she ended and he began.

So he kept his eyes open, pinned on hers, and said, "It, um…it's not a good time for this, Lila."

She expelled a quiet sound of disbelief. "It's always a good time for this."

Joel said nothing, only continued to meet her gaze, hoping she would just let it go.

But of course she didn't. Not that he blamed her. Had the tables been turned, he wouldn't have reacted any differently. She tilted her head to one side, moved her body in a way that sent a shudder of heat from his chest to his groin, and started to push the zipper of his jeans lower.

"Lila, don't," he said again.

"Why not?" Although she didn't push her hand any lower, she didn't move away from him either. Not that Joel was moving away from her, he reminded himself. No wonder she wasn't taking him seriously. "It's pretty obvious we both want to," she added.

He couldn't deny that, so he just repeated, "It's not a good time."

"Why not?" she asked again. "After the night we had, we deserve to blow off a little steam."

It was exactly what Joel needed to hear to assure him he was doing the right thing. "And that's all it would be, right?" he asked. "Blowing off steam?"

Something darted across her expression at the question, making her smile falter, but it moved too quickly for him to identify quite what it was. "Of course," she said. "What else would it be?"

"And in the morning we'll just wake up and get back to work?"

She nodded again, but her smile fell some more. "Sure."

He nodded dispassionately. "Yeah, well, I don't think it's a good idea for us to get involved," he said lamely.

"We're not going to get involved," she told him. "We're going to have sex."

It was exactly the opening Joel needed, he told himself.

So why didn't he take it? But instead of explaining to her the promise he'd made to himself, he only repeated, "It's not a good idea to mix business with pleasure."

"In this business," she said, "you have to take your pleasure where you find it."

With no small effort, he circled his fingers around her wrist and withdrew her hand from his zipper. But he couldn't quite keep himself from placing a brief, chaste kiss at the center of her palm before settling her hand in her lap. His gaze never leaving hers, he yanked up his zipper and buttoned his jeans, trying not to wince at the discomfort of still being so fully erect. Lila's shirt was still pushed high enough on her torso to reveal the lower curves of her breasts, and since she was doing nothing to rectify that, Joel reached over and, with great, great regret, tugged the little shirt back into place. Then he dropped his hands into his own lap and met her gaze again.

"You're serious," she said softly, incredulously. "You're really not going to put out."

He chuckled a little anxiously. "Not on the first date," he said. "I'm not that kind of boy."

She eyed him with much interest. "You sure kiss like you're that kind of boy."

He said nothing in response to that. He was too busy swelling with manly pride.

Lila scooted over a little, so that their bodies were no longer touching, then crossed her arms over her midsection. "Okay, Joel, what's up? I think I deserve an explanation. You were as eager as I was a minute ago." She dropped her gaze blatantly to his groin. "You're still eager," she added. She looked at his face again. "What gives? Since, obviously, you won't."

He expelled a long, frustrated sound. "Look, I just think it will make things difficult if we add this to an already stressful situation, that's all."

"There are those—me—who would argue that having sex might alleviate some of that stress."

"And there are others—me—who think having sex might just create more. More stress, I mean," he hastily added. "Not more…sex."

She said nothing in response to that, only smiled, as if she had absolutely no problem with there being more sex.

Fine, Joel thought. He'd just tell her the ugly truth.

"Look, Lila," he began, not caring if he called her by name now. They'd done a lousy job of staying in character since the assignment began, and he was tired of trying to be someone he wasn't—in more ways than one. "I did used to be that kind of boy, long ago, in a galaxy far, far away. I had a very full and active sex life. I know you probably find that hard to believe," he couldn't help adding, "that a geek like me ever had a girlfriend, but trust me. I did."

"I don't find that hard to believe at all," she told him.

But she didn't elaborate. Dammit. So he continued, "In fact, although I was a late bloomer, I more than made up for it once I was finally…ah…plucked."

Her smile broadened at that, but again she said nothing.

"And I was pretty indiscriminate when it came to partners," he admitted. "Ultimately, it got to the point where women stopped being women and became something else instead."

She eyed him thoughtfully now. "What did they become?"

"A receptacle," he said simply. "A place I could put part of my anatomy into and feel better."

Now Lila looked confused. "And that was a problem because…?"

He sighed. "Because there comes a time in a person's life when sex isn't enough to make you feel better."

She looked even more confused when he said that.

"I don't expect you to understand," he told her. "A lot of people think there's no such thing as too much sex. But I just reached a point where the more sex I had, the emptier I felt. So I decided to…take a break from it for a while."

She narrowed her eyes at him. "And by take a break you mean…?"

"I mean I decided I wouldn't have sex again until I met a woman who would bring more to my life than physical gratification."

She studied him in silence a moment longer. "And just when did you make this decision?" she finally asked.

Oh, he'd really been hoping she wouldn't ask that. He hesitated for a moment, then admitted, "Almost five years ago."

She expelled a single, incredulous sound at that, her eyes going wide, her mouth even wider. "You haven't had sex for five years?"

"*Almost* five years," he qualified. Not that it was much qualification.

"*Five years?*" she repeated even more incredulously.

"*Almost.* Look, I didn't *mean* for it to be five years," he told her. "But I just haven't met a woman who was anything special." *Until now,* he added to himself.

Her expression changed drastically at his remark, and he realized how badly he had misspoken. By turning down her offer with the explanation he'd just given, he'd just told Lila he didn't think she was special, either. But he didn't know what to say to counter it. If he told Lila he thought she *was* special, extremely special, more special than any woman he'd ever met…

Oh, hell. He didn't know how she'd react. She might be flattered. She might laugh in his face. One thing she wouldn't do, however, was feel anything reciprocal.

"Lila, I didn't mean that the way it sounded," he said quickly, knowing it was too little, too late.

"No, it's all right, Joel," she said, lifting both hands before her as if she were trying to ward him off…or maybe build a brick wall. "I know I'm not the kind of girl guys take home to meet Mom. And I like it that way," she added with complete conviction.

He knew that. It was one of the reasons he thought she was so special. Because she was so self-aware and so utterly comfortable with that self.

"But I understand your point," she continued. "Well, actually, I don't," she said immediately, backpedaling. "It's only been a little over five months since I had sex, and that's been pretty…" Her eyes suddenly went wide, as if she were surprised by her own revelation. "I mean, uh… That's probably more information than you need, huh?"

Actually, it was information Joel appreciated. Knowing it had been a while since she'd been with anyone made him feel strangely…good.

"I just meant I can't imagine going five years without

sex," she hurried on. "But if that's the decision you've made, I'll respect that. Even if, you know, I think it's nuts."

"Thank you," he replied lamely. "I think."

They sat there looking at each other for another silent and very awkward moment, then Lila stood. "Um, I guess I should turn in," she said. "I, ah, have to start my new job tomorrow."

For a split second Joel honestly had no idea what she was talking about. Then it all came crashing back, like two tons of grossly neglected covert operations. Oh, yeah. Lila was scheduled to start her phony-baloney job at the coffee shop tomorrow. The coffee shop they were supposed to infiltrate because some of Sorcerer's e-mails had gone there, and he'd received others from that location in return. Joel had completely forgotten, because he'd been too busy thinking about how he had to quit thinking about Lila.

Forget about finding Sorcerer. The way Joel was running this operation, they'd be lucky to find a shiny new penny.

"Ah, yeah, right," he said, hoping he didn't sound as stupid as he felt. "And I need to go through all those files I downloaded from DUC house tonight. That'll take the better part of my day."

With one last, not especially happy, smile, she murmured a quiet good-night, then headed to her bedroom. As her door was swinging closed, something hot and heavy twisted in Joel's chest, and he almost—almost—called out to her to wait. But he reminded himself just how badly he was handling this assignment already, and told himself it would be stupid to say another word to Lila tonight—about anything. And then, finally, the door latch caught with a soft *click* behind her, and she was effectively closed off from him.

Physically, anyway. Mentally and emotionally, he had accepted by now, she would always be with him. Which, he knew, completely blew his chances for ever finding a special woman. Because no woman in the world would ever be special compared to Lila Moreau.

CHAPTER ELEVEN

"GOOD MORNING."

Iris shot up in bed with a gasp at the sound of the warm greeting, her heart pounding, her pulse racing, her brain screaming at her to flee, and had to quickly remind herself that she was perfectly safe. Which, except for the sound of the warm greeting, was the way she'd been waking up pretty much every morning for the past eight years. Well, except for yesterday, when she had awoken to the same warm greeting.

Shoving her hair out of her eyes, she saw Nick standing at the door of the suite behind a room-service trolley that had evidently just been delivered, the air between them redolent with the delicious aroma of a meal someone else had prepared. She returned his smile and inhaled a deeper, slower breath, releasing it with infinitely more satisfaction.

"Good morning," she replied dreamily.

Because this had to be a dream, right? It wasn't normal to feel this good, just by virtue of having woken up and drawn breath.

She told herself the only reason she felt so good was that she'd had two consecutive nights of solid sleep, something that almost never happened. She'd never been a sound sleeper to begin with, and since leaving home, the condition had only worsened. Over the past eight years, she'd moved a dozen times, to a dozen different states, and had stolen a new identity every time. She'd altered her looks, her voice, her lifestyle, her habits, everything, so that every last trace of Trisha Harrington would be gone. Three years ago she'd finally decided she'd put enough time and distance between herself and her family that she could risk staying in one place and being one person long enough to earn a degree that would enable her to support herself honestly and without having to look over her shoulder all the time.

She swiveled in bed to put her feet on the floor, shoving her hair back from her face as she rose. Nick looked yummy as usual in his dark blue robe and pajama bottoms, the garments flowing like silk over his body. Probably because they were silk. Duh. His dark auburn hair was rumpled from sleep, and the lower half of his face was shadowed by a night's growth of dark beard. The hair on his chest was dark, too, spanning his torso up and down and from side to side, disappearing into the drawstring waistband that dipped just below a luscious-looking navel. Her fingers curled involuntarily into her palms as she wondered what it would be like to touch him.

She was surprised he hadn't come on to her yet. He didn't seem like the kind of man who would share his hotel suite with a woman and not demand something from that woman in return. And even being the bundle of nerves she was about such a thing, Iris had decided she would agree if he did. But he'd only told her she was welcome to stay in the suite as long as she wanted, and he'd given her plenty of privacy. He'd left yesterday morning shortly after she woke, and he hadn't been back yet when she'd returned from her afternoon classes. He'd finally arrived around dinnertime and ordered room service for them both, and although they'd shared some quiet conversation, it had only touched on superficial subjects. He'd not mentioned her family at all.

But then, neither had she. Maybe he was waiting for her to be the one to bring it up, she thought. Or maybe it wasn't that important to him. Which was weird for a guy whose goal in life was to steal the world blind. A million five might not be a huge amount compared to what he'd get pillaging the global economy. But greed was greed, and a million five was no small change.

He was such a bundle of contradictions, she thought as she watched him push the trolley into the sitting area. Ruthless and relentless in his pursuit of money and power, but kind to, and even protective of, her whenever the guys gave her a hard time. Just who was Nick Darian? And what were the chances he might abandon the former behavior to focus on the latter?

Pretty slim, she immediately decided. He seemed as focused on his hunger for wealth and power as she was on her determination to elude her family. Not that she hadn't realized from the start how intent he was on this taking-over-the-world thing. Today, though, for some reason, it bothered Iris more than it had before.

"Sleep well?" he asked as she came to a stop beside him.

She nodded. "Better than I have in a long time, actually."

"Well, they say confession is good for the soul." He began to remove the metal covers from bacon and eggs and a platter of fresh fruit, then looked up at her and smiled. "Not that I'd know anything about that myself."

She smiled back, but the gesture felt hollow. "I didn't confess anything," she said as she reached for a slice of cantaloupe. "You found out about who I am all by yourself."

He tilted his head to one side as she nibbled the melon, as if he were trying to look at her from a different perspective. "But don't you feel better having shared the truth with someone else?"

She thought about that for a moment. "In some ways, I guess."

"But in others?"

She met his gaze levelly. "In some ways, I'm more scared now than ever before."

Nick hesitated for a moment, then said, "You *can* trust me."

She wished she could believe him. For now, she only asked, "How did you find out who I am? I've spent eight years erasing everything about Trisha Harrington. There shouldn't have been any way for anyone to find out who I am."

He shrugged without concern. "I have my ways."

"That mysterious contact in your mysterious organization," she guessed.

He nodded.

She shook her head, laughing lightly. She'd thought he'd made all that up. She'd figured he was just one of those guys who had to embellish everything they said about themselves so they'd sound more important than they really were. The kind who said they were former Green Berets when they'd actually been drummed out of the Boy Scouts. Or the ones who claimed to be part of a groundbreaking medical research team based on the amount of mold growing in their refrigerators.

Iris—and Chuck and Donny and Hobie, too, she knew—had figured Nick made up the shadowy government agency he used to work for because he wanted the rest of them to be impressed. Wanted to compensate for not knowing as much about what they were doing as the rest of them did. Now it looked as if maybe he was just who he said he was. Or had been, once upon a time. Because no one should have been able to find out the truth about Iris without some kind of heavy-duty search capabilities behind them.

"And what's the name of this group again?" she asked.

He smiled. "I never told you their name the first time," he said. "And I won't now. It's not important, Iris. What's important is that I still have someone there who can do things for me."

"Like checking up on me, Chuck, Donny and Hobie," she said.

"Like that, yes. Among other things."

She said nothing for a moment, then, "You invaded our privacy."

He laughed outright at that. A full-bodied, completely uninhibited laugh that rippled through Iris like a finger running down her spine. Then again, she supposed her comment was pretty funny, considering what they'd been doing to other people for the past few months—and what Iris had been doing to other people for years, she reluctantly reminded herself. Stealing their names, their personal information, their savings. Their lives, their financial plans for their offspring, their very trust in their own judgment.

It was the only way she'd known how to support herself, the only way she'd known how to survive. She'd been a whiz with computers since receiving her first one for her tenth birthday. Hacking came as naturally to her as breathing, and she'd had no other skills to earn her way. Stealing from people who already had plenty hadn't seemed like a big deal when the alternative was too terrible to consider. And she figured anyone she stole from eventually got their lives back in order. Her life would never be in order as long as there was a chance her family would find out where she was.

But they hadn't, she told herself now. It had been eight years, and she hadn't even had any close calls. It had been a while since she'd really *needed* to steal anything from anyone. Lately she'd only been doing it because… Well, because she'd been doing it for so long, she'd stopped thinking much about it. And because it had won her cachet into a small circle of friends—even if they were a bunch of assholes sometimes. Okay, a lot of times. Okay, all the time. And, too, because of Nick. Then again, if Donny, Hobie and Chuck were her only friends in the world—and God help her, they were—maybe it was time to rethink her social situation.

She frowned. "Nick?"

"Yes?"

"How much longer are we going to keep this up?"

He was clearly puzzled by the question. "Keep what up?"

"The stealing, the virus building…" She chuckled. "The taking over the world."

Now his expression grew wary. "Until we've succeeded in doing it," he said.

She expelled a soft sound she hoped was light and airy.

"Oh, come on. You don't honestly think you're going to take over the world."

"No. But I intend to hold it hostage until I get what I want."

"But don't you have enough? I mean, we must have scammed tens of millions of dollars by now."

"Yes, we have."

His admission both sobered and panicked her. She truly hadn't thought about any fixed number, had thrown out that "tens of millions" on what she'd thought would be a way wide guess of the actual figure. Chuck and Hobie and Donny must have been putting in a lot more hours on this than she had. And if they truly were responsible for the theft of that much money, then there had to be a lot of people in law-enforcement looking for them and trying to stop them. And if they found them—*when* they found them, she made herself admit—their faces would be splashed all over the news.

All those years of running and trying to hide from her family would be for nothing. Because the minute the Harringtons realized where their missing daughter was, they'd go right to work on getting her released from custody—and returned to them. Her family had more corrupt lawyers and judges and politicians in their pockets than Iris could count. Local, state, federal, it didn't matter. The Harringtons *would* get her off. They *would* force her return to the family fold. And her father would make damned sure she married Michael Covey this time.

Swallowing the terror she felt rising, Iris said, "You know, Nick, even divvied up between the five of us, that's a lot of money."

"Yes, it is," he agreed. "But it's not *enough* money."

She'd been afraid he would say that. "Well, how much is enough?"

He grinned. "I'll let you know when we have it."

She started to say something more, but Nick prevented her by asking, "Why did you run away from your family?"

She knew Nick wouldn't be satisfied until he learned the truth about her. The whole truth. Strangely, she didn't mind giving it to him. Maybe he was right. Maybe confession was good for the soul. If nothing else, if he knew the truth about her situation—and if he cared about her, even a little, which she was beginning to think he did—then he might be even less inclined to contact her family and turn her in.

"Coffee?" she asked. "This is kind of a long story."

He poured a cup for each of them, and as he closed his fingers around his mug, he asked, "How does a family of cutthroats like the Harringtons produce a daughter as lovely as you?"

Something warm and fluid splashed through her midsection at the question. No one had ever called her lovely before. Not even back when she was lovely. The whole Goth thing was just another attempt to hide who she was, but Nick's words, spoken so sweetly, actually made her *feel* lovely. Even in the black tank and pajama bottoms, even with the black, chewed-off fingernails.

"The whole time I was growing up," she began, "I thought I was living a totally ordinary life. I mean, I knew my family had a lot of money, but there was nothing about our life that even hinted at what the Harringtons actually did for a living. My father went off to work every day, and came home every night. My mother seemed like this typical society wife. Even when I was old enough to look at the stuff going on around me and start thinking some of it was a little suspicious, I guess I just decided not to see the facts."

"What kind of stuff?" Nick asked.

She shook her head. "I don't know. There was just this… vibe."

He arched his eyebrows at that. "A vibe?"

She nodded. "Yeah, just…this weird sort of tension or something that I never picked up on as a kid. I started noticing that whenever I walked into a room, conversations got quiet. And once I started high school, a lot of the kids stopped wanting to come to my house, and none of the guys would ask me out. I just figured nobody liked me. Now, of course, I realize everyone was just being smart enough not to get too close."

Nick studied her in silence for a moment. Then he said, "I didn't have many friends in school, either. Well, except one," he amended after some thought. "But we eventually drifted apart."

"I didn't even have one," Iris said.

"Must have been lonely."

She glanced away. "Yeah, well, I guess it was sometimes. But I sort of just created my own little bubble to live in, where I could tell myself that my life was totally normal and I had lots of friends and there were plenty of boys who had crushes on me. Besides, compared to what a lot of kids have to grow up with, my life really wasn't so bad." She looked at him again. "Until…"

"Until what?"

Iris sighed heavily. "My sixteenth birthday. That was when my father sat me down to have a talk with me. I thought he was going to outline some dating rules—like that was even necessary, since no one was asking me out—or tell me how smoking was bad for me and not to drink and drive. Instead, he told me all about the history of the Harringtons and their business, and what would be expected of me in the future."

"The facts of life, as it were."

She nodded slowly. "Yeah. He and my grandfather had my life all mapped out."

"And where did the journey lead?" Nick asked.

Iris laughed, a strangled, joyless sound. "In addition to learning how to run one of the biggest crime syndicates in the country I'd also have to marry Michael Covey, a guy handpicked by my grandfather, and the biggest sleazebag on the planet. With wealth and privilege comes obligation, my father told me. And my obligation was to my family. My parents said they'd announce the engagement when I turned eighteen, and Michael and I would get married when I was twenty. In the meantime, I wasn't allowed to ever go out with any other boys, and I would have to start getting to know Michael better."

Even today, her revulsion nearly strangled her when she recalled those, thankfully infrequent, times with Michael, when her parents invited him to dinner or whatever so that Iris could grow more accustomed to the idea of spending her life with him.

Yeah, like that was going to happen.

"He was twenty-eight years older than me," she continued. "And he had more kills under his belt than anyone in the family. At that point, I'd never even kissed a boy. And this guy was supposed to be my first, my last, my only." She inhaled deeply and released the breath slowly, feeling the quaver in it, even a decade after the fact. "He made my flesh crawl, Nick. I didn't want…I couldn't…" She sighed again. "I couldn't. So the day I turned eighteen, the minute I could legally do it, and before my parents had a chance to announce the engagement, I took off. And I never went back."

She wasn't sure what made her tell him the rest of it, since it was something she'd never told anyone else. In spite of that, and much to her surprise, she heard herself say, "But here's the best part, Nick. You'll love this irony." At least, she hoped he would. "By being forced into an unannounced engagement with some creep who might have ended up being the only man I was ever intimate with—or, at least, whatever passes for intimacy with creeps like him—I ended up never being intimate with anyone."

There. It was out. She'd told him the sad truth of her life. At twenty-six, she had to be one of the world's oldest living virgins. There was probably some primitive tribe in the Amazon somewhere that still practiced human sacrifice that would love to get their hands on her. Twenty-six-year-old virgins had to be riper than just about anything you could serve up to the gods.

She waited for some reaction from Nick, but he only continued to look at her as if she'd just told him what her shoe size was. All he did was lift his coffee to his lips and look at her expectantly, as if he were waiting for her to go on.

Maybe he hadn't understood, she thought. Maybe she should have spelled it out a little better. "I've never been with anyone, Nick," she finally said. "I'm still a virgin."

Okay, that got a response from him. Unfortunately, it mostly involved a lot of choking and coughing and spitting coffee.

"What?" he said when he was able to manage it, grabbing a linen napkin from the tray to dab at the coffee stains on his pajama bottoms. "You're *what?*"

"I've never been intimate with anyone," she said again.

"Well, neither have I," he told her. "But that doesn't make me a virgin."

"Yeah, well, what I haven't done *does* make me a virgin," she told him.

He continued to dab at coffee that he'd already wiped up, focusing way more attention on the task than it actually needed. He couldn't even look at her. Man, she really was a freak of nature. Finally he replaced the napkin on the tray and met her gaze evenly.

"You've really never been with a man?"

She shook her head. "Or a woman, either."

He smiled at that, and something about it made her feel a little better.

Until he told her, "That's not what Chuck and Hobie and Donny say, you know."

The statement confused her. "What would they know about it? Why would they even care?"

"They talk quite a lot when you're not around," Nick said. "And sometimes they talk about you."

This was news to Iris. And not necessarily good news, either, knowing those guys as well as she did. Although she wasn't sure she wanted to know, she asked cautiously, "What do they say?"

She could tell Nick was trying to hold back a smile—but not very hard. "Well," he began importantly, "among other things, they each claim to have…been intimate…with you."

Iris's mouth dropped open at that. "They what?"

"Only, they meant intimate the way you mean intimate. Not the way I mean intimate."

"Those liars!" she exclaimed indignantly.

Now Nick let the smile go full-blown, and she could see that it was one of vast amusement. "In fact," he continued, "they claim that, on one particularly memorable occasion, they were all…intimate with you…at the same time."

Now Iris felt the blood drain from her face. "They didn't," she said, her voice hollow. Those little pricks. And here she'd been thinking they were her *friends?* Okay, yeah, she'd known they weren't the kind of friends you'd ask to be in your wedding—or, you know, *at* your wedding—but she hadn't thought they'd think that little of her.

Instead of being as horrified as she was, however, Nick began to laugh in earnest. "I can't believe I actually believed them," he said. "As if those losers stood even half a chance of having any kind of…intimacy…with a woman like you."

Iris was about to snarl something in outrage about the three of them when Nick's words registered and stopped her. Mostly because they made something warm and fizzy go *pop* in her brain, chasing away all the bad thoughts. First he'd called her lovely, and now he was saying she was worthy of better men than Chuck and Donny and Hobie. Which, okay, wasn't maybe such an amazing compliment, but the way he'd said it, he made it sound like one.

He chuckled for another moment, then looked at her in a

way that made the warm fizziness travel from her brain to her chest, then down to her belly, then lower still, to settle in a place where she'd never quite felt warm fizziness before. Well, all right, she'd felt warm fizziness there before, but not like this. Usually, when Iris thought about sex, it was in some hazy, uncertain, slightly fearful way. Now, thinking about it with Nick, the haziness and uncertainty were still there, but the fear was totally gone.

His laughter faded off, and very softly he asked, "Why are you telling me this about yourself, Iris?"

She shrugged, the gesture feeling in no way casual, and stared into her coffee. "Like you said. Confession is good for the soul."

"So it is," he agreed in that same quiet voice. "And do you feel better now, having confessed this?"

She thought about that for a moment and was surprised to hear herself answer honestly, "Yeah. This time I think I do."

When she looked up again, Nick was smiling at her in a way she'd never seen him smile before. "Interestingly, Iris," he said, "I think I feel better now, too." He quickly added, "What are you doing for dinner this evening? Perhaps you and I could go out for a bite."

She tried not to look too stunned by the invitation. Nick never invited any of them to go out anywhere with him. And dinner? That was just so…intimate.

"I have to work at the coffee shop this afternoon," she told him. "But I get off at five. Dinner sounds…" *Intimate,* she thought. "Fun," she said.

CHAPTER TWELVE

JAVA JACKIE'S, LILA'S newest—and most temporary—place of employment, was decorated in typical nouveau Bohemian. The mustard-and-brown walls were covered with framed Art Deco posters depicting coffee beans in varying degrees of production, and the kidney-shaped tables were big enough to seat two, maybe three electrons in their artsy, leopard-print chairs. Both the patrons and the employees were a bit... quirky. And Lila wasn't sure if it was a good thing or not that she felt right at home the moment she began her shift.

Although she would be keeping a careful eye on the clientele, there were three other Waverly students working with her, all of whom were worthy of consideration, and one of whom had specifically made it onto the official OPUS list. Iris Daugherty's background check hadn't contained anything remarkable, other than that she was unusually bright and had been a high achiever in high school. But she was a known associate of Chuck Miller, which made her more than a little suspicious. And not just because Chuck was probably engaged in criminal behavior. No, Lila found her suspicious simply by virtue of being an associate of Chuck Miller. Not that it was in any way a virtue to hang out with that little son of a bitch.

Inescapably, Lila's thoughts turned to the events of the night before. But they weren't thoughts about what had happened in Chuck's room. That was something that was easily forgotten. It was Joel's words at the apartment later that still weighed heavily.

I just haven't met a woman who was anything special.

She wondered how long it would take for those words, spoken in Joel's deep, velvety voice, to leave her. And she wondered why they were still hanging around in the first place. And she wondered, too, why every time they echoed in her head, it felt as if someone was tearing another little hole in her heart. She didn't give a damn what anyone thought of her. And she sure as hell didn't want to be special to anyone. Even to a guy like Joel who, okay, was kind of special himself.

She didn't want the same things he did, she reminded herself. She didn't want the home and hearth in the 'burbs that he'd professed to wanting himself. She could no more be a soccer mom than she could perform a lobotomy on herself. Hell, to become a soccer mom *would* be to perform a lobotomy on herself. She didn't begrudge anyone who aspired to a traditional life filled with barbecues and SUVs and school uniforms. But to try to live a life like that herself?

It would kill her. If not physically, then certainly spiritually.

She liked who she was. She liked the life she lived. Yeah, maybe she'd had some problems with her job over the past year. Maybe there had been days when she'd wondered if it was all worth it. And maybe there had been times when she'd felt a little empty inside and thought that there must be something more. Still she wouldn't change anything from her past, even if she could. Because her experiences, even the bad ones, were what made her the woman she was today. And that woman had no desire for the things Joel Faraday desired. That woman shouldn't even be wanting a man like him.

So why, even after what he'd said to her the night before, did she still want him so much?

"Hi, I'm Iris. You're Jenny, right?"

The brightly offered greeting brought Lila's thoughts back around where they needed to be—on the assignment. Funny how they kept veering away from that. She smiled at the young woman who had joined her behind the counter, noting that she was dressed entirely—as was virtually everyone in Java Jackie's, including Lila—in black. Having scoped out the shop the day before and noted the proclivities of its inhabitants, Lila had made sure she would fit in.

"Yeah, Jenny Sturgis," she introduced herself. She extended a hand and the other woman, though clearly surprised by the gesture, shook it.

"You're still in training?" Iris asked.

Lila nodded. "Yeah, it's my first day. But I've worked jobs like this before."

Iris nodded back. "There's not a lot to it."

She gave Lila a brief rundown on how to find and run everything, letting her wait on the first few customers to get the hang of things. The stream of people was fairly steady for the first hour, but by midafternoon things had slowed to nearly a crawl, giving the two women a chance to talk as they tidied up. Their conversation revolved mostly around classes, music and movies, and then, inescapably, boys.

"So you dating anyone?" Iris asked.

"Actually, I'm living with someone," Lila replied, staying true to the history of Jenny Sturgis.

"No way," Iris said with a smile. "You gonna marry him?"

"Oh, God, no," Lila told her quickly.

Iris laughed. "Not the marrying kind, huh?"

"No, I'm not," Lila told her. Which she actually didn't know for sure about Jenny, but what the hell.

Iris's expression shifted to puzzled. "No, I meant him. He's not the marrying kind. Most guys aren't, right?"

Lila found the remark curious. Not that she disagreed, but Iris didn't seem as if she'd had the right kind of experiences in life—which would actually be the wrong kind of experiences—to come to such a conclusion so soon. "Actually, he *is* the marrying kind," she told Iris. "But I'm not."

"So then…he wants to marry you?"

"No, no," Lila replied quickly. A little too quickly, judging by the look on Iris's face. "I mean…" She hesitated. Just what did she mean? And why had she answered for herself instead of Jenny? For all she knew, Jenny wanted to be the very soccer mom Lila didn't.

Why was she having so much trouble staying in character for this assignment? Whatever role Lila was told to assume, she assumed it brilliantly. And once she got in character, she stayed that way until the assignment was over. She walked, talked, dressed, thought, ate and played like whomever she was supposed to be. Always.

Until now.

It wasn't just today that she was having trouble being Jenny Sturgis. She hadn't been Jenny since… Well, now that she thought about it, she realized she'd never really taken on the role of Jenny completely. Even though Jenny Sturgis should have been one of the easiest roles she'd ever assumed, Lila hadn't been able to assume it.

Or else she hadn't wanted to.

Realization dawned on her then, like a Louisville Slugger to the back of the head. It wasn't that Lila hadn't been able to become Jenny Sturgis. It was that she hadn't wanted to. For some reason, on some level, she'd wanted to be herself for this assignment. But why this one? The only thing different this time was—

Joel.

Whap went the Louisville Slugger a second time. Lila hadn't wanted to be Jenny this time because she'd wanted to be herself with Joel.

Hell of a time for a revelation, she thought, noting that Iris was beginning to look as confused as Lila felt. She told herself she'd think about all this later, and somehow managed to return her attention to the woman she was supposed to be investigating.

"So why are you living with this guy," Iris said, "if he wants to get married to someone, but not to you, and you don't want to get married at all?"

Now was as good a time as any to turn the tables, Lila thought. So she muttered something about her guy just being a really great guy and asked Iris, "Why do you think most guys don't want to get married?"

She shrugged. "I don't know. I guess 'cause none of the guys I know is the marrying kind."

Good thing, too, Lila thought, since her closest friends

were losers like Chuck Miller. The thought of that guy pro-creating was enough to keep a person awake nights.

"So are you dating anyone?" she asked in an effort to keep the conversation on Iris.

"No. Yes. I don't know," the other woman replied in a rush of words.

"You don't know if you're dating anyone?"

Iris smiled a little shyly. "Well, there is a guy. And we are going out tonight for the first time."

"Oh, he's a *new* guy," Lila said.

"Actually, I've known him a few months. But tonight's the first time we're actually going out on a date. It's really kind of weird that I even like him," Iris added. "I mean, we have hardly anything in common. And he's way older than me."

"How much older?" Lila asked, her interest piqued.

"Maybe twenty years?" Iris said, sounding both amazed and almost apologetic for going out with someone that much older.

Roughly the same age as Adrian Padgett, Lila thought. And Adrian was notorious for liking much younger women.

"And he's, like, Mr. Suit," Iris added. "The really expensive kind. He's got a ton of money. Not that that kind of thing is all that important to me. But it's another thing I'm usually not all that crazy about when it comes to guys."

Adrian Padgett had a lot of money, Lila thought further. And he spent a good bit of it on tailored suits.

"But he's not like a lot of rich guys," Iris continued. "He's very sweet."

Okay, not sounding much like Adrian now. "So what is he, like a stockbroker or something?" she asked.

Had Lila been anyone else, she probably wouldn't have noticed the very slight, very brief shadow that fell over Iris's features at hearing the question about what her boyfriend did for a living. But Lila did notice it. And it told her more than anything else Iris had said so far. Immediately, she went on alert.

"He's a businessman of some kind," Iris said vaguely. "Investor or something. I can never understand all that finance stuff."

"Tell me about it," Lila said, rolling her eyes. "My father is a businessman, too, but I couldn't for the life of me tell you what his job involves."

The verbal side route about Jenny's father had been intended to deflate Iris's sudden wariness, and it worked like a charm. She smiled the sort of smile people share when they discover the common bond of cluelessness.

"I can't imagine dating a guy like my dad, though," Lila added, hoping to squeeze out more information. "He's so ultraconservative and old-fashioned and everything. Not to mention he's losing his hair, and he's all flabby and out of shape. I like guys buff and gorgeous."

"Oh, he's totally in shape. And totally gorgeous. He's like…" A dreamy look came over her face as she thought about him. "Like that guy who used to play James Bond."

Alarm bells that were nearly deafening began to go off in Lila's head. What an interesting choice Iris had made to compare her beloved to. Her answer to Lila's next question would be critical. "Which one? Pierce Brosnan or Timothy Dalton?"

Iris shook her head. "No, not them. The one a long time ago."

"Roger Moore?" Lila asked.

Again Iris shook her head. "No, that's not it. I can't remember his name. Something Irish."

"Sean Connery?"

"That's the one. He looks like Sean Connery. They have the same smile."

Sean Connery was actually Scottish, but Lila wasn't going to pick nits. She had something far more important pounding in her brain at the moment. The first time she'd laid eyes on Adrian Padgett, she'd thought he looked vaguely familiar. It wasn't until sometime later that it finally hit her. He bore a vague resemblance to a younger Sean Connery.

Especially when he smiled.

Of course, there were probably a lot of men out there who bore a resemblance to Sean Connery and had similar smiles. And people who were smitten often saw the object of their affections in a more flattering light than was actual. So it was entirely possible that the object of Iris Daugherty's affections didn't look a thing like Sean Connery. It was entirely possible that the man with whom she was so entranced was not Adrian Padgett.

Then again, it was entirely possible that he was.

"Sean Connery, huh?" Lila asked, revealing none of the excitement that was humming just beneath her skin. "All tall, dark and handsome?"

"Tall and handsome, yes," Iris told her. "But his hair's actually kind of brownish with red highlights, and his eyes are this gorgeous amber."

The excitement zinging through Lila went downright

atomic at that. Not many men had amber eyes. But Adrian Padgett did. He also had dark auburn hair.

"So what's this guy's name?" Lila asked, knowing the reply wouldn't be *Adrian Padgett,* since Adrian was much too smart for that, but thinking it might be close. He'd often used variations on his name, or names that mirrored his initials, in the past.

"It's Nick," Iris said. "Nick Darian."

Darian. An anagram of *Adrian.* And another word for *Jackpot.*

Lila knew without question that the love of Iris Daugherty's life was the same man she'd been hunting for years, the man she and Joel had come to Cincinnati to find. Now all Lila had to do was figure out how to get Iris to lead them to him. Unfortunately, before she had a chance to ask anything more, Waverly's quick recall team came into the shop for an afternoon confab, and the two women didn't have another spare moment to chat. The coffee shop was so busy, in fact, that Lila didn't even notice when Iris was relieved by another employee and left for the day.

With no small frustration, Lila finished her shift like a good little employee, since she didn't want to draw attention to herself by bugging out early. Her thoughts, however, were completely consumed by the case. Finally. And the more Lila thought about how close they were to capturing Sorcerer, the more agitated she became. And not just her thoughts became frantic.

It was always like this when she began the final sprint toward an assignment's conclusion—her body and brain both reacted anxiously to whatever made all the pieces of the puzzle fall into place. Her mind darted in a dozen different directions at once, all five senses became hyperaware, her body hummed with expectancy until she could feel the anticipation in every pore. It was as if her body knew it needed to be supercharged for what was to come, and it was gearing up now.

Unfortunately, her body always got way ahead of itself. Even being as close as they were, it could potentially be days before she and Joel got their hands on Sorcerer. In the past, to alleviate the tension, Lila had used sex as an outlet. Unfortunately, she'd been without a sex partner for months. And the idea of finding some stranger to fit the bill was in no way appealing.

Of course, there was Joel, she thought immediately. But Joel had imposed a boundary that he, at least, wouldn't cross. She'd have to find some other way to burn off her tension. Waverly had a gym, she recalled. Not nearly as much fun as romping in bed with an able-bodied male, but it would have to do. After she finished her shift at Java Jackie's, she'd drive to the campus to tackle the weight room. A couple of hours ought to do it. Then she could go home to Joel with a reasonably clear head, a reasonably satisfied body and reasonably well focused energy. And then they could plan their attack.

Depending on how long it took them to track Sorcerer, Lila figured she'd probably be seeing a lot of the Waverly weight room over the next couple of days. Which was just as well. Because she wasn't *special* enough for Joel.

CHAPTER THIRTEEN

JOEL HAD JUST UNCOVERED some very interesting information in the data he'd mined out of Hobie Jurgens's computer when he heard the front door slam shut and Lila's voice call out, "Joel?"

He noticed right off that she hadn't used her customary greeting of "Hi, honey, I'm home," and wasn't sure he wanted to think about why not. The intimacy of the "Hi, honey" comment had been a joke before, because there was no intimacy in the comment. But now...

Well, since the kiss—and then some—that the two of them had shared last night, the intimacy was all too real. Or might have been. Had he not put the brakes on what could have happened.

"In here," he called out, nudging the memories of last night out of his brain. He was getting used to having to do that, since memories of the way Lila had felt in his arms had been creeping into his thoughts all day. Good thing he was getting so much practice. He had a feeling he was going to be battling memories of that for the rest of his life.

He tried to focus on the lines of code scrolling across the screen of his laptop, shaking his head at the ingenuity that had gone into the programming. Hobie was a genius, no two ways about it. If the kid hadn't been working on the wrong side of the law, Joel would have suggested to his superiors that he be recruited by OPUS. It had taken most of the day for Joel to hack his way into Hobie's files, and boy, what he'd found once he got there. The beginnings of a computer virus unlike anything Joel had ever encountered.

He was convinced now that Hobie was working in conjunction with Sorcerer. Which meant Donny Grawemeyer and Chuck Miller doubtless were, too, because the three of them were virtually inseparable. It was interesting, because Joel would have suspected that Chuck was the dominant member of the group, and maybe he was, as far as personalities went. But after studying the contents of Hobie's hard drive, it was clear he was the real brain. With a little more tweaking and refining, the virus he was designing could indeed take out half the planet before it was stopped. Probably Hobie was still working on it because half the planet wasn't enough. If Joel and Lila didn't find Sorcerer soon, this baby was going to go off in all their faces.

He heard the rustle of her approach beyond his bedroom door and, damning himself for primping even as he did it, ran a hand through his hair to straighten it and checked to make sure his clothes matched and his buttons were properly aligned. Yep, the burgundy oxford shirt and blue jeans were presentable enough for the occasion, which tonight, considering what he'd just discovered, would be brainstorming a new strategy. Looked as if he and Lila would be ordering in for dinner.

Of course, the moment he got a look at her, leaning in his bedroom doorway, he began to think about other things they could do if they stayed home tonight. She looked, as always, sexy as hell. Her black jeans, ripped at one knee, hugged slender thighs, and her black T-shirt revealed a hint of creamy flesh between it and her waistband, along with a scant peek of her breasts above the deeply scooping neck. As he watched, she tugged a rubber band from the ponytail at the back of her head and shook out her hair, the gesture releasing the aroma of freshly ground coffee. Even that was sexy, because it made him crave something lush and exotic and potent, and that was Lila to a T.

But there was something else about her tonight, too, some barely leashed vibe that hadn't been there when she left this morning. Her face was flushed, as if she'd been exerting herself physically, and a fine sheen of perspiration mottled her forehead. He noticed now that the front of her shirt was damp, too, a faint V of moisture making the fabric of her shirt a shade darker between her breasts.

"You okay?" he asked. "You look like you've been running or something."

"I stopped by the Waverly gym to hit the weight room for a little while."

The announcement surprised him. It seemed an odd side trip for her to make on the way home. "In your street clothes?" he asked.

"Mmm-hmm," she replied, the murmur sounding a little strained for some reason.

He narrowed his eyes at her. "Why?"

"Just feeling a little antsy," she told him. "I had some extra energy I needed to work off."

She looked as if she hadn't worked off much of it, he

thought. One leg was bent slightly, and that foot was perched on its ball, moving rapidly up and down. She'd linked her hands loosely together over her belly, but her thumbs were hammering against each other as if she couldn't keep them still. Even her eyes seemed alive, darting from one thing in the bedroom to another...though never quite settling on Joel. Her whole being seemed to be overflowing with...something. Something restless and potent and barely contained.

"Do you feel better now?" he asked, not a little cautiously.

She shook her head, the movement jerky and anxious. "Not really, no. This, ah...this happens to me on the job sometimes," she told him, her gaze still ricocheting around the room. "I get this overabundance of adrenaline or something. Just have to do whatever I can to burn it off. Sometimes working with weights will do it. Sometimes it takes, um...something else. I'll be fine. Eventually."

He sensed it then, as if a huge, invisible wave slammed into him, knocking him down and jerking him out with the undertow. It wasn't just adrenaline rushing through Lila. It was something much stronger. Something much more primitive. Something much more arousing.

Something much too contagious.

"Wh-what?" he stammered, pushing the thought away. Mostly because it was a thought he couldn't afford to have right now. Or ever. "What's the matter?"

She continued to fidget, but her gaze finally connected with his. And stayed there. "There's only one degree of separation between us and Adrian Padgett," she told him.

Something hot exploded in Joel's belly at hearing the announcement. "How do you know? Did you see him?"

She shook her head. "But Iris Daugherty can take us to him. She and I had a nice little chat at work tonight about boys. She seems to have rather a crush on a man who sounds a lot like Adrian."

"Did she mention him by name?"

"No. He's going by Nick Darian. But the description fits. And Darian is an anagram for Adrian." She added with a half-hearted smile, "And my spider sense is tingling."

With the force of a jackhammer, by the looks of her. Her entire body seemed to vibrate with whatever had her so agitated. And hers wasn't the only one, he realized. Something in him started tingling, too. And talk about your jackhammers... Only, the sensation steaming through Joel like a locomotive had nothing to do with their proximity to Sorcerer. This was a sensation he recognized too well, even if he hadn't felt it for years. As turned on as he'd been by Lila last night, it paled compared to what was raging through him now. Last night he'd been able to control his feelings. Barely. He wasn't sure he'd succeed a second time. Not when he felt like this.

"Where is he?" he asked Lila, trying to stay focused on what should have been important.

"I don't know," she said.

She pushed herself away from the door frame and began a slow journey into the room. One step. Two. Three. Four. Then she halted, as if she'd suddenly realized she was moving toward him and had to make herself stop.

"I didn't get a chance to find out," she said. "But Iris Daugherty is our link, Joel, I know it. We need to get someone on her right away."

"I'll phone home tonight and arrange it," he said, using the term field agents used for contacting OPUS. Not that it mattered, since he and Lila had fallen completely out of character by now. And he had a feeling they were about to fall even more.

They watched each other in silence for a few long moments, and with each ensuing one, Joel felt the level of awareness ratchet higher. The heat, too, cranked higher. Along with every last one of his senses. He noted every detail on Lila's body, from the way her flesh was flushed above the neckline of her shirt to how her nipples had pebbled against the fabric. He heard her breathing coming in short, shallow breaths that seemed to mimic his own suddenly ragged respiration. He smelled the trenchant remnants of her workout mingling with the coffee now, an earthy aroma that surrounded him until he could almost taste the salt that must linger on her skin. Even his sense of touch seemed more sensitive, his fingertips growing hot as he skimmed them restlessly over the denim of his jeans. And he couldn't help wondering if he touched Lila that way, would his hands burst into flame?

Stupid question, he told himself. The way she was looking at him now, his entire body was about to burst into flame.

He inhaled a deep breath and released it slowly, thinking it might slow his rapid heart rate. But it came out thready and unsteady, and only made his pulse race more. "I, ah...I've made a, um...a breakthrough at my end, as well," he finally said.

He turned the laptop so that Lila could see what he'd discovered, telling himself it was *not* because he wanted her to finish her trek across the room to get a better look at it, something that would put her within touching distance. There would be no touching, Joel told himself. None. They had work to do. Lots and lots of work. Important work, too, by God. Really, really important. Whatever this weird current was arcing between them, it was only because they were so close to finally grabbing Sorcerer. It wasn't because of... anything else.

She completed the handful of steps necessary to put her right beside him, then bent forward a little so that she might see the screen better—or something. The aroma of coffee was stronger now, but not strong enough to mask the scent that was intrinsically—erotically—hers. Joel closed his eyes and swallowed hard. He need only lift his hand a few inches to open it over the small of her back. A few more, and he could tumble her right into his lap. And then he'd get a lot more than his hands involved.

"What is it?" she said as she studied the collection of letters and numbers and symbols on the screen. Her voice was soft, breathless and thick with something he told himself he should just try to ignore. "I don't get it."

Which, of course, was the problem, he thought. Neither of them was getting it, which was why he kept noticing things like how the rosy bloom on her flesh had deepened, and how her breathing was growing more frayed, and how her luscious scent was starting to intoxicate him, and how easy it would be to have her in his lap, and then he could fill his hands with her breasts and fill her mouth with his tongue and fill herself with himself.

She glanced away from the screen and stood straight

again, then looked down at Joel. And immediately her expression began to change, from mildly curious to thoroughly confused to hopefully uncertain to profoundly aroused.

And then, in a voice that was soft and rough and needy, she said, "Joel?"

He couldn't have stopped himself from doing what he did next any more than he could have halted a speeding locomotive with one hand. Still sitting, he settled both hands on her hips and tugged her closer, then pressed his open mouth against the bare flesh of her abdomen just above her navel.

She sucked in a breath at the gesture, but immediately dropped her hands to his head, tangling one in his hair and opening the other over his cheek. Then she bent to touch her forehead to the crown of his head and curled her arms around his shoulders. It was all the encouragement Joel needed. More than he needed, really. Just having Lila in the same room with him was enough. Having her in the world was enough. He knew in that moment that no matter what happened in the days ahead, no matter what happened after this assignment was over, no matter where she went or what she did, or where he went or what he did, he would always want Lila Moreau. Because what he felt for her was unlike anything he had felt for a woman before. She was indeed special. And she had indeed become a part of his life. Even if she stayed for only a little while, she would be with him forever.

It didn't matter how she felt about him, he decided as he nudged her shirt higher and opened his mouth over her bare torso. It only mattered how he felt about her. He wanted her. He needed her. He might very well have fallen in love with her. And there was no reason he shouldn't—couldn't—have her.

He pushed her shirt higher still, revealing the taut, elegant musculature beneath a filmy bra the color of good champagne. She wasn't the silk-and-lace type, but the garment was sexy anyway, sweeping low on her breasts to reveal their upper halves, as smooth and supple as fine silk. She removed her shirt the rest of the way herself, tossing it carelessly aside, then returned her hands to his hair. She pushed the dark tresses back over his scalp as he dragged a long line of open-mouthed kisses across her belly, as if she wanted to watch him while he kissed her. He closed his eyes and moved his head lower, rubbing his lips lightly over the band of flesh above her waistband, dipping his tongue into the delectable dent of her navel, loving the soft gasp that escaped her when he did. Then his fingers were working at the button and zipper of her jeans, freeing the former and lowering the latter, until the tiny triangle of her underwear became visible beneath.

She groaned softly, her fingers tightening in his hair. Joel pushed his hands up over her back, marveling at the shallow bumps and swells of muscle he encountered. The recognition of her physical strength aroused him even more, and he skimmed his hands higher, deftly unfastening her brassiere, which tumbled down over her arms. As she shifted to free herself of the garment, he covered her breasts with both hands, squeezing gently, loving the way they fit so perfectly in his palms. She sighed at the contact, as if she realized, too, just how well she and he went together.

She lowered herself into his lap, straddling his thighs,

scooting herself forward over the hard ridge of his cock that was by now surging against the heavy denim of his blue jeans. Still cupping one luscious breast in his hand, Joel moved his head forward, opening his mouth wide over the taut nipple and dusky aureole, pulling both deep inside to press his tongue hard against her soft warmth. She gasped again at the quickness of his possession, looping both arms around his neck and burying her fingers in his hair again, as if she wanted to possess him, too.

For a long time he only sucked hard on her flesh, palming her other breast zealously, reveling in her responding murmurs of delight. Her fingers skimmed down his neck and over his shoulders, settling on the buttons of his shirt, freeing them one by one before pushing it from his shoulders completely. Her hands roved up and down his bare arms now, over his chest, his shoulders, his neck, his jaw, then back into his hair before starting the journey all over again. Finally she dropped her hands between their legs and pushed at the zipper of Joel's fly, tugging it down until she could tuck her hand inside his jeans.

His cock surged against her fingers in welcome, and she immediately cupped her palm over the head, rubbing, stroking, pushing, until Joel jerked his head from her breast to catch his breath. The moment he did, she levered herself off his lap and dropped to her knees in front of him and, freeing him from his boxers, covered the head of his cock with her mouth. The thrill that shot through him then was exquisite, all heat and fire and barely restrained eruption. So long. It had been so long since a woman had touched him, teased him, tasted him. And never had one been so eager to have him as Lila was then.

"I want all of you," she panted against his swollen flesh, pushing now at his blue jeans. "Every last inch."

Joel stood long enough for her to jerk his clothes down around his knees before collapsing into the chair again. Then Lila bent over him once more, curling her fingers around the base of his shaft and tracing her tongue around the head. He made a hazy promise to himself to return the favor later, then sat back to enjoy the ride.

And what a ride it was, pushing him to unimaginable heights, speeding him around sharp curves and through mind-blowing loop-de-loops. By the time Lila crawled into his lap again, this time completely naked, Joel wasn't even sure where his body ended and hers began.

Oh, wait. Thanks to what she did next, he did actually know that. Because she curled her fingers around his cock and covered his mouth with hers, thrusting her tongue deep inside as she stroked him once, twice, three times, four. Then she dipped her head close to his ear and said, "Let's go to bed. We're going to need more room."

He wasn't sure how he managed it, but somehow he was able to finish undressing and find his way into his bed with Lila beside him. For a long time they only lay naked side by side, their limbs entwined, their mouths joined, each of them exploring as much of the other's body as they could reach. Then Lila pulled away a little and, smiling at him in a way he liked very, *very* much, urged Joel onto his back.

When she straddled his waist, he dropped his hands to her hips, gripping them firmly and pulling her toward his chest. She seemed to understand what he wanted, because she rose on her knees and moved forward, climbing over his shoulders and bracing a knee on the mattress on each side of his head. She gripped the headboard as he lifted his head from the pillow, looking down to meet his gaze full-on as he touched his mouth to her sex. She hissed a sound of pleasure at the contact, but she never stopped watching him.

Her expression changed as he licked her tender flesh, however, softening and going slack with every stroke of his tongue against her. She tasted dark and musky and hot, an irresistible combination, and when she finally closed her eyes and threw her head backward, he closed his, too, to better savor the experience. He darted his tongue deftly between the damp folds of her flesh, slow, then fast, then slow again. Then he slipped his long middle finger into her slick canal and ate her more voraciously.

She rocketed upward at the invasion, but he followed her, driving his finger deeper, and licking her harder. She cried out a half dozen times, her body jerking in unison with the sounds, then went completely still, save the shudder her orgasm sent through her. Then, with a final groan of *complete* satisfaction, she collapsed atop him. Carefully Joel withdrew his finger, noting her soft sigh of pleasure when he did. Then, even more carefully, he turned them both so that they lay alongside each other on the bed.

For a long, long time he only kissed her, softly, tenderly, his hand on her breast, hers on his cock, each of them stroking the other with slow, gentle caresses. They hadn't finished, of course, but Joel knew she needed some time to regroup. No matter. Just touching Lila brought him infinitely more pleasure than even the earthiest coupling with any other woman had.

She finally ended the kiss, but she continued to caress his cock as she said, "I think it's only fair that I should tell you that I never come more than once. That was why I was trying to hold it off when you…ah… When you…um… When you…uh…"

Joel smiled as he watched her speak, unable to believe what he was seeing. Lila Moreau was blushing. She was stumbling over words he would have thought her very comfortable with. He hadn't thought her capable of either.

"When I what?" he said, still grinning.

"When you…you know…"

"What, you can't even say it?"

She shook her head.

His grin broadened. "Lila Moreau? Can't talk dirty?"

Her blush deepened. "Not with you," she said.

The words surprised him. "Why not?"

She ducked her head. Very softly she told him, "Because it's not dirty with you."

The thrill that shot through him then was nearly overwhelming. He told himself not to read anything into her comment. But something inside him…splintered at hearing what she said. Then whatever it was burst open completely. And then it spilled happiness and a strange kind of completion through his entire system.

"What is it with me, then?" he asked quietly.

But she only shook her head and repeated what she'd said before. "I can't come again, Joel," she repeated. "I never have more than one orgasm. And we haven't even…" She sighed, obviously impatient with her lack of articulation. "We haven't even…finished. But I want us to…finish. I just don't want you to think I'm not enjoying myself because I don't have another orgasm. Believe me, I'll enjoy myself plenty."

He smiled at that. "You'll enjoy it even more when I make you come a second time."

"You won't make—"

He moved his hand between her legs and fingered her gently but thoroughly, loving the sound she made, because it was so similar to the ones she'd uttered just before climaxing that first time.

"I will," he told her with utter confidence.

And he proceeded to do just that.

More than once.

WHEN LILA AWOKE, the room was bathed in the pewter light of very early dawn. She lay on her belly half atop Joel, who lay on his back beside her, her hand opened over the center of his chest so that she felt the slow, easy thump of his heartbeat beneath her palm. The arms he'd wrapped around her before the two of them fell asleep still embraced her, and his head was turned toward hers. Her left arm was draped over his hard torso, her left leg was nestled between both of his, and she marveled that, even in sleep, he was fully erect. She smiled. That boded well for later.

She opened her hand wider, loving the feel of his dark hair against her palm and his warm flesh beneath her fingertips, and wondered why it felt so good to wake up like this. This was new to her, this postcoital touching. Normally, once Lila came, she went. Orgasms were great, but she hadn't been lying to Joel when she'd told him she normally never had more than one. And usually one was enough to tide her over until the next one. Usually, after experiencing that physical release, she wanted nothing more from a man for a while. But even though she'd touched and tasted every inch of Joel during the night, she still wanted to be with him. Still wanted to explore him. Still wanted to marvel at all the ways their bodies fit together.

She just wanted to keep looking at him. Touching him. Being with him. She had no idea why.

He began to stir, as if even her one soft touch had been enough to rouse him. When he opened his eyes and saw her gazing at him, he smiled, a delicious, toe-curling smile that made her think everything in the world was just about perfect. And although Lila knew better than most people that the world was a far from perfect place, something about Joel just then made her feel as if perfection was still possible. And, if she was lucky, only moments away.

"Good morning," he murmured in a satisfied voice that made a ripple of pleasure curl through her.

"Good morning," she replied in much the same way.

He lifted a hand to her hair, pushing it lightly over her shoulder. Then he traced his finger along her collarbone, dipped it into the divot at the base of her throat, skimmed it along the line of her jaw. Gentle, tender touches, every one. But every one set a fire wherever his skin made contact with hers.

There hadn't been much gentleness or tenderness in Lila's life, and she still wasn't sure how to react to it. As a child, she had yearned for it, but as an adult, she'd been philo-sophical. Adults outgrew the need for gentleness and tenderness, she'd always told herself. Gentleness and tenderness made adults vulnerable. Made them weak. In her line of work, gentleness and tenderness could even get a person killed. She wasn't a gentle, tender person, and she hadn't thought a man with such traits could be attractive.

But Joel was both, and he more than attracted her. She just couldn't quite get a handle on exactly what it was he made her feel. Other than, at the moment at least, incredibly aroused.

"We should probably try to get some work done today," he said—gently, tenderly—as he pushed his hand into her hair and sifted the dark tresses over his fingers.

"We should," she agreed as she skimmed her hand along his chest and over his neck.

"We got a little sidetracked before we could finish sharing the details of our respective discoveries yesterday," he added. He brushed his fingertips over her cheekbone, then along her lower lip.

"Yeah, we did," she agreed before lightly nipping the pad of his thumb as it went by.

He smiled. "We should get right to it, then," he told her. He dropped his hand to her breast, drawing his thumb slowly along the lower curve.

"We should," she concurred, pushing her hand down the length of his torso.

She kissed him then, rolling her tongue into his mouth, only to have him meet her halfway with his. As they kissed, they continued to caress and stroke each other.

They were lying side by side again, clinging to each other, gasping for breath, groping for coherent thought.

But the thoughts that bubbled to the top of Lila's head were anything but coherent. In fact, they were ridiculous. Because they all seemed to involve her and Joel together as a unit, and in ways that had nothing to do with the assignment they were supposed to be completing. Like coordinating, not covert operations, but grocery lists. And instead of the two of them trying to figure out how to take out the bad guys, she saw them trying to figure out whose turn it was to take out the garbage. In place of deciphering secret codes, they were programming their new TiVo. Even when she pictured them in bed together, it wasn't to see them panting with hunger, but sipping coffee and sharing the Sunday paper.

Harmless scenes, not hazardous ones. Domestic bliss, not dangerous liaisons. Lives of absolute contentment, not desperate achievement. Of serenity, not ferocity. Lives plural, she marveled further, not life singular. The realization of the direction in which her thoughts had traveled stunned Lila to the point where she could only lie on her back and gaze at the ceiling and wonder who had placed a pod from outer space by her bed while she was sleeping. Because an invasion by body snatchers was the only explanation that made any sense. Never in her life had Lila Moreau entertained ideas of sharing that life with anyone, never mind in ways that involved grocery lists and Sunday papers. Unless it was to be relieved that her life included none of that crap.

But it wasn't relief she felt now. It was…something else. Something she dared not try to identify.

"What are you thinking about?"

It was the last question Lila wanted to hear anyone ask

at the moment. That it was Joel asking only made her feel that much more…

Oh, God. Terrified, she realized. She only recognized the emotion now because she had felt it so often as a child. It had been decades since she'd been frightened of anything. But now she was terrified by a question of less than a dozen words. She, Lila Moreau, the most ruthless, most fearless, most dangerous woman in the world, had been brought down by five simple words.

Then she realized it wasn't the question that had her so scared. It was the answer.

So she lied when she told him, "I'm thinking that as nice as this is, it's not what we should be doing right now."

She glanced over at Joel in time to see what had been a radiant smile go dark. And she fought the urge to say something—anything—that might bring it back again. Instead, she told him, "We have an assignment we need to complete. ASAP."

He nodded without much enthusiasm. And she told herself she was only imagining the sarcasm in his voice when he said, "Right. I keep forgetting you're working on a schedule here because you have to be at a wedding in six days to stand up as best man for your former partner."

Actually, that hadn't been why Lila was thinking they needed to finish up as soon as possible. In fact, she wasn't even thinking they needed to hurry in order to save the world. No, it was only her sanity she was worried about saving at the moment. They needed to bring in Sorcerer quickly so she could stop being plagued by thoughts like the ones that had invaded her brain this morning.

Only after Adrian Padgett was in OPUS's custody would her connection to Joel Faraday be severed. And only after her connection to Joel was severed would she stop thinking about things like grocery lists and appliances and coffee in bed. Only then would she stop entertaining ridiculous ideas like how nice it would be to stay with him after the assignment came to a close. Like, for instance, forever. Only then could she go back to feeling like herself again. Like the ruthless, fearless, dangerous—*solitary,* dammit—woman she was. The woman she liked, dammit. The woman she wanted to be, dammit. The woman who was perfectly happy alone, dammit. The woman who didn't need anybody.

Dammit.

CHAPTER FOURTEEN

"OH, MAN, IT'S TOO BAD you missed the party, Iris. You woulda loved it."

"Yeah, they dumped Chuck in the middle of the living room like a bag of dirty laundry."

"Yeah, dirty laundry without any pants or underwear in it!"

"Hey, I said shut up, you dicks, or I'll tear you both new ones!"

From her position on the sofa in Nick's suite, Iris rolled her eyes at Hobie and Donny, both seated on the floor, as they concluded with much laughter the story of Chuck's party de-pantsing two nights ago. Chuck sat in a chair on the other side of the suite, deliberately having separated himself from the rest of them, his face tightened by anger and embarrass-ment…and something else that transcended both.

Served him right, the little prick—in more ways than one, evidently, Iris thought with some small satisfaction. Which, she thought further, would be all that Chuck would be able to provide with his little prick. She just wished Hobie and Donny could have suffered a similar indignity. After what Nick had told her the guys said about her, it was all Iris could do not to smack the crap out of all three of them. The only reason she hadn't was that she didn't want to compromise their project, and because Nick had assured her the guys had said what they had only to try to win points with him. Not that that had made her feel any better, but she didn't want to make waves at this point, either. The sooner they finished building the virus for Nick, the sooner she could part ways with those assholes. And, you know, smack the crap out of them before she left.

Still, she couldn't help smiling as Hobie and Donny added a few more details about just how itty-bitty Chuck's widdle weewee was. As entertaining as it must have been, she was glad she hadn't gone to the party after leaving the suggested three-way between her roommate and her roommate's sleazy boyfriend. She'd had a much nicer time with Nick than she would have had at DUC house. In fact, the past few days with him had been some of the most enjoyable she'd had in years.

She just wished she knew what the past few days with him had been about. Although she'd spent a third night in his suite last night after they returned from dinner, he hadn't pressed her for anything sexual, and she'd once again slept on the sofa bed in the living area. He hadn't even kissed her good-night, something that had surprised Iris, considering the nice time they'd had together, and considering the way she'd seen him looking at her on more than one occasion. There was no mistaking his attraction to her. And he'd treated her to plenty of innocent touches, placing his hand at the small of her back as he followed her to their table in the restaurant, draping an arm casually across her shoulders as they strode to his car, brushing a strand of hair behind her ear when the evening breeze nudged it over her forehead.

But he hadn't pursued anything more, even though she'd tried to make clear her interest. Maybe he was put off by her virginity, she thought. Maybe he was afraid she would take too seriously anything that happened between the two of them. Not that that would have anything to do with her virginity. Not that she wasn't already taking seriously everything that happened between them.

She glanced over at Nick now and saw that he was in no way amused by the report of Chuck's humiliation. Seated at the desk with his fingers steepled together, he was alternating his gaze between Hobie and Donny, who were closest to him, and Chuck on the far side of the room. But he was looking at all of them as if they were silverfish that had just crawled up from the bathtub drain. Because it was Sunday, he'd forgone his usual suit in favor of more casual attire—though, in Iris's opinion, his khakis and navy polo still made him look formal and reserved, even if he had left the shirt untucked. And his dark expression did nothing to alleviate the image.

Chuck's expression wasn't much different, but he was glaring only at Hobie and Donny. "You dicks tell that story one more time, to one more person, I swear to God, I'll kill you."

"But it's such a great story!" Donny objected, clearly unbothered by the threat. "I could tell it a million times."

Hobie nodded his blond head enthusiastically. "Yeah, I never woulda guessed you had such a wee willie winkie, Chuck. What'd you do with the rolled-up sock you usually shove down your pants? Musta come as a huge surprise to the lady when she got a look at the real thing."

"Nah, it was a *tiny* surprise," Donny countered, laughing

again. "A surprise about *th-i-i-i-s big*." He held up his thumb and forefinger about a millimeter apart.

"You mean *th-a-a-a-t small!*" Hobie cried, doubling over again.

More uproarious laughter. More Chuck glaring. More Nick looking disgusted.

"It was shrinkage!" Chuck finally shouted, loud enough that Iris was fairly sure everyone on the hotel's housekeeping staff heard. Even the ones who were off for the evening. "It happens to everybody. Haven't you seen that *Seinfeld* episode?"

"Everyone's seen that *Seinfeld* episode," Hobie told him. "And every guy who has a needle dick just uses it for an excuse. *I've* never had a problem with shrinkage."

Iris rolled her eyes again. Yeah, 'cause how could something that's barely there to begin with get any smaller? Not that she had any personal knowledge of Hobie's Incredible Nonshrinking Member. It was just obvious, that was all.

"Me neither," Donny joined in. "I've never had that problem, either."

Ditto, Iris thought. In fact, now that she thought about it, small physical endowments would explain a lot about this group. She looked at Nick and decided it explained why he was so different from the other guys, too. Not that she had personal knowledge of his supersize member, either. It was just obvious, that was all.

"You are so lame," Chuck told the other guys.

"Better than being so limp," Hobie replied.

"And a needle dick," Donny added helpfully.

"I am *not* a—" Chuck began. But he cut himself off with an exasperated sound.

Although, Iris thought, maybe *cut himself off* wasn't the best phrase to use here. All things considered.

"That was one smokin'-hot babe who took you down, though," Hobie said, his voice so reverent, he could have been talking about the Second Coming. "I usually like 'em blond and blue-eyed, but I gotta say, she makes a strong argument for brown-eyed girls."

"I don't think her eyes are really brown," Donny said thoughtfully. "I talked to her for a while, and you could tell she was wearing those colored contacts."

"Naw," Hobie disagreed. "If someone was gonna wear colored contacts, why would they pick brown? Hell, do they even *make* colored contacts in brown? Besides, her hair was dark, and dark hair and eyes always happen together."

"You are so fulla shit," Donny said. "I got a cousin with black hair and blue eyes. She was wearing contacts."

"Well, it doesn't matter," Hobie told him in an I'm-blowing-you-off-now voice. "She was smokin' hot, no matter what color her eyes were." Then, to Chuck, he added with a smile, "Too bad she doesn't like needle dicks."

Shaking his head and looking at no one now, Chuck said in a voice Iris had never heard him use before, one that frankly chilled her, "Man, if I *ever* get my hands on that bitch and her dick of a boyfriend, I'll kill 'em both."

"Yeah, and how you gonna do that, Chuckie?" Donny asked jovially, clearly not having noted the menace in Chuck's voice that Iris had. "She's just some chick you met in the library. And after what happened at the party, you can bet your ass she's not going to come looking for you again."

Iris had been sneaking peeks at Nick during the exchange—but, of course, she was always sneaking peeks at Nick when the group was together—and had noted the way his expression changed as the guys' remarks moved from one subject to the next. At first he'd looked disgusted by the story. Then, as the group had talked about the mystery woman's hotness, he'd become more interested. Though Iris told herself she had *not* felt a twinge of jealousy at how he'd become interested in the story only because of the introduction of a hot babe into it. Strangely, however, it was when Hobie mentioned the possibility of contact lenses that Nick's attention had really become honed on the conversation. By the time Donny uttered the words "come looking for you again," Nick's eyes had narrowed and his lips had parted fractionally, as if there was something he wanted to say, but he wasn't quite sure how to say it.

Finally, though, he repeated, "Looking for you again? Is that what you said, Hobie?" He directed his next question at Chuck. "Why was she looking for you the first time?"

All three guys looked at Nick, seeming surprised to find him in the room. Which was pretty much the way they always looked at him. Iris knew they didn't take Nick very seriously. Certainly not the way she did. Not that she would expect any of them to be interested in him the way she was. But they weren't interested in him in any other way, either. Sure, they gave the guy credit for organizing their group into something more than just a bunch of slackers looking to make mischief for fun and profit. Nick had focused them into a whole new direction, where making mischief for fun and profit was also promising to make them rich.

But the guys knew—and so did Iris—that Nick was only

the glue holding them all together. And maybe he was the map by which they were guided, too. But he wasn't the brains. He wasn't the brawn. He wasn't even the doer, truth be told, since the guys and Iris were always the ones creating and sending out the viruses and doing the hacking. Nick was the planner. He was the guy who found the targets. The one who watched their backs. He was important to the group, for sure. But he wasn't essential. They all knew it. Probably Nick knew it, too. It was why he tolerated them when he so obviously disdained them—at least the guys.

Now the guys looked back at Nick with puzzled expressions. When none of them said anything, he repeated his question. "What makes you think she was looking for you a first time? *Was* she looking for you, Chuck? You specifically, I mean?"

"Dude, it was just a figure of speech," Hobie said. "I don't think she was really looking for Chuck that first time."

Donny nodded. "Yeah, she just wandered into the computer lab one day when he was working. Needed some help with some of her homework or something. If Duncan had been working that day instead of Chuck, she woulda ended up at a party at TKE house."

"And happier," Hobie said. "Since everybody knows those TKE guys are hung like horses."

"Shove it, Hobie," Chuck said in that same voice that had sent a chill through Iris.

Finally, finally, the guys seemed to pick up on the threat lacing the third man's voice, because they both stopped laughing mid-guffaw and threw Chuck a look that was more than a little concerned.

Nick seemed in no way bothered by Chuck's sinister turn himself. "Are you sure?" he asked. "That she wasn't looking for you specifically that day?"

Chuck's puzzlement turned to something else then, something Iris wasn't sure she wanted to identify. Mostly because it looked like something really, really scary. "What do you mean?" he asked.

"I mean did she just show up out of nowhere at the library that day? Or is she someone you've seen around campus before?"

The three guys exchanged looks, then all shook their heads and replied that no, none of them had encountered her before the party Friday night, or, in Chuck's case, at the library the day before.

Nick looked at Iris. "How about you? Any smokin'-hot brunettes among your circle of female friends?"

She shook her head. But then, she didn't have a circle of female friends. She didn't have a circle of friends at all. Especially now that she knew Chuck and Donny and Hobie thought so little of her. Iris wasn't exactly a social person. Nor was she predisposed to trust people. Chuck, Hobie and Donny might have had their faults, but—until recently, anyway—she'd trusted them as much as she'd ever trusted anyone. She'd known them for three years now, and—until recently, anyway—none of them had ever screwed her over. But even with their having lied about her to Nick—assholes would be assholes, after all—in Iris's book, the time she'd spent with the three of them was pretty much the same as childhood sweethearts celebrating their seventy-fifth wedding anniversary.

"But it's a big campus," Hobie said in response to Nick's question. "She coulda been around and we just never saw her."

Nick sat forward in his chair, dropping his hands into his lap now and studying each of the guys in turn. "Is the campus so big that you don't notice a smokin'-hot babe when you see one?" he asked. "Waverly's not exactly overrun with them. Most of the students are male, and most of the female students are pretty forgettable-looking."

Iris's back went up at that, her chin instinctively lifted and an indignant heat exploded in her belly.

"Present company excluded, Iris," he added belatedly, moving his attention to her.

She had thought he would try to further patronize her by saying more and falling all over himself to apologize, but his voice was matter-of-fact, and his gaze was steady, and no apology was forthcoming. He didn't look apologetic, either, which she decided must mean he didn't feel apologetic. And if he didn't feel apologetic, then it was because he didn't think he had a reason to apologize. Which meant he was telling the truth when he said "Present company excluded" and wasn't trying to backpedal his way out of anything. So he must really not have been including her in that "forgettable-looking" comment.

Or else it meant he was an even bigger dick than what the TKE guys were packing and didn't care about her response to his statement at all, and she had placed her trust in a fourth man who thought very little of her.

She nodded disconsolately, dropped her gaze to the floor and blew out a weary breath. "Yeah. Right. Thanks. Whatever."

When Nick said nothing, she glanced up again to see him smiling at her in a way that indicated he really was genuinely sorry. "Truly," he told her. "Present company completely excluded."

She nodded, feeling a little better. Okay, feeling a lot better. But she said nothing more, so Nick turned his attention back to the guys. "And what did you say her name was again?"

The guys all exchanged glances. "I don't think we did, did we?"

Nick's eyes narrowed with his impatience. "What was her name?" Although he didn't say it aloud, Iris could still hear the "you little assholes" with which she was sure he'd wanted to conclude the question.

"Jenny something," Hobie said.

"Sturgis," Chuck immediately added. "Jenny Sturgis."

Iris, too, sat up straighter at hearing it. "She works with me," she said. "At Java Jackie's."

Nick turned back to her again, his eyes alive now with the sort of fire she'd been hoping to see in them when he looked at her. Only this time, the fire was for the smokin'-hot babe Jenny Sturgis, and not for Iris. "How long has she worked there?" he asked.

"She just started yesterday," Iris told him.

Nick smiled at that, but it wasn't the sort of smile she would have expected him to have for a smokin'-hot babe he was interested in sexually. It was more the kind of smile he would have for someone whose neck he wanted to wring. "What else can you tell me about her?" he asked.

Iris drew up her shoulders in what would have been a

shrug if she'd released them, but she was too nervous to relax even that much. "Nothing. It was pretty busy yesterday. We didn't have a lot of time to talk."

"And when you did, what did you talk about?"

Iris swallowed with some difficulty. "Um, you," she confessed.

Nick closed his eyes for a moment and shook his head slowly. "Oh, Iris," he said softly. "You didn't tell her where I was staying, did you?"

She shook her head vigorously. "No. No way. I only told her..." She swallowed hard again. She wasn't about to tell Nick she'd been talking about him as her potential guy. "We were just talking about guys we knew," she hedged. "And I mentioned you. I mentioned all of you," she lied, turning to look at the others. "It was just, you know, girl talk. Nothing major."

He looked as if he wanted to ask her more, but turned back to the guys instead. "And the rest of you?" he asked. "What do you know about this Jenny Sturgis?"

Hobie and Donny looked at Chuck. Chuck looked at Nick. "Not much," he replied. "Like they said, she came into the library when I was working and needed some help finding some stuff on the Net. So I gave her a hand. We started talking. I could tell she was digging me, so I invited her to the party."

"And you didn't think that was odd?" Nick asked.

"That she was digging him?" Hobie asked, stifling another giggle. "Hell, yes, it was odd."

Nick didn't even acknowledge the other man's remark. What Iris found interesting was that Chuck didn't, either.

To Chuck, Nick clarified, "You didn't find it odd that a student at a tech school like Waverly needed help finding something on the Internet? Just what kind of SAT scores did she have?"

Chuck said nothing. But his expression had elevated from angry and embarrassed to enraged and malevolent.

Hobie obviously didn't notice, because he laughed and said, "Chuck was too busy searching her to notice anything else."

Donny, just as clueless as his friend to Chuck's state, added, "Yeah, he was too busy checkin' out *her* Net."

"And browsing her Web," Hobie continued.

"Fingerin' her mouse," Donny said with a chuckle.

"Defragging her."

"Takin' a byte outta her Apple."

"Naw, man. Outta her ASCII." Though Hobie gave the abbreviation its phonetic pronunciation of ass-key, naturally.

"Workin' on his RAM," Donny continued, thrusting his fist forward—evidently having forgotten how much smaller Chuck's member was. He should have thrust his pinkie forward instead.

"Looking for a place to shoot his upload," Hobie added.

"Yeah, too bad about his tiny hard drive," Donny concluded, generating new bursts of laughter all around.

"She was digging me," Chuck replied adamantly, ignoring the other two. Which, Iris thought, should have told them how far his fury had ratcheted. "We hit it off. I didn't think about why she'd need help."

"And now that you do think about it?" Nick asked.

A look came into Chuck's eyes then that was nothing

short of murderous. And again Iris had to battle a twinge of fear at seeing it. "Now that I do," he said, "it seems kind of strange."

"Like maybe she *did* come into the library looking for something—or maybe you—specifically?"

"Maybe," Chuck said.

Nick smiled, and there was something in his expression, too, that gave Iris pause, something that made her wonder if maybe he wasn't exactly who—or what—she'd first thought him to be.

Very softly, very evenly he said, "So now, Chuck, the question is, what are you going to do about it?"

THIRTY MINUTES LATER, Hobie and Donny had taken off, leaving Adrian relieved to be rid of them and alone with Chuck and Iris to ponder the puzzle of the mysterious Jenny Sturgis.

Well, Adrian and Chuck were pondering that. Iris, Adrian saw, had seated herself in front of the television, joystick in hand—or whatever the hell joysticks were called these days, since Adrian was too unhip by their standards to know—playing a game. One he'd watched the boys play on a number of occasions. It seemed to involve an excessive amount of car chases and crashes, except that the goal of the game seemed to be *causing* the crashes, not avoiding them. The player was rewarded for every act of destruction, then given bonus points for additional, even more heinous acts. Running down a traffic cop, say. Or careening into the window of a day-care center. Or hurtling through the local humane society, sending puppies and kittens flying. Points were deducted, on the other hand, for things like buckling up or using a turn signal or maintaining a safe speed.

And they said today's youth culture was too immersed in violence, Adrian thought as he watched Iris play. Well, gosh.

To his surprise, however, although Iris did indeed bring on the dangerously high speeds as she drove through the city, she slowed down when she passed the day-care center and humane society, and she carefully skirted the traffic cop. She just kept speeding through the urban landscape until she passed the city limits, then she headed into a more bucolic countryside where she drove some more. Slower now. Farther and farther away from any potential big point targets like scouts helping old ladies across the street and homeless people living in boxes. There was no potential for chases now. Nothing to crash into. No explosions of animal shelters. No fiery deaths of preschoolers. Just slow driving through the country. Though she stopped to allow a long line of baby ducks to cross the highway.

Of course, Adrian already knew Iris was burdened by a conscience. He knew she had an aversion to violence. And he knew she was second-guessing all the mayhem the group had been wreaking on the Net. In spite of her shortcomings, he very much enjoyed having her around. Because he was beginning to think maybe those things weren't such short-comings, after all. Iris was one of the rarest creations on earth, so rare, in fact, that Adrian had begun to think hers was an extinct species—a decent human being. He couldn't remember the last time he'd encountered anyone up close who always tried to Do the Right Thing. *On purpose.* Even when that someone was just playing a video game.

Oh, wait. Yes, Adrian could remember the last time he'd encountered someone like that up close. And she might very well be getting close to him again. Because he had reason to believe that this Jenny Sturgis, the smokin'-hot babe who'd come out of nowhere on the Waverly campus, and who wore brown contact lenses, and who had dispatched three large men, leaving one in a half-naked heap on the floor, was a woman he knew rather well. Or, at least, had known her that way once.

Lila Moreau. Agent for his former employer, OPUS. Reputedly the most dangerous woman in the world.

Adrian believed it. Though not necessarily because of her actions or behavior. But because of what she could make men like him do and the ways she could make men like him behave.

One night. That was all he'd had with her. But it had been completely unforgettable. So unforgettable that he'd trotted out the memory on a fairly regular basis in the years since it had happened. And that was saying something for a man who generally considered women to be—

Well. For a man who didn't consider women at all.

He glanced at Iris then. Most women, anyway.

But Lila Moreau was the sort of woman who wouldn't allow herself to be forgotten. She had proved to be not so much Adrian's nemesis as his rival. They were well matched, the two of them. In many ways they were two of a kind. Once he'd realized she worked for OPUS—not long after that unforgettable night—he'd found out everything he could about her. And he'd been surprisingly unsurprised to discover that the backgrounds and upbringings of them both bore many parallels. Yet she'd chosen the path of Doing the *Right* Thing, while he'd chosen the path of Taking *Every*thing. With a side trip down The Rest of the World Be Damned Way.

Strangely, however, as thoroughly interwoven as their paths had been since meeting, Adrian hadn't seen Lila in person for years. He'd *thought* he was seeing her last month in Cleveland, of all places, but the woman he had been so certain was Lila was actually her twin sister, Marnie Lundy— a woman none of them had even known existed until about a month ago. Well, OPUS had known. They just hadn't seen any reason to tell anyone about Marnie's existence—not even the twin sister from whom she'd been separated as an infant. Even Adrian's contact within the organization hadn't had any prior knowledge that there was another Lila Moreau in the world—or, at least, someone who resembled her. Enough that OPUS tried to use Marnie as bait to lure Adrian out of hiding by having her pretend to be her sister.

Thankfully, his contact was able to relay the plan to him before he had indeed been reeled in, and he'd been able to slip away before they caught him. Unfortunately, it had also been before he'd had a chance to recover a document he very much wished he'd been able to recover: an encoded "novel" written by a retired OPUS archivist who went by the code name of Philosopher. Ironic, since the man's brain was less a think tank of ponderous consideration and more a fun house of frivolous delusion. Too many years in service to OPUS could do that to a person, Adrian supposed.

Philosopher hadn't been so deluded, however, that he hadn't been able to piece together a good bit of Adrian's comings and goings over the years. In fact, in his retirement he'd made Adrian's comings and goings his hobby, and he'd identified behavior patterns and penchants Adrian himself hadn't even realized he had. Enough that Philosopher's "novel" had helped OPUS enormously in their hunt for him.

As evidenced by the fact that Lila Moreau was now close enough that she had made personal contact with every member of the group Adrian had surrounded himself with. Knowing Lila as well as he did—or, at least, knowing her reputation as well as he did, since he didn't think anyone could really *know* Lila Moreau in anything other than the Biblical sense—she could be knocking on the door to his suite any moment.

"Do you know where she lives?" Adrian asked Chuck now.

Chuck shook his head. "I only saw her that day in the library and that night at the party."

"Any chance you'll see her again?"

"Doubtful, after what happened last time."

"The attempted rape by you and your friends, you mean?" Adrian couldn't help injecting. Nor could he help the contempt that colored the question. Actually, he probably could have helped that if he'd wanted to. He just didn't want to.

Chuck sat up. "It wasn't rape. She was up for it."

Adrian bit his lip to keep himself from saying the obvious. Then he wondered why he was sparing a despicable abomination like Chuck and replied, "Pity you weren't up for it, too."

"It wasn't rape," Chuck insisted again.

"Only because you were prevented from going through

with it," Adrian pointed out. "What the hell were you think-ing?"

Chuck squirmed enough that Adrian knew he understood perfectly what had almost happened at the party. What he had almost done. "I was drinking," Chuck said. "We all were. Jenny was, too."

"As if that excuses it," Adrian sneered.

"Hey, what the hell do you care?" Chuck demanded, going on the offensive. "Since when did you become the almighty defender of truth and justice? You're not exactly Mr. Sensi-tive when it comes to women."

Good point, Adrian thought. Just why *did* he care that a bunch of drunken thugs had assaulted Lila? Had assaulted anyone? He should have been bothered by Chuck's actions because they had threatened to draw attention to him, and therefore to the work they were doing—and to Adrian himself. Instead, he was bothered because Chuck's actions were repugnant and had endangered someone. Someone who, ironically, was trying to keep Adrian from carrying out a plan he'd put in motion years ago, and about whose welfare he should be in no way concerned.

Just what the hell was the matter with him these days?

He glanced over at Iris again, who had stopped playing the video game and was now gazing back over her shoulder at Adrian, as if she, too, were interested in his response to Chuck's statement.

Still looking at Iris, Adrian said, "There are some women in the world, Chuck, who are stronger than we men. In trying to overcome or control them, we simply illustrate how very weak we are. You need to learn to respect women like that.

You need to respect all women. Because you never know when one like that will show up in your life. And you never know her effect on you until it's too late." He looked back at Chuck. "Not to mention you behaved like a pig."

Adrian thought again about what Chuck and his two friends had tried to do to Lila. And he thought about someone else—three someone elses—trying to do the same thing to Iris, and succeeding. But where Adrian had been outraged by the act committed against Lila, he was enraged by the thought of it happening to Iris. Lila could take care of herself, as evidenced by the outcome of her own episode, even if she'd had a bit of help from the alleged boyfriend, who was doubtless another OPUS operative. Had Iris been cornered in the same way…

"Chuck," Adrian said softly, "get the hell out of my suite."

"What?" the other man said, clearly surprised by the sudden command.

Adrian looked him full in the eye. "I said, 'Get out.' You need to locate Jenny Sturgis and this boyfriend of hers. And you need to do it now. And then you need to let me know where they are." Not to mention he was making the air in the room stink.

"B-but how am I supposed to do that?" he asked. "If she's who you say she is, she's not gonna be in the Waverly directory. Why don't you get your secret agent contact to find out where she's staying?"

"Because I suspect at this point that my contact will find the amount of available information is limited."

Which, alas, Adrian thought, was doubtless true. Otherwise, he would have been notified long ago by said contact that Lila specifically was in the area, and precisely where she could be found at any given moment. Which could only mean OPUS was being very, very careful in dispensing information these days, deliberately revealing only enough to make Adrian's contact—and Adrian—feel as if they were still on top of things. Which could likewise only mean that he and his contact were *not* on top of things. At least not as much as they had thought. That in turn could only mean that the end was in sight.

If Lila had gotten this close to him without his even knowing it was she who was this close, then he'd definitely lost his edge. And his advantage. And, quite possibly, the game.

He waited for that to sink into his brain, waited, too, for the trickle of anger and frustration that should start seeping in right on its heels. But all he felt seeping was a mild sort of disappointment and resigned kind of fatigue. And then maybe, just maybe, a hint of relief.

Interesting.

"Oh, you're a smart little prick," he told Chuck in his mock fatherly voice. "I'm sure you'll think of something. Now, get out."

Chuck sputtered a few more things about how he always got saddled with all the work and how was he supposed to even know where to start looking and other such whiny complaints, but he finally picked himself up and left the suite. Adrian continued to look at Iris, but after one final, inscrutable look at him, she returned her attention to the images on the TV screen, again just driving her game car through the game countryside, enjoying the game scenery, as if she were trying to find a spot to have a game picnic.

She was still smarting, he supposed, from his thoughtless comment about the female student body of Waverly not consisting of any attractive female bodies. And for the second time in mere moments, Adrian found himself experiencing a reaction he'd never experienced before. He felt bad about hurting Iris's feelings. Even though he hadn't done it deliberately. He, a man who had gone out of his way in the past to hurt some people's feelings, suddenly found himself feeling guilty about having done so inadvertently.

Just what the devil was going on?

He told himself Iris was a nice person who didn't deserve to have her feelings hurt. But so were a lot of other people he didn't give a damn about. He told himself it was because she was his partner in crime, and partners in crime owed it to each other to watch each other's backs and take care of each other. But he knew that was ridiculous. There truly was no honor among thieves, and one's partners in crime were no more trustworthy than one's most mistrusted enemies. Besides, he'd screwed over partners in the past—one of whom had been his best friend once upon a time. And he'd done it without remorse. Well, without *too* much remorse. What made Iris any different?

Aside from her being a virgin, he meant.

Oh, he'd really been trying not to think about that since she'd told him. And he'd *really* been trying not to think about why she'd told him in the first place. And he'd really, *really* been trying not to think about why he found the idea of her being a virgin so incredibly attractive.

Normally, Adrian wouldn't have wanted to be bothered with a virgin. He was an uninhibited, adventurous, enthusiastic lover, and he expected his partner to be his equal in that regard. He liked his sex earthy and fierce and prolonged. He didn't want to be an instructor. Nor did he want to be a gentleman. And he certainly didn't want to be patient.

With Iris, though, somehow the prospect of being all those things was rather…intriguing. And although he considered himself a thoroughly enlightened male of the twenty-first century, he'd be lying if he didn't admit to feeling a primitive—but not at all unpleasant—thrill at the prospect of being the first man to make love to her. Perhaps even the only man to make love to her. Which was beyond madness, because Adrian had never wanted to be anyone's only.

So why did he rather like the idea of being Iris's? Even more astonishing, why did he find himself rather liking the idea of Iris being the only one for him, too?

If he'd had more time, he could have wondered about all that at length, but time was a luxury he could no longer afford. Lila Moreau—who, he was surprised to realize, wasn't haunting him nearly as much as she used to when he thought about her—was closing in on him and his merry band of…

He sighed. His merry band of assholes, he had to admit. Good God, what had he been reduced to? When had he ceased to be the one in charge of his own destiny and started having to rely on the work of—he sighed again—assholes to build his empire? And just what kind of empire was it going to be, anyway, if it was built by—he sighed a third time—assholes?

Later, he told himself. He'd think about that later. Right now he had other, more important things to think about.

Strangely, though, instead of mapping out a strategy to deal with Lila and whoever her current partner happened to be—since Adrian knew her regular partner was currently in the Hamptons with his fiancée, planning his wedding to a woman who was completely neurotic—Adrian's thoughts turned again to Iris. And the next thing he knew, he was sitting beside her on the floor, picking up a second joystick—or whatever the hell joysticks were called these days, since Adrian was too unhip by his cohorts' standards to know—and joining her for a drive in the game-generated countryside.

For a long time neither of them said a word to each other, only enjoyed the virtual scenery as their cars drove along, side by side, neither moving ahead, neither falling behind.

Finally, though, still watching the screen, Iris said, "That was nice, what you said to Chuck."

"About him being a pig?" Adrian asked. "He'd beg to differ, I'm sure."

She laughed softly, and there was something in the sound that sent a thrill of heat through his entire body. Strange. He hadn't felt something like that since… Well, he didn't think he'd ever felt anything like that.

"No, I mean about some women being stronger than men."

"Ah."

"Do you believe that?"

Adrian sighed, but continued to watch the cars on the TV. "There was a time when I would have laughed myself silly had someone said the same thing to me. Now, though…" He looked over at Iris, meeting her gaze unflinchingly. "Now I absolutely believe it."

She studied him in silence for a moment, her car having stopped moving on the screen. "Sometimes the things you say make me think your life growing up wasn't so great." His bark of laughter must have been all the response she needed. Because she continued, "That bad, huh?"

"My mother was a prostitute," he told her without hesitation, not even questioning why he did. He was reasonably certain he knew what his motivation was. He just didn't understand it. Nor did he bother to try. "I didn't know it when I was very young, but by the time I was a teenager, I figured it out. Thanks in large part to my treatment by other people in town and some not particularly nice things said by the other boys at school. I never knew my father," he added matter-of-factly. "We were very poor. Our house was ugly. I never got the dog I wanted for my birthday. Someone stole my bicycle when I was eight and I never got another one. Shall I go on?"

He waited for Iris to give him one of those oh-you-poor-baby pouts, but she only shook her head. "No. That's okay. It's probably not the kind of thing you want to talk about, huh?"

Her response surprised him. Most women who'd found out considerably less about him wanted to, in effect, kiss his boo-boo and make it all better. As if his past were something that could be improved by the proper placement of a woman's mouth. There were, actually, many things that could be improved with that. Alas, one's past wasn't one of them.

"As a matter of fact, no," he said. "I'd just as soon not."

"That's cool," Iris said. Then she perked up some. "You want to play the new Xenosaga?"

CHAPTER FIFTEEN

JOEL WAS IN HIS BEDROOM at his computer, still trying to decipher the finer points of Hobie's virus—and doing his best *not* to think about what had happened with Lila the night before, which was probably why he was having so much trouble trying to decipher the finer points of Hobie's virus— when he heard the knock at the front door. Lila had gone to the Waverly library, where Chuck had been scheduled to work a Sunday-afternoon shift, and it was too early for her to be back. Besides which, she wouldn't bother knocking. Unless, of course, she was feeling as tentative as he was about what had happened last night. Not that there had been anything tentative about what had happened last night, he couldn't help thinking further.

And just what *had* happened last night? Other than that he'd broken a five-year-old promise to himself. And other than that he didn't even give a damn that he'd broken that five-year-old promise. And that he'd had the most incredible sex of his life. And that he'd awoken in the morning with the realization that he wanted to have more nights like that one. Lots and lots of nights, in fact. Countless nights. Endless nights. Nights that lasted the rest of his life.

Oh, man, was he in it. Deep. If he kept this up, he was

going to start thinking he was in love. With Lila. Who was anything but a rest-of-his-life kind of woman.

The knock sounded again, louder this time, with more urgency, demanding a reply. Joel started to rise, then hesitated. Considering the velocity at which developments in the case had progressed over the past twenty-four hours, he decided it would probably be best to err on the side of caution. Would that he had been more cautious about the quickness with which things had developed between him and Lila during the same period, he might not be having so much trouble deciphering Hobie's virus. Or his own emotions, for that matter.

Withdrawing his 9 mm from the desk drawer, Joel stood, tucked it into the waistband of his jeans near his hip and rearranged the shirt tail of his baggy dark blue T-shirt to hide it. Then he crept in his stocking feet to the front door, never making a sound. He was just about to put his eye to the peephole when a third knock sounded, thundering this time as if the person on the other side of the door was using the side of his fist as hard as he could. A glimpse through the peephole revealed Chuck Miller standing on the other side, hands on hips, weight shifted to one foot, as if he were getting tired of waiting for a response.

What the hell?

How had the other man found out where he and Lila were staying? And what the hell was he doing here now? Why wasn't he at work?

"Hey, Ned!" Chuck called almost amiably through the door. "I know you're in there, dude. And I know you're right on the other side. C'mon, man, open the door. We need to talk about what happened the other night. I wanna apologize to you and Jenny. And I need to know there's no hard feelings and that you guys aren't gonna, you know, call the cops on me."

Joel told himself to keep pretending there was no one home. He knew better than to believe a guy like Chuck, who couldn't possibly have an apologetic bone in his body. Still, he had the 9 mm, he reasoned, and there was a chance, however small, that having a little chat with the guy might help further the investigation somehow. In spite of his reassurances to himself, however, he hesitated.

What would Lila do? he asked himself.

Oh, well, that was easy. She'd open the door and beat the hell out of Chuck.

Or maybe not, he thought further. She wasn't one for reacting blindly. When she kicked someone's ass it was as a last resort. Or because, you know, the ass in question deserved it. Which, of course, Chuck did, but if there was some potential, however questionable, that the guy might be able to provide any new info—whether voluntarily or otherwise—maybe Joel should try talking to him. If it looked as if Chuck was going to be a problem, then Joel could just beat the hell out of him.

Figuring his dilemma was solved, he opened the door.

And immediately realized that not only was Chuck going to be a problem, but Joel's problems had just begun. Because, like an idiot, he hadn't thought about the possibility that Chuck might not be alone. It hadn't occurred to him that both Hobie and Donny might be with him, hiding on each side of the front door so they couldn't be seen through the peephole.

Therefore he hadn't considered the fact that he could potentially be overcome when the three of them forced their way into the apartment and surrounded him. Which, it went without saying, they did. Then they closed the door behind them and gazed at him as if they resented having had to come over in the first place.

So Joel, being the gracious host, took the initiative and demanded, "What the hell is this about?"

Chuck evidently realized then that Joel towered over him by a good eight inches, because he straightened out of his bored slump and squared his shoulders. Not that that helped much, but if it made Chuck feel better, who was Joel to criticize?

"You and I need to talk," Chuck repeated.

"So you've said. But I'm guessing it's not because you want to apologize, as you claimed."

Chuck grinned at that, a toothy, menacing grin that made Joel want to hit him even more than he already wanted to hit him. "Apologize for what?" he asked. "Not only was that bitch asking for it, but if you hadn't interrupted, she would have had the night of her life."

Joel's fingers curled reflexively into fists, but he forced himself not to react. Yet.

"Is she home?" Chuck asked when Joel remained silent. "'Cause me and the guys were thinking maybe we could give her another go. And this time you could watch and see how it's supposed to be done."

Joel's fingers curled tighter, but he somehow managed to keep himself in check. "She's not here, Chuck," he said, surprised he was able to keep his voice level and bland. "Lucky you, since if she was here, you'd have your dick in a cast by now." He smiled as he added, "Course, they'd have to go to the pediatric wing to find one small enough to fit a baby's pinkie first."

Chuck's smile fell, and he took a swing at Joel, but Joel easily dodged it by taking a step back. Hobie and Donny, however, stepped in, each grabbing one of Joel's arms and holding tight. When they did, his shirttail lifted just enough to reveal the 9 mm nestled at his waist, which Chuck naturally noticed.

"Well, well, well," he said with delight as he withdrew it and held it aloft for the others to see. "What have we here?" He eyed Joel with something akin to glee. "Who the hell walks around their own apartment packing? The only guys who do that, I figure, are either up to something they shouldn't be or else they're big pussies." His smile went lethal. "So which are you, Ned?"

Joel figured it would probably be best at this point to just keep his mouth shut and figure out how to turn the situation around. Chuck wanted to get a rise out of him, and if Joel reacted, he'd be giving the guy what he wanted. So he said nothing, only continued to meet Chuck's gaze levelly, keeping his expression bland. Sure enough, Chuck's smile fell again, and he didn't try to provoke Joel any further.

He did, however, tuck the gun into his own waistband and say, "I think I'll have a little look around."

Joel remembered then that his computer screen was currently filled with the particulars of the virus he'd downloaded from Hobie's computer. He had no idea if Chuck would be able to discern that by looking at it, but if Hobie saw it, he doubtless would. There were other things in Joel's room, too, that might indicate to Chuck what he and Lila were doing, and he hastily scanned his memory to recall what he'd been working on earlier in the day. He'd had Sorcerer's dossier out, but he was pretty sure he'd put that back in his briefcase and locked it. But—damn—he hadn't returned Iris Daugherty's school records to his briefcase. The file was closed, but it was sitting on his desk beside the computer.

Joel dug frantically into his brain, trying to think of something to say that would keep Chuck from entering his bedroom. But God help him, his mind was a complete blank. So he did what millions of brainless men before him had done. He began to fight. Hard. Hobie and Donny were both shorter and more wiry than Joel, but there were two of them. And although Joel caught them by enough surprise that he was able to free himself and get in a few punches, it wasn't long before they had him by the arms again, this time twisting them behind his back in a way that, if they pushed much harder, could have broken some bones.

The sound of the scuffle brought Chuck out of the bedroom, and he was carrying Iris's file, open now, when he returned. He scanned the contents—which really weren't incriminating, except for the fact that if Joel was a student, he shouldn't have access to them—then looked up at Joel with a smile.

"Got a thing for Iris, Ned?" he asked. "That smokin'-hot Jenny's not enough for you? Ya ask me, once a guy had a piece 'a that, he wouldn't need the other white meat."

Joel kept his tone level as he replied, "Yeah, well, you wouldn't know anything about that, would you, Chuck?

Since the time you tried to taste her, she left your meat out for a whole party to enjoy."

Instead of reacting angrily to the remark, Chuck said, "Yeah, well, next time I taste her, she's gonna melt in my mouth. And if you're nice, there might be a little piece of her left for you. After Hobie and Donny get their turn. And maybe some 'a the guys at the frat house. They're still pretty disappointed about how that whole thing turned out."

"Gee, if they thought they were disappointed not to get a turn with Jenny," Joel said, "imagine how they're going to feel when she serves them their own nuts on a silver platter."

"If she can still walk after we're through with her," Chuck said.

Okay, so much for being self-contained and stoic, Joel thought. That was for pussies. Harnessing all the rage he'd been tamping down ever since that night at the frat party, he heaved himself forward, out of Hobie's and Donny's grasp, and lunged at Chuck.

Never in his life had he tried to fight three men all by himself. Even that night at the frat house, he'd had Lila fighting by his side. And before that night at the frat house, Joel had never engaged in physical combat with even one man before. Since Lila had come into his life, though, he'd gotten seriously in touch with his inner caveman. And not just when it came to fighting. Truth be told, he'd kind of liked getting to know the guy, too. Which was good, because he really needed his primitive side at the moment.

Even so, Joel struggled as he fought the three men. But whenever he felt himself beginning to succumb, he thought again about how Lila had looked when he'd burst into the room at the frat house, and about what Chuck had threatened to do just now, and the rage came again, and the power came again, and Joel let the caveman take over, and was suddenly perfectly willing and completely able to tear apart and disembowel anyone who threatened his mate.

He had no idea how long he fought like that, nor did he realize how much damage he did. Not until the sound of a single gunshot penetrated his frenzy enough that he was able to realize what was going on. And what was going on was that Joel had Hobie pinned beneath Donny and Donny pinned beneath himself. He had a vague recollection of having had Chuck by the hair a moment ago, too, and having slammed his head into the floor. The evidence of that was clear when he looked up to see Chuck gazing back at him with a bloodied lip and a huge red contusion on his forehead. Unfortunately Chuck also had the gun trained on Joel, and his hand was shaking, as if even he wasn't sure whether or not he would shoot again.

"What the hell is the matter with you?" he shouted at the pile of men on the floor. Though the question, Joel thought, was probably directed at him in particular.

"Nothing's…the matter…with me," he panted, surprised to realize how much trouble he was having catching his breath. "But I imagine…at least a handful…of my neighbors…have called the police by now…about that gunshot. And once they get here…there might be one or two things… the matter with you."

The understanding of what he'd done dawned on Chuck like a rabid badger at his groin. "Grab 'im," he said to Hobie and Donny, evidently not thinking about how hard that was going to be since they were both still pinned under the guy they were supposed to be grabbing. Once he did, he shook the gun at Joel again. "Get up. Get up, or I swear to God, I'll blow your head off."

Until that moment, Joel would have sworn Chuck was incapable of carrying out such a threat. But there was terror in his eyes, and he'd taken a fairly decent blow to his head. Maybe more than one—Joel honestly couldn't remember. Hell, just the way the guy's hand was shaking could potentially cause the gun to go off. So he did what Chuck told him to, rising slowly and stepping away from the other two men, hoping he was right and that at least one of his neighbors had called the police. Provided one of his neighbors was home. And provided they recognized the sound as a gunshot and didn't assume it was a car backfiring or an out-of-season firecracker.

"Grab 'im," Chuck told his friends again, once they were standing.

They were almost as dazed as he was, but they did as Chuck instructed. And all the while, he kept the gun pointed at Joel's forehead, his hand in no way steady.

"Look, Chuck, just take it easy," Joel said, trying to both calm him down and buy some time.

Chuck tightened his grip on the gun and steadied his hand a little. But Joel wasn't sure if that was better or worse. "Don't tell me what to do, man. Do *not* tell me what to do."

"Fine. I won't tell you what to do. But it might be a good idea if you guys left."

"Oh, we will," Chuck assured him. "We're heading out right now. And you, you dick, are going with us."

IF HE HAD TO BE HELD hostage, Joel thought an hour later as he worked at the leather belts binding each of his wrists to the arms of a chair, he supposed he could do a lot worse than the Four Seasons Hotel. Escape was as close as the telephone. All he had to do was dial room service and ask them to send up a rescue party and a bottle of Dom Pérignon, and add it to the tab of his host, since he knew his host so well. It was, after all, a logical assumption to conclude that his host was Adrian Padgett. No way could Chuck and his loser friends afford the Four Seasons. And no way would they have kidnapped Joel unless it was because his and Lila's cover was blown.

He tugged at the belts fruitlessly, even knowing his efforts would be, well, fruitless. Yeah, that rescue party from room service was looking better all the time. It was just too bad about the belts binding his limbs. And the three captors, one of whom was potentially psychotic. And the gun, which was definitely loaded.

But except for the potentially psychotic one, even his captors didn't seem as menacing now as they had an hour ago, because Hobie and Donny were seated on the floor in front of the TV pitting Princess Peach against Ganondorf in Super Smash Brothers. Chuck, though, was still a little twitchy. But he'd at least laid down the gun and turned his attention to something other than Joel once he was confident his captive was effectively secured. Maybe Chuck and the boys couldn't restrain themselves, but they were damned good at restraining someone else. There were belts wrapping Joel's ankles to the chair, as well, though not the cheap crap kind these guys would buy—otherwise Joel might have escaped by now. Not that Chuck seemed to understand the purpose of a belt in the first place, since the guy's pants exposed half his ass. These were high-end accessories the boys had retrieved from a closet filled with expensive-looking suits and dress shoes lined up neatly on the floor.

Clue number two that Joel was currently being held against his will in the hiding place of the man he was supposed to have in restraints by now himself.

This wasn't going to look good on his report.

But where was Adrian Padgett right now? he wondered. Yes, it was helpful to know where the guy had been holed up most recently—and didn't it just figure he'd have the balls to do it in Cincinnati's finest luxury hotel?—but it would be more helpful to find him here now. Though it would have been better if, you know, Joel had surprised him here while he was alone. It would also have been helpful if Joel wasn't inescapably bound while making these discoveries. And it would be most helpful of all if Lila were here with him. But since there was little chance she'd be able to figure out where he was…

He bit back a frustrated sound. Lila had been right about him all along, Joel thought. He wasn't suited to work in the field. Even a slacker like Chuck Miller had been able to imprison him with fairly little effort. Joel hadn't put up a struggle or tried to draw attention to himself, even as they'd escorted him across a crowded hotel lobby, because Chuck had had the 9 mm pressed to the base of his spine, the weapon hidden by Hobie and Donny, who flanked him. Lila, Joel was certain, would have had all three of them on their knees within moments of their arrival at the apartment.

Because Lila had all the makings of a good field agent.

Field agents had to think on their feet and make split-second decisions. They had to be able to evaluate a situation in an instant and figure out how to work it. Their brains had to operate at lightning-fast speed, processing a million pieces of information at once. Joel was superb at thinking, but he was accustomed to doing it in a much more controlled environment. He excelled at considering facts and analyzing data and drawing conclusions. His brain was more suited to the leisurely, logical perusal of one thing at a time. He was used to working in an entirely different way than Lila. And his way wasn't the right way when it came to doing her job.

Still, he thought, the two of them together made a good team. And not just professionally, either. He just wished there was some way to make her understand that, too.

Later, he told himself. He could think about that later. Right now he had to figure out how the hell he was going to get out of this, so that there would be a later for him to think about.

Although he was technically outnumbered, Joel knew that, ultimately, the person who had the gun was the one in control of the situation. Right now no one had it. But it was closest to Chuck, who sat at the desk on the opposite side of the suite. He'd dropped the weapon onto an end table by the sofa, only a few steps away from where he sat now. Between him and Joel was not only the sofa and TV and another chair in the living area, but a small dining set minus the chair to which Joel was currently bound. Not to mention Hobie and Donny.

Those two were completely caught up in their game, however, and might remain distracted enough not to pose a problem if Joel could work quickly. Chuck, too, had his attention focused on something other than Joel at the moment, as his gaze was fixed on one of a stack of file folders he'd discovered in a desk drawer when he'd started rifling through it to look for something shortly after sitting down. So Joel continued to work at the belts, hoping maybe if he were careful enough, he could loosen them. Hey, they were made of smooth, flexible—slippery—leather. There was a chance, however small, that he might be able to extricate himself.

For a good ten minutes he worked at the straps without rousing the attention of any of his captors. Then, suddenly, Chuck shouted out, "You dick!"

As far as Joel was concerned, he could have been addressing just about anyone in the room. Hobie and Donny seemed to take the moniker personally, though, because both of them looked over and said, "What?"

Chuck glanced up, confusion warring with anger in his expression. "No, not you," he said to Hobie and Donny, who then looked over at Joel…who immediately stopped working at the belts. "No, not him, either," Chuck added impatiently. "Nick."

For a minute Joel wasn't sure who Chuck was talking about, then remembered Nick was the name Adrian Padgett had most recently assumed. And now Chuck thought he was a dick. Wow, there was a shocker.

"Dude, what are you talking about?" Donny asked. But he'd already returned his attention to the game, as had Hobie.

Chuck stood, still holding the file, and began to make his way toward the others. Then, seemingly as an afterthought, he went back and retrieved two more. There was one file left, still closed, on the desk, but he didn't bother with that one

and instead strode to where Hobie and Donny sat, something that put more distance between himself and the gun.
Of course, Chuck had also put himself between Joel and the
gun. Still, it was worth noting.

"Look at this," Chuck said as he held out one of the files
toward Donny. "I found some files in the desk. They're
Nick's. But they're about us."

"What?"

Chuck threw the file at him. "It's your life story, man.
Even about how you wet the bed until you were thirteen."

"That's a goddamned lie!" Donny shouted, jumping up.
"I stopped when I was twelve." He grabbed the file from
Chuck and began to flip through it, shaking his head slowly
as he read over each page. "Jesus, he's really done his
homework. He's even got the name of the shrink I saw when
I was seven, after my old man died."

Now Hobie jumped up, too. "What's mine say?" he asked
eagerly as he strode to Chuck. "Does it have anything about
how I kicked ass at the surfing competition in Rincon when
I was fifteen?"

Chuck tossed a second file at Hobie. "Fifty-eighth on a
roster of sixty isn't kicking ass, dumbshit."

Judging by the color Hobie's face turned just then, Joel
was able to determine that yes, as a matter of fact, the file
did cover the competition in Rincon.

"But, hell, Hobie," Chuck continued, "you never told us
about the fire you set at your middle school. Way to go, bro."

"It was an accident," Hobie mumbled as he snatched his
file from Chuck.

"That's not what the superintendent of the Raleigh, North Carolina, school system says."

"Son of a bitch is a liar."

So, Joel thought. Sorcerer had felt compelled to look into the backgrounds of his partners in crime, doubtless using his contact at OPUS to do so. Damn. The guy didn't trust anybody. Which was probably why he'd gotten as far as he had and eluded them for as long as he had. Trust was a good thing among friends and lovers and coworkers. Among thieves and liars and slackers, however, it was doubtless too expensive an investment.

When Joel saw that all three of the men were engrossed in their respective files, he increased his efforts to loosen his bonds. His hands had begun to perspire, making them and the belts damp, and he tried to use the moisture to both stretch the leather and lubricate his wrists. He was making some meager progress when a soft beep from his right announced the use of the key card in the door of the suite, something that caused him and his captors to turn their attention simultaneously in that direction.

But Joel doubted that their hearts were racing as fast as his own. Finally, he thought. Finally, finally. He was going to come face-to-face with the man he'd been studying for years. The man he'd been pursuing for almost a week.

But it wasn't Adrian Padgett who stepped through the door. It was Iris Daugherty, dressed completely in black, from her high-tops to the knit cap embroidered with the circled *A* symbol for anarchy. She looked first at Joel, tied to the chair, then at her comrades, then back at Joel, tied to the chair. Her mouth dropped open and she immediately pushed the door closed and stormed toward her friends.

"What the hell do you think you're doing?" she demanded. She pointed at Joel. "Who the hell is that? And why the hell is he tied to a chair? *What the hell is going on?*"

"Where's Nick?" Chuck replied, ignoring her questions.

"He stopped by the bar for a drink. He'll be up in a minute." She shook the arm still extended at Joel for more emphasis. "Who the hell is that?" she asked again.

"You might be more interested in what's on the desk over there, Iris," Chuck told her. "Nick's been checking us all out. He's got files on all of us. Pretty confidential information some of it, too. The dick."

Joel noted that Iris seemed in no way surprised by the revelation. Interesting.

"Hey," Hobie said, closing his own file and making his way toward the desk, "let's see what Nick found out about Iris. I bet *she* didn't wet the bed 'til she was thirteen."

"Twelve," Donny corrected him.

Iris darted after Hobie, but she wasn't quick enough to reach the file before he did. Instead of expressing curiosity about its contents as she tried to grab it from him, she said, "It's none of your business, Hobie. Give it back."

"Give it *back?*" he echoed as he held it over his head, out of her reach. "I didn't know you had it in the first place. What's up, Iris? You already seen this stuff?"

"No…I…I mean…of course not," she said. But there was enough stammer and hesitation—and anxiety—in her voice to suggest she was lying about that. "Give it to me, Hobie," she repeated.

But Hobie tossed it to Chuck on the other side of the sofa. Iris was circling the big piece of furniture to try to retrieve it when her gaze lit on the gun that was sitting in clear view on the end table.

"Holy shit," she said, stopping in her tracks. She looked first at Chuck, then must have realized he would just blow her off again, so turned to Hobie instead. "Jesus, Hobie. Where did you guys get a gun? What the hell is going on?"

By now, Chuck had opened Iris's file and was reading it over himself. When Iris realized it, she vaulted toward him and tried to grab it, but he spun out of her way and kept reading.

"Whatsa matter, Iris?" Hobie taunted her as she fought to claim her file. "Afraid we're gonna find out you didn't get your period when all the other girls did?"

"Or that you wrote fan letters to Screech?"

Joel watched Iris struggle with Chuck until she finally managed to curl her fingers over one side of the file and give it a good pull. But Chuck retaliated by bending his free arm and backhanding her across the face with what appeared to be every bit of strength he possessed.

Her feet went out from under her, and she fell back onto the sofa like a rag doll, lifting a hand to her jaw. The room went completely still after that, except for Chuck, who continued to read over her file as if nothing had happened. Both Hobie and Donny stood silent with their mouths open, gaping first at Chuck, then at Iris. Joel's fingers curled involuntarily into fists and he jerked harder at his restraints—unfortunately to no avail.

"Jesus, Chuck," Donny finally said. "Why'd you do that?"

But Chuck didn't answer, too caught up was he in reading over whatever he'd discovered in Iris's file.

Hobie, to his credit, moved to the couch and held out a hand to her. "Are you okay, Iris?" he asked.

She ignored his hand, but pushed herself up to standing, her hand still cupped over the right side of her face. She rubbed it once, then dropped her hand to her side. Even from as far away as he was, Joel could see that her cheek was already bright red. She'd probably have a nasty bruise before long.

"Yeah, Hobie, I'm okay," she said softly.

Joel wasn't sure, but he thought her gaze dropped for a moment to the gun before she completed a few steps backward that took her out of swinging distance of Chuck.

"Why'd you hit Iris, Chuck?" Donny asked again.

But again Chuck ignored the question. Instead, he said, "You guys aren't going to believe this, but Iris is worth a million and a half bucks."

"What are you talking about?" Hobie asked.

Finally Chuck looked up from the file. When he turned to look at Iris, who bore the clear evidence of his assault, there wasn't an iota of apology or regret on his face. Instead, he smiled. "Iris has been holding out on us," he told the others. "She's not just some worthless little bitch after all."

CHAPTER SIXTEEN

ADRIAN HAD USED THE excuse of needing a drink to separate himself from Iris so that he could call his contact at OPUS to see if he could learn anything about the comings and goings of Lila Moreau. Not much to his surprise, he learned nothing. So before returning to the room, when he detoured to the bar to get a snifter of Armagnac that would further his ruse, he realized it wasn't much of a ruse at all. He really did need a drink. So much so that the glass was half empty by the time the elevator doors folded open on his floor. Maybe he'd just call room service and have them send up an entire bottle. It was turning out to be that kind of day.

It wasn't just because he knew Lila Moreau was out there closing in on him. And it wasn't that Iris had informed him that Hobie had hit a snag on the virus they were building that could set the work back days. Perhaps weeks. What troubled Adrian was that when he considered the repercussions of both bits of news, he realized he just didn't care.

He was tired of having to depend on a bunch of pathetic little gits to build a virus he didn't know how to build himself. He was tired of waiting for the completion of a project he was beginning to suspect wouldn't come close to living up to his expectations anyway. He was tired of looking at the same hotel suite day after day after day. He was tired of seeing the Cincinnati skyline out his window night after night after night. He was tired of room service, tired of having his movements hindered, tired of Chuck and the boys, tired of what his life had become. But most of all, he was tired of being Adrian Padgett, aka Sorcerer, aka Number One on the OPUS Most Wanted List.

He was tired. Period. Tired and restless and irritable and confused, and in no way certain what he even wanted anymore. He was a man approaching midlife who had been reduced to relying on boys half his age, whom he didn't even like or respect, for his own happiness. Happiness that he was beginning to think would never, ever come.

When had everything gone awry? he asked himself as he approached his suite. When had the lust for unlimited wealth and power ceased to be the focus of his existence? When had it ceased to be desirable? Lately he'd begun to wonder what he'd even do with unlimited wealth and power if he had it. If he succeeded in what he planned, he'd be hunted for the rest of his life, by representatives of every country on the planet. He wouldn't be safe anywhere, wouldn't be able to stay in any one place for any length of time. He'd be alone for the rest of his life. And what kind of life was that? He couldn't buy or bully himself peace of mind, even with unlimited wealth and power.

The thoughts halted him as he was about to insert his key card into the door. Not the parts about never being able to stay in one place and remaining alone for the rest of his life, because those things had always been givens, and neither had ever bothered him before. Adrian had always intended to move around constantly and remain alone. He'd always been certain that was what he wanted. And he'd never worried about peace of mind, because he'd always thought a peaceful mind would drive him mad. He'd never wanted peace of mind. Not once.

Until now.

The very fact that such thoughts had even entered his brain—and with negative connotation, no less—spoke volumes as to his current state of mind. Which, ironically, was in no way peaceful. Somehow, at some point over the past few years, Adrian had started having second thoughts about what he was doing. And he'd begun to regret the idea of never being able to settle down. Of being alone. For the rest of his life.

No, not over the past few years, he realized as he inserted the key card into the door. Over the past few *months*. It had only been since coming to Cincinnati that he'd begun to feel this strange ambiguity over what he was doing. Only since collecting his current band of merry hackers and slackers. Only since Iris had become so—

The thought concluded abruptly at the sight that greeted him when he pushed open the door to his suite. The first thing he saw was a man he didn't recognize tied to one of the dining chairs with four of his best belts. Then he stepped inside and saw the rest. Iris sitting on the sofa flanked by Donny and Hobie, who were each holding one of her arms and who both looked very, very anxious about something. But Iris looked worse. And not just because she was clearly terrified of something. But because someone had obviously hit her hard enough in the face to discolor her flesh.

Adrian was completely unprepared for the swell of rage

that surged up inside him at the sight of her flawless skin marred by such violence. Iris Daugherty was the most gentle person he had ever met, the only person he knew who he could say with all confidence had never hurt a fly. She was a rarity among human beings—inherently good. That anyone would strike her for any reason made Adrian want to strike back. Hard.

"Who hit Iris?" he asked by way of greeting the rest of the men. The calmness in his voice belied the rage that continued to well up from that dark pit in his belly he thought had emptied a long time ago.

Chuck, who had been standing with his back to Adrian, spun around at the sound of his voice and said, "Yo, Nick, you—"

"Who hit Iris?" Adrian demanded again. Again his voice was quiet, but this time he couldn't quite prevent the sliver of fury that crept through.

He turned to the man in the chair, thinking perhaps he was the most likely suspect, though somehow Adrian already knew who was responsible. Nevertheless, he asked, "Was it you?"

The man shook his head, but said nothing.

"Then why are you tied up?" Adrian asked him. "For that matter, who are you and why are you here?"

As soon as he uttered the question, however, he knew the answer to it, as well. Chuck had made good on Adrian's instructions that he find Lila. Except that it wasn't Lila he'd brought back. Not surprising, actually, since Lila wouldn't be foolish enough to be captured by Chuck. Her new partner, however, obviously had a lot to learn.

"You're gonna love this, Nick," Chuck said.

Oh, Adrian doubted that. Still looking at the man in the chair, he asked, "What am I going to love, Chuck?"

"This is the guy who was with Jenny at the party Friday night," Chuck said. "Friend of mine who works at Java Jackie's scored Jenny's address from her application there, so we went over to the apartment to have a little talk with her and found him there instead. And guess what?"

"What?" Adrian asked wearily.

"This dick's got all kinds of information about you on his laptop," Chuck said. "And the rest of us, too. We brought it with us when we brought him here. And his briefcase, too, which I haven't been able to open yet. But I put both of them over—"

"Who hit Iris?" Adrian asked again, turning to look at Chuck.

Strangely, he didn't even care that Chuck had somehow managed to capture one of the people who'd been trying to catch him. He didn't care that by having this man here, they'd just turned the tables on OPUS—and Lila. He didn't care that the ball was now in his own court to do with whatever he wanted. All he cared about was Iris.

Chuck seemed to realize that, because his smile fell a little. "Nobody hit Iris," he said. "She fell."

Adrian nodded slowly and echoed, "She fell. I see." He looked at Iris then, at how the entire left side of her face between her eye and her chin was red. At how she was looking back at him, silently pleading with him to…do something.

"You know, Nick," Chuck said with great self-importance,

long since he'd felt it. Nothing had frightened Adrian for decades, not really. And never in his life had he felt fear like this. This wasn't fear for himself. This was fear for something else. Some*one* else. Someone for whom he had come to feel a great deal. He was afraid for Iris. For her safety. Because knowing Chuck as well as he did—alas—Adrian knew where this conversation was heading.

"We already called the number you had in the file to report her whereabouts," Chuck said.

Ah, he'd been mistaken. The conversation had already arrived. "Did you?" he asked, schooling both his features and his voice into a blandness he was nowhere close to feeling, because the knots in his belly now were nearly cutting off his circulation.

"Yeah, they got somebody flying down from Toledo to pick her up," Chuck said. "Ought to be here in a couple hours."

Adrian thought quickly. Two hours. That should be enough. Barely, but enough. "And you think you're going to split the money three ways and leave me nothing, is that it?" he asked. "I may not be quite the engineering protégés you three are, but I can do basic math."

Iris's face went white at his remark, save the angry bruise that was beginning to form. Clearly, she thought Adrian was planning to let the boys get away with what they'd done. Clearly, she thought Adrian was taking exception only because he wanted to be cut in on the reward himself. Clearly, she thought he was an unspeakable little bastard.

There was a time—not long ago, in fact—when she would have been right. He used to be an unspeakable little bastard.

But not now. Not anymore. Because Adrian was tired of being that man.

More to the point, Adrian was through.

Chuck shrugged. "Well, we figure it's the least you can do for being such a dick and not trusting us and having us all checked out. This way, there will be no hard feelings."

"Oh, of course not, Chuck," Adrian assured him. "Why would I have any hard feelings?" He began to walk toward the small group, slowly, then veered to the right, as if to make his way around the sofa to the desk on the other side. As he walked, he continued, "The three of you have helped me make a lot of money. And you've been such charming company for me, lo these last three months. I now know more about animated hedgehogs and…" He lifted a hand to tap his forehead, feigning memory loss as he slowly continued to make his way around the sofa. "Oh, what is that other interesting animal you all like so much in that game?"

"An echidna," Donny supplied helpfully.

Adrian smiled and pointed a finger at him. "That's the one." He continued to walk. "And then there were those wonderful games where you all blew the bejesus out of law enforcement officials and brutally raped sorority girls. My God, who wouldn't love the world you play in? I learned so much from you boys."

By now Adrian had made his way to the other side of the sofa, having passed the end table where lay a gun that had come from only God knew where. At this point, all Adrian cared about was that it was there. Because he scooped it up and, with the expert skill that had never left him, pointed it at Chuck's forehead.

And then he said, "You unspeakable little bastard."

Chuck's expression went slack at the sudden turn of events, but he said nothing and made not a single move.

"You pathetic little miscreant," Adrian continued. "You odious little toad. You revolting little Caliban. You scabrous little vermin. Or to put it in terms you might be able to understand, Chuck, you dick."

Hobie and Donny had craned their heads around at his outburst, and when they saw Adrian standing there with the gun trained on Chuck they, as one, dropped their mouths open in surprise. Both jumped up from the sofa and began to back up, so Adrian levered the gun in their direction and said, "Move again, and I'll shoot you both in an area most men consider exceedingly important. The fellow you have strapped to the chair over there can tell you that I am an excellent shot and will have no trouble picking off—" he pointed the gun at Chuck again "—all three of you before you can get even halfway through the admonition, 'Chuck, you dick, look what you've gotten us into.'"

"True fact," the fellow strapped to the chair over there called from the other side of the room. "He was awarded sharpshooter honors every year he worked for OPUS. Chuck really was a dick, getting you into this."

Without Adrian's even having to ask, Hobie and Donny lifted their hands palms out. And both remained rooted where they stood.

Chuck, too, lifted his hands, but being a dick, he took a step toward Adrian. Adrian, in turn, cocked the gun and pointed it at Chuck's groin. Chuck stopped. Oh, Adrian did so love it when that whole cause-and-effect thing worked the way it was supposed to.

"Whoa, Nick," Chuck said. "I was just joking. We'll cut you in on the money for Iris. Won't we, guys?"

Hobie and Donny both nodded vigorously.

"I mean, three hundred and seventy-five gees will still buy a really nice Lamborghini. Maybe not the Murciélago, but for sure the Spyder."

Adrian smiled. "That's much too nice a car for a cockroach like you, Chuck. I'm afraid you're just going to have to do without. Because none of you will be collecting that money. In fact, none of you will be collecting another cent. Save what they're paying in federal prisons these days for the tiny-minded labor you'll all be doing for a while."

Chuck emitted an incredulous sound, as if he couldn't believe Adrian would turn on him, even though he'd just turned on Adrian himself. Incredible, Adrian thought. For someone who had an IQ in the range of Mozart, the kid was as bright as a melba toast.

"Well, that's not fair." Chuck spat out the words. "You can't keep all of it for yourself. And you can't turn us in, because we'll rat you out faster than chili through a Chihuahua."

"Nick."

Iris's voice was soft when she said his name. No, not his name, Adrian thought. Someone else's name. Someone he was tired of being. He didn't dare look at her when he replied, so, still holding the gun on the boys, he said, "Adrian. My name is Adrian, Iris. Adrian Padgett."

"It is?" She sounded genuinely surprised that he had given them all a false name. Which only went to show how innocent she remained, in spite of all she'd been through.

"You're not Nick Darian?" she asked.

He shook his head. "I am not."

He did brave a glance at her then, long enough to see the devastated look on her face. So he hastily returned his attention to the trio of boys.

"You lied to me," she said.

"Yes."

"You're not any of the things you told me you are."

"Actually," Adrian said, "everything I told you about myself—save my name—was true. In fact, you're the first person I've been able to tell the truth to since…" He sighed with much fatigue. "Well. For a very long time. Perhaps even for the first time."

"Are you going to let my family take me back?" she asked.

"No, Iris. I'm going to take you home."

He looked at her again, and saw her eyes filling with tears. It took a moment for him to understand her reaction. So, hastily, he clarified, "I'm not taking you back to your family, Iris. I'm taking you home."

She obviously still didn't understand, because her eyebrows knitted downward in confusion. "Where's home?" she asked.

He grinned and looked back at the boys. "I have no idea. I guess we'll find out when we get there."

JOEL WAS STILL TRYING to process everything that had happened in the last fifteen minutes when Adrian pulled a garment bag and carry-on from the closet and began to stuff it with his clothes. By then, Donny, Hobie and Chuck were all tightly bound with duct tape, courtesy of Iris Daugherty, who had pulled a roll of it out of her huge black tote bag to bind each of them to the three remaining dining-room chairs while Adrian held the gun on them. And if Chuck had cried out in pain more than Hobie and Donny had when she jerked his arms behind him, to the point where Iris had taped his mouth shut, too, well, hey, who was Joel to say anything?

Ultimately, she'd taped Hobie's and Donny's mouths, too, and now all three of them sat completely helpless—and figuratively emasculated, which Joel had to admit was kind of gratifying to see—in the middle of the suite. Not that Joel was one to point a finger, since, not only were his hands still bound to his chair, making such a gesture impossible, but his hands were still bound to his chair, making such a gesture moot. He was still as much a prisoner as the others were. And he still had no idea what Adrian intended to do next. Except, you know, stuff all his clothes into his luggage.

Which actually told Joel rather a lot. He'd gotten to know Sorcerer-AKA-Adrian-Padgett fairly well over the past few months, even if he'd never met the guy personally. And he knew Padgett was, among other things, fastidious and vain. The fact that he was so carelessly shoving thousands of dollars worth of clothing into his bags without bothering to fold them indicated he was in a massive hurry. Strange, since Joel wasn't in any position to alert OPUS to his whereabouts, and his three amigos posed as much threat as a trio of trussed-up turkeys. Iris, too, he noted, was scurrying around the room like a whirlwind collecting what was left of Adrian's belongings, cramming them into the bags with even less concern than he.

Obviously their rush had something to do with Chuck's

comments about Iris being worth a million and a half dollars and someone coming to get her. The remark had been just one of many things that had Joel's head spinning, especially since it had sounded as if the million-five was a reward. But OPUS's background check of Iris Daugherty had indicated she was from a working-class neighborhood in Columbus, Ohio, and her father was currently unemployed. Nor had she ever been arrested for anything. Whatever was in the file Adrian had received from his OPUS contact, it was information no one else in OPUS had been made privy to. It was just one more thing Joel and Lila were going to need to figure out. As if there weren't already enough loose ends on this case to weave a carpet.

And not just with the case, either. There were even more loose ends with whatever was going on between Joel and Lila. Or, at least, with Lila. Because one thing had become crystal clear to him over the past twenty-four hours. He was in love with her. He must be. What he felt for her, even after knowing her a short time, was infinitely stronger than anything he'd ever felt for anyone else. Since meeting her, he'd been reduced to his most basic masculine responses, and elevated to the highest human joy. And in between, he'd come to realize that the day—any day—was made better just by having Lila in it. He wanted every day to have her in it. Every hour. Every moment. And he wasn't sure how he was going to enjoy the days ahead without her.

Because he feared Lila hadn't responded to him the same way. Or, if she had, she wasn't willing, or even able, to acknowledge it. She'd spent her life pulling away from other people. And, truth be told, he didn't blame her. Pulling away was probably what had kept her sane. What had kept her going. What had kept her alive. Had he had to suffer the same kind of upbringing she'd had to weather, he probably wouldn't be half as well-adjusted as she.

But that kind of life was over for her, and had been for some time. As an adult, Lila was strong and focused and confident. She'd made a life for herself that might not be conventional, but it was damned sure meaningful. She just didn't want to share it with anyone. Or else she was afraid to. And maybe that was what it all boiled down to, Joel thought. Lila Moreau wasn't as fearless as she thought.

His thoughts halted there, because Adrian and Iris had finished their packing, and were clearly preparing to leave. Before going, however, Adrian moved to the desk and picked up the phone, punching in enough numbers to let Joel know it was a local call. When whoever was at the other end of the line answered, Adrian said, "Hello, sweetheart, long time, no chat." There was a pause as the other person replied, and whatever they said made Adrian smile a broad, very happy smile. "Yes, I've missed you, too. It's a shame we keep missing each other the way we do. We've gotten so close to meeting face-to-face again so many times, and then… Ah, well. Still, it *is* good to hear your voice, Lila."

CHAPTER SEVENTEEN

"CUT THE CRAP, ADRIAN," Lila said into her cell phone.

She was seated at the foot of the Waverly library steps, where she'd been seated for the past thirty minutes, waiting for Chuck Miller to show up for his shift in the computer lab and wondering where the hell he was. She told herself she shouldn't be surprised to be receiving a call from Adrian. The guy loved to taunt whoever was tracking him at any given moment, and he had to have figured out by now—either through his contact or simply because he was Adrian Padgett—that Lila was close to finding him.

But she was surprised to hear from him. The voice coming to her from the other end of the line was one she hadn't heard for years, one that had been able to, at one time, pebble her flesh with goose bumps. The first time she'd heard it, those goose bumps had been a result of the sexual awareness and anticipation he'd roused in her. After that first time, hearing his voice had generated goose bumps because of the challenge he presented. Hearing it now…

Huh. That was weird. Hearing Adrian's voice now had no effect on Lila at all. It was still deep and velvety and erotic, still self-possessed and defiant. But there was something else there, too, now. Fatigue. Disenchantment. Even—she was amazed to realize it—fear. Adrian sounded different now. He sounded...human.

"Still the charming way with words, I see," he said. "You always did know how to reduce all of life's big moments to a handful of words. One of which was almost always... Well, not *crap*," he said, sounding as if he was the one who was surprised now. "My, my. You've cleaned up your vocabulary, Lila. You must have met a nice boy."

"You are so full of crap, Adrian."

Even if he was right. But it hadn't been a nice boy who'd cleaned up Lila's vocabulary. That had been a result of her sister Marnie's influence. Even though the two of them had had only one evening together to get caught up before OPUS had sent Lila after Adrian again, it had been enough to make Lila realize how rough around the edges she was when compared to polite society, and had made her rethink much of what she'd become in that regard. Of course, Joel was also polite society, she reminded herself. And like Marnie, he'd made Lila rethink much about herself, too. But unlike Marnie, what Joel had made Lila rethink had nothing to do with surface things like social niceties. Joel had hit her much deeper than that.

"What do you want, Adrian?" she demanded. And after voicing the question, Lila realized it was one she should probably be asking herself, too.

"I want to help you," he said.

"Of course you do," she cooed. "After all, you've made it your life's work to help OPUS, haven't you?"

There was a slight pause on the other end of the line. Then, very earnestly, he said, "I'm serious, Lila. I want to help you. And believe me, at this point you need my help."

Every scrap of mischief had left his voice as he'd spoken. He really did sound serious. Lila had never heard him sound serious before. This was serious.

"I've been forced to make a change in my plans," he told her.

Oh, that didn't sound good. "What kind of change?"

"A change for the better."

"For me or for you?"

He hesitated another scant moment before replying, but even that scant hesitation spoke volumes. She'd never known Adrian Padgett to hesitate before, not even for an instant.

"For both of us," he finally said.

Lila shifted the phone to her other hand, mostly because she needed a couple of seconds to digest that. "How can it be better for both of us?" she asked.

"We can discuss that part later," he said. "Once I've worked out all the details."

"But—"

"Right now I have someone here who wants to talk to you."

There was the sound of a phone being transferred to someone else, then a voice that had become all too familiar over the past few days. And it was a voice that raised goose bumps a hundred times faster than Adrian Padgett ever had. "Lila?"

"Joel?"

Her fingers convulsed on the phone as she uttered his name, her heart constricting with terror at the realization that he was with Adrian. Terror rolled in her belly, too, and air fled her lungs in a whoosh so fierce it dizzied her. It was all she could do to ask shallowly, "Are you okay?"

"I'm fine," he hastened to tell her. "I'm tied up, but I'm fine."

"Did he hurt you?" she demanded. "I'll kill the son of a bitch if he laid a finger on you."

It was with no small surprise that Lila realized what she said was true. Never had she felt homicidal before. Sure, she got angry, and more than once she'd reacted too hastily to that anger. But those reactions had still been focused and carried out with great care. Had Adrian done anything to harm Joel, however, she knew that not only would she react blindly, but she wouldn't regret a moment of whatever she ended up doing.

"I'm fine," Joel repeated. "But—"

"He's fine." Adrian's voice came over the phone again. "But as he said, he's a bit tied up. You'll need to come and get him."

"Where are you?" Lila demanded, her heart still pounding. Her entire body was trembling now in response to her fear. Her palms were damp and her face was hot, and she thought for a moment she might even throw up. And she knew her condition wouldn't change until she saw Joel for herself and knew he was safe.

"*I* will be gone by the time you get here," Adrian assured her. "But you can find—" Lila heard his voice shift away from the phone as he asked, "I'm sorry, I don't believe I caught your name. What a dreadful host I've become." She heard Joel's muffled reply, then Adrian's voice, still away from the phone but more clearly now, saying, "Virtuoso? Are you serious? What kind of code name is that? Who's assigning code names these days? They should be shot. How can anyone feel threatened by someone named Virtuoso?"

Oh, if he only knew, Lila thought.

"Anyway," Adrian continued, his voice coming clearly again, "Mr. Virtuoso would appreciate it very much if you came to get him at the Four Seasons Hotel. Suite 2442. I'll put out the Do Not Disturb sign so no one will bother him between now and then. Oh, and when you get here you'll find I've left a few more little presents for you, as well. Nothing destructive, I promise," he added, anticipating her next question. "Well, not anymore, at any rate. Ta-ta, Lila. We'll chat again. Soon."

"Adrian, wait, I need to know if—"

But he'd already severed the connection. There was only silence at the other end of the line.

In one swift, fluid gesture, Lila snapped closed the phone, gathered up her backpack and sprang from the concrete step where she'd been sitting. If she hurried, she could be downtown in less than half an hour. She just hoped Joel would still be there—safe—when she arrived.

NOT ONLY WAS JOEL safe by the time Lila arrived, but he was wandering around the hotel suite consulting with four other OPUS agents who had responded when she'd alerted the local office to what was going on. The "few more little presents" Adrian had referred to, she saw now, were Chuck, Hobie and Donny, all taped up nicely. Unfortunately— though not surprisingly—Adrian was nowhere to be found. What *was* surprising—and more than a little interesting, as far as Lila was concerned—was that Iris Daugherty wasn't around, either. What was most interesting of all, however, was Lila's reaction to all of it.

Simply put, she didn't care about any of it except for the fact that Joel was safe. Not that Adrian was still on the loose. Not that there might still be a potentially disastrous virus floating around out there. Not that Chuck Miller looked even smaller than his little peepee all trussed up as he was. Just that she was within touching distance of Joel again, and that he was looking at her as if he very much wanted her to touch him. Even better, he looked as if he wanted to touch her, too.

So, heedless of the other two agents in the room, Lila strode directly to him, threw her arms around his neck, snuggled—yes, *snuggled*—her entire body against his and said, "Thank God you're okay. I don't know what I would have done if he'd… If you'd… If anyone had…" She couldn't finish the statement. Because she couldn't finish the thought. If anything had happened to Joel… Well. It was just unthinkable, that was all.

He hesitated not a moment in wrapping his arms around her and pulling her closer still. "Gee, you sound like you were kind of worried about me."

"No way," she said, pushing herself harder against him. "I was *incredibly* worried about you."

He said nothing in response to that, only skimmed his open hands lightly over her back and bent to settle his cheek against the crown of her head. There was nothing sexual in the embrace. As close as they were, and as intimately as they were touching, there was nothing arousing about it. Lila didn't think she'd ever held a man without it being some kind of prelude to sex. But in this embrace there was only serenity and familiarity and…affection, she told herself. Because she did feel…affection…for Joel. Hey, he was her partner. Of course she'd have…affection…for him.

Someone cleared his throat gently, and Lila was surprised to discover it was Joel. She removed her head from his chest and looked up to find him looking back at her as if he had something very important he wanted to tell her. All he said, though, was, "We need to coordinate on everything that's happened."

Boy, did they, Lila thought. Then she realized he was talking about the assignment, not about the two of them. She gave herself a good mental shaking, forced herself to drop her hands to her sides and took a step away from him. The assignment, she reminded herself. The job. That had to come first, right? Of course it did. The job always came first. Even if she did care more about Joel at the moment.

"Right," she said. "So tell me what happened, and then we can figure out what to do next."

He filled her in on how he'd gotten to the Four Seasons and everything he'd learned during his brief confinement. And after they made clear to Chuck and Hobie and Donny just how serious their situations were, the three men began to talk all at once, each vying to see who could reveal the most information first and buy himself the most legal favors.

"This could take a while," one of the other OPUS agents finally said. "We should take them in and question them all separately."

"We'll expect a full report tonight," Lila said. Then she turned to Joel. "Any sign of the virus?" she asked.

He shook his head. "Sorcerer never mentioned it when he was here, and he and Iris cleared out everything when they took off. Except," he added with a curious smile, "my briefcase. Chuck brought it with him from the apartment when they brought me here, but Adrian never even glanced at it."

Interesting, Lila thought. But something else interested her even more. "Adrian and Iris left together?" she asked.

Joel nodded. "Funny thing, too," he said.

"What?"

"I got the feeling they were going to stay together. As in, disappear together."

"Along with the virus," Lila said.

Now Joel cocked his head to the side a bit. "Yeah, but I'm not sure we should be as worried about that as we were before," he told her. "Call me crazy, but I don't think the two of them are all that interested in the virus anymore."

This, too, surprised Lila. "No?"

"No. I think they were a lot more interested in something else."

"What?"

Joel grinned. "Each other."

"What?"

"Long story," Joel said. "I'll fill you in on the way back to the apartment, after we've finished up here. There is one thing, though," he added.

"What's that?"

"We should be able to locate his source in OPUS," Joel said.

"How?"

"Sorcerer evidently collected *a lot* of information about Chuck and the gang. Information that only his contact in OPUS could have uncovered. And it was information that the source didn't relay to anyone else, or you and I would have had it. No one in OPUS can run searches like that without leaving a trail. So all we have to do is find out who ran searches on Chuck, Hobie, Donny and Iris, and we'll have our leak."

"It'll be that easy?"

He nodded. "Yeah. It will. I can take care of it myself."

"There's one other thing, too," Lila said.

"What's that?"

"Adrian told me on the phone that he and I would chat again."

"So he did," Joel said, obviously remembering. "And he doesn't make idle promises, does he?"

"Never. And I'm betting it won't take him long to contact me," she added. "His time is running out. He's smart enough to figure out we'll be able to ID his contact at OPUS now. So that contact won't be able to give him any more one-step-ahead-of-the-agents information. He knows we're gaining on him. And he knows I'm good enough to get him. So if he's going to contact me, it will be soon. And then, if he has his way, it will all finally be over."

Joel met her gaze levelly. "So now we just have to figure out how to make sure it ends in our favor instead of his."

ACTUALLY, LILA THOUGHT NINETY minutes later as Joel closed the apartment door behind them, they had a lot more to figure out than that. At least, *she* did. Like how she was supposed to act around Joel now. Now that she realized how terrified she was by the prospect of losing him, but still couldn't see how he would fit into her life if he stayed. Now that she understood how good the two of them were together, but still couldn't imagine being shackled to someone else—even someone she…had affection for.

Lila just couldn't imagine including someone else in her life. She didn't even know how to share her life with someone else. She'd been alone for so long. In many ways, she'd always been alone. And she'd always expected to stay alone. And she'd *liked* knowing she would be alone. Alone, she didn't have to be responsible for anyone else. She didn't have to worry about anyone else. Didn't have to take care of anyone else. Alone, she didn't have to fear for anyone else. She could do whatever she wanted, whenever she wanted to do it. She hadn't wanted anyone else to mess that up.

But when she'd discovered the existence of her sister six months ago, Lila had begun to reconsider all that. Because it was then that she'd realized she *wasn't* alone. There was someone else in the world to whom she would be connected forever, whether she and Marnie met again in person or not. And then, when they had met in person…

Well. Lila had begun to rethink everything after that initial meeting with her sister. Who she was, what she was, the purpose of her life…and, inescapably, OPUS's place in all of it. Because OPUS was responsible for much of what Lila, and her life, had become.

They had known about Marnie—and Lila's father, too— years before Lila found out about them. Yet they'd never told Lila about her family's existence for fear that it might take away some of her edge. They'd worried that if Lila had someone to care about in the world, someone who would care for her in return, it might make her less willing to take risks, might make her more tentative, might keep her from being the superagent they wanted her to be, the superagent she'd in fact become. So they hadn't told her about Marnie and her father. By the time Lila had discovered their existence, her father was dead. And when she'd realized what OPUS had done, what they had denied her, it had pissed her off. Badly.

But the funny thing was, they were right. Since she'd learned of Marnie's existence, Lila *had* lost her edge. No, not lost it. Abandoned it willingly. The presence of someone else in her life to care about, who cared about her in return, did indeed make a huge difference. And it wasn't just Marnie she was thinking about.

Joel turned away from the front door as that last thought uncurled in Lila's head. Before he could say a word, and not questioning why she did it, she launched herself at him, looping her arms around his neck and covering his mouth with hers. He didn't question why she did it, either, just roped his arms around her waist and pulled her closer, kissing her back with equal fire, equal passion, equal…affection.

They moved more slowly when they made love this time, taking longer to arouse and pleasure each other, as if they both knew they did indeed have more time. And although Lila still wasn't convinced of that, although she was still completely uncertain how things between the two of them would play out—or maybe it was because of that—she didn't try to hurry them along. When they made love again, the desperation and voraciousness that had been present the first time was gone. It was almost as if they wanted to get to know each other better this time, as if it were important they learn about each other's wants and desires and preferences.

Afterward, they fell into a seamless slumber in Joel's bed, with Lila wrapped in his arms and her entire body curled into his. Her last thoughts before sleep claimed her were mostly about how good it felt to share a bed with someone else, and how nice it felt to share the night with someone else, and how much she looked forward to waking up in the morning and sharing a day with someone else, too.

So it was with some surprise that she awoke in the middle of the night instead. Especially when she realized she and Joel were no longer alone.

As she jackknifed up in bed, she clenched the sheet to herself with one hand and switched on the bedside lamp with the other. It took only a second for her eyes to adjust to the light that spilled into the room, so she immediately saw Adrian Padgett squinting back at her. Never before had she seen him in such a state. His khaki pants and navy polo were rumpled, his face was unshaven, his hair was uncombed and faint purple crescents smudged both eyes. He looked exhausted and flustered and…scared, she marveled.

In spite of that, "You know, a forty-watt bulb is plenty sufficient for a bedside lamp," he said by way of a greeting.

The young woman standing beside him was bothered by the light even more than he was, to the point of holding a hand in front of her eyes to shield them from the glare. But that wasn't why it took a moment for Lila to recognize her as Iris Daugherty. It was because she looked nothing like the young woman Lila had come to know. The black clothing had been replaced by generic student wear of blue jeans and a slouchy blue sweater, the black cosmetics and facial jewelry were gone and her hair had been dyed a pale blond. The transformation should have made her look more fragile and less intimidating than the Goth wear. Instead, her strength and conviction were almost palpable now.

Joel was a little slower to wake than Lila, since even after a week of being in the field—had it really been only that long?—he still wasn't accustomed to being in a position of having to be on constant alert. But when he finally pushed himself up in bed and nudged his hair out of his eyes and realized what was happening, he, too, snapped to attention, tugging up his side of the sheet, too.

"What the hell…?" he demanded.

Okay, so maybe he still hadn't quite realized what was going on, Lila thought. 'Cause it was pretty freakin' clear to her. They'd been caught not with their pants down, but with their pants off, something that didn't happen to even the greenest OPUS agent. Something that never would have happened to Lila, either, she thought, if she'd been focused on her professional duties instead of being sidetracked by all the developments in her personal life. It was becoming more and more apparent that she couldn't have both. OPUS was right. Having people to care about in her life prevented Lila from doing her job. She was going to have to make some decisions. Soon.

For now, however, for obvious reasons, she did her best to focus on the job. Her eyes never leaving Adrian's, she finished the question Joel had begun, "What the hell is going on, Sorcerer?"

Adrian expelled a weary-sounding sigh. "Oh, come on, Lila. After everything we've been through together, don't you think you could call me Adrian?"

"All right. What the hell is going on, Adrian?"

He hesitated only a moment before announcing, "I want to turn myself in."

She actually chuckled at that. "No, really. What the hell is going on?"

He draped an arm around Iris and pulled her close, but there was something in the gesture that made Lila think it wasn't because he was trying to protect her, but because he needed her physical nearness to sustain him. Iris in turn wrapped an arm around his waist and leaned her entire body into him, as if she were perfectly willing to give him such sustenance. It was the weirdest thing. Had Lila not known better, she would have sworn it was Iris, not Adrian, who was the stronger of the two at the moment.

"I want to turn myself in," he said again.

He actually seemed serious, Lila marveled. He honestly seemed to be turning himself in. She looked over at Joel, who looked back at her, clearly as skeptical as she. Then they both turned back to Adrian. "You really want to turn yourself in?" she asked.

"I really do."

"Just like that?"

He nodded. "Just like that."

"No threats to do anyone bodily harm?"

"No."

"No shoot-outs?"

He shook his head.

"No car chases through the city?"

"I'm afraid none will be necessary."

"No explosions?"

"Not a one."

She gaped at him. "Well, that sucks."

He shrugged again. "What can I say, Lila? Cinematic spectacle is not my forte."

"Well, it's not mine, either, but come on. No agent worth her salt likes to just have the bad guy show up in the middle of the night and turn himself in. It's embarrassing."

He smiled. "Face it, sweetheart. I've eluded OPUS for too long. This is the only way you'd ever bring me in. But look at it this way." He hurried on when she opened her mouth to object. "I won't tell you the name of my contact in the organization, and when you finally figure out who it is, perhaps that person will lead you on a merry chase, and you'll have more gunfire, squealing tires and exploding buildings than you can shake a stick at."

"We already found her," Joel said.

Which was true. Once Joel had called the home office and given them the information about the files on Chuck and the others, they'd located Adrian's source within moments. Then they'd called Lila and Joel back with the ID before they even left the hotel.

Adrian seemed in no way surprised by the quickness with which they'd worked. Though he did seem genuinely regretful. Somehow, though, Lila got the impression it was as much because he'd dragged someone else into his schemes as it was that she had been caught. "I guess I should have realized you would. She's a nice girl, though. You shouldn't have any trouble getting her to talk."

From what little Lila had heard, his contact actually did sound like a nice girl. A young woman in the research department who'd been with OPUS for almost five years and should have known better than to get mixed up with Adrian. But then, Lila had seen for herself how persuasive—and seductive—the guy could be. Nice girls were generally the most susceptible to him, which was probably why she'd never been swayed to the dark side herself. Iris, too, was a nice girl who had succumbed to him.

Although, looking at the two of them together now, it was almost the other way around. As if Adrian had been the one to succumb to Iris. As if Iris was *so* nice, some of it had inevitably rubbed off on Adrian. Who would have thought that that was what it would take to undo the guy? Someone whose goodness completely overshadowed his badness.

"I want to turn myself in," he said for a third time.

"We both do," Iris added.

Adrian's face—his whole body, in fact—went soft at her words. Soft, Lila marveled. Adrian Padgett. Because of a nice woman to whom he had succumbed.

When Adrian spoke again, it was with significantly more emphasis. "As I said, I *want* to turn myself in. We both do. Unfortunately, we can't."

Okay. All right. It was all making sense now. Lila should have seen this coming from a million miles away.

"Stop jerking us around," Joel said. "Just say whatever it is you need to say. Don't play games with us."

When Adrian replied, he spoke not to Joel, but to Lila. "I assure you, I am finished with games. For good. I truly would turn myself in, if circumstances were different. But it's not just me I have to worry about anymore. There's someone else I worry about now, too. Even more than I worry about myself."

Lila didn't need to ask who.

"For extremely good reasons," Adrian continued, "Iris has to stay in hiding. For the rest of her life. And although she's done a very good job of that for eight years, I'm better at it. Between the two of us, she'll stay well hidden forever. She'll stay safe."

"And so will you," Lila said pointedly.

He dipped his head forward in acknowledgment of that. "I don't blame you for thinking I have only my own interests at heart," he said. "But neither do I care that you think that. I know, and Iris knows," he added, pulling her closer, "what the truth of the situation is. It benefits us both to disappear," he agreed. "But believe me when I say it's no longer my interests that mean the most to me."

Lila wasn't sure if she'd ever believe that. But there was definitely something different about Adrian. Something that hadn't been there before. Something that made her think that maybe, just maybe, he was telling the truth.

"You may disappear," Joel said, "but you'll always have people looking for you. OPUS will never rest until they have you behind bars."

Adrian continued to look at Lila when he replied. "I was hoping perhaps if I gave OPUS what they wanted, they might leave Iris and me alone. For good."

"But it's you OPUS wants," Lila pointed out.

"Perhaps," he said. "What I think OPUS wants even more, however, is the little project I've been working on most recently."

Something hot and heavy hummed in Lila's midsection at the words. "The virus?"

"The virus."

"You actually built it?" she asked.

"I didn't," he admitted. "Hobie built the framework, then he and Iris filled it in and nearly finished it. They hit a small snag, but Iris has been working nonstop to get it working. An hour ago, she finished."

"It works?" Lila asked.

This time it was Iris who replied. "It'll work," she said. "Obviously we didn't test it, but…" She nodded with all confidence. She spoke with even more as she added, "If it's unleashed, it will be absolutely devastating. But here's the thing. I altered some of the programming to allow the user better control of it. It can wipe out as much—or as little—as the one who sends it out into the world would like to wipe out."

"Just think," Adrian added. "Whoever has it in their possession could use it to cripple just about any enemy to the country they'd like. Even those pesky third-world terrorists who rely on computers to get so much done. The Office for Political Unity and Security would have a *very* powerful weapon on their hands, one that wouldn't physically harm a soul. *If* Iris and I turn it over. And we'll only turn it over if they promise to pretend we no longer exist."

Lila wasn't sure what to say in response to that. So she said nothing. Neither did Joel. When she looked over at him, though, she could see he wasn't sitting there idly. He had one of those looks on his face that indicated he was giving great thought to something. So she said nothing that might distract him.

When neither of them replied to his proposed bargain,

Adrian spoke again. "So what do you say, Lila? Iris and I are forgotten in exchange for the virus."

"They won't go for it, Adrian," Lila told him. "You've done too much damage. You're responsible for a man's death."

His eyebrows arrowed downward at that. "I never intended for anyone to be killed," he said softly.

"But someone was."

"It was a terrible mistake."

"It was an execution. An execution that never would have happened if you hadn't deliberately leaked classified information to the wrong people."

"Had I known what those people were capable of, I assure you, I never would have said a word. If I could take back what I did, I would. But I can't. I can only say that I never intended for anyone to be harmed. I'm greedy, Lila, not vicious. But even my greed has its limits."

She supposed she did believe that. Adrian had betrayed people's trust, and he'd exploited people's weaknesses, and he'd extorted and flat-out stolen millions of dollars. But he'd never shown any capacity for violence, and he did seem to embrace a certain obscure morality. True, it was a morality that benefited him over everyone else, but she'd never known him to physically harm anyone. Nevertheless, he had committed crimes, and he should pay for them.

Unfortunately, Lila couldn't guarantee that he *would* pay for them any more than she could guarantee OPUS would let him go. Because OPUS, too, embraced a morality that benefited them over everyone else. And if getting their hands on a virus like the one Iris had created to unleash on their enemies meant looking the other way with regard to Adrian's crimes, they might very well do it.

"Neither Joel nor I is in a position to make guarantees like the one you want us to make," Lila said. "That will be up to much higher-ranking officials than either of us."

Adrian smiled his knowing smile. "Lila, you're in a position to make OPUS do whatever you want. You always have been. You know it as well as I do. If you make this guarantee, it's as good as done."

She said nothing to indicate agreement or disagreement with the statement. Even though she knew he was right. Instead, she said, "I'll have to consult the others first and get back to you. Where will you be staying in the meantime?" she asked.

He laughed outright at that. "Nice try," he told her. "You have one hour," he added. "I'll call you in sixty minutes and you can let me know their decision. Regardless of what happens, Iris and I will be gone by the time the sun comes up. The only thing left to decide now is whether or not OPUS gets their virus, and whether or not Iris and I will be free."

"You'll never be free, Adrian," Lila told him. "There will always be someone looking for you."

He shook his head as he pulled Iris close again. "Someone's already found me," he said. "I'm not lost anymore." Lila started to say something else, but he cut her off. "Don't bother getting up. We can find our own way out."

And before Lila or Joel could make a move, they did.

CHAPTER EIGHTEEN

THE HIGHER-UPS AT OPUS went for the deal. Lila told herself she shouldn't be surprised, considering some of the morally questionable things those guys had done in the past, but she was. She had still held out some small hope that they would do the right thing and make Adrian's payment for his crimes their priority. Instead, they'd done what she supposed they considered the greater good—taking out of circulation a weapon that might have been used against the country otherwise, a weapon the country might now be able to use on their own enemies instead.

All hail the greater good.

In spite of her disappointment, she would have been lying if she hadn't admitted that there was a part of her that was strangely satisfied by the outcome. She knew she had excellent instincts—she couldn't have been OPUS's best agent without them—and her instincts told her that Adrian had indeed turned over a new leaf, and that it was due in large part to Iris Daugherty's entry into his life. He *had* been different the last time she saw him. And he had turned over to OPUS a perfectly well functioning, totally devastating virus that he might have used himself. His reasons for wanting to disappear had as much to do with Iris's welfare as his own—perhaps even more.

He just wasn't the same man Lila had started pursuing years ago. He wasn't Sorcerer anymore. He wasn't even Adrian Padgett. He and Iris both would assume new names now. New identities. A new residence. A new lifestyle. A new life.

A new life, Lila thought again as she looked over at Joel, who was seated across from her in the same government jet that had carried them to Cincinnati from Washington just over a week ago. His dark hair was tucked behind one ear, making his face clearly visible, but his gaze was fixed on the laptop in front of him. He had his glasses on and was dressed in a beige oxford shirt, the cuffs rolled back to his elbows, the shirt tucked into brown trousers. He looked as if he was already slipping back into archivist mode, even though Washington was still hundreds of miles away. In a few moments they'd be taking off, though, going in the opposite direction from the one they had flown before. This time they were headed back.

At least literally. Figuratively, Lila knew she would never be able to go back. Just as Adrian was a different man from the one she'd started chasing years ago, the woman chasing him was different, too. When she and Joel arrived in Washington, nothing would be the same as when they'd left it. Especially not Lila. So much had happened in the week since she'd met Joel Faraday. The criminal she'd been tracking for years didn't seem so criminal anymore, and he was no longer hers to pursue. The organization she'd thought she would devote her life to serving had, for a second time, jerked the rug out from under her. Before that she'd met a sister she hadn't known she had. Had learned that her biological father wasn't some faceless jerk who had bedded and abandoned her mother. She'd met a man who—

Joel turned his head to look at her then, smiling when he saw that she was studying him so intently.

"What?" he asked, his smile warming his mouth, his eyes, his entire face. "What are you thinking about?"

So much, Lila thought. There was just so much. Too much. Too much for her not to feel overwhelmed by it. So she dropped her gaze to smooth out a nonexistent wrinkle in her baggy charcoal pants, and straightened the dark red shirt that needed no straightening. Then she replied softly, "I'm leaving OPUS."

When Joel said nothing in response, she glanced up again. But she could tell nothing of what he was thinking by his expression. And all he said when he finally did speak was, "Why?"

Oh, where to begin? she thought. Oversimplifying it egregiously, she told him, "It's not the organization I thought it was."

To his credit, he chuckled—once—at the comment. "It's not the organization anyone thinks it is, Lila. Hell, half the time I don't think OPUS even knows what kind of an organization it is."

"Oh, they know," she replied immediately, not quite able to keep the edge out of her voice. Then she relented. "And I suppose, deep down, I did, too. I just didn't care before."

"Before what?"

She dropped her gaze back into her lap. "Before I realized I'm not the machine they want me to be. At least, I'm not anymore. That machine wouldn't have cared that it was being controlled through lies and manipulation. That machine wouldn't have cared that a criminal it had spent years trying to bring down got away without so much as a slap on the wrist. That machine wouldn't have cared that OPUS didn't tell it about its sister and father, and it wouldn't have lain awake at night wondering what it missed out on by not having that information. And that machine wouldn't have cared about—" She halted before she could put voice to her feelings about Joel. Because, honestly, she still wasn't sure about her feelings for Joel.

"It wouldn't have cared about what?" he asked.

But all Lila said was, "I'm not a machine. I'm a human being. With a brain and a heart, and everything that comes with both of them. All the fear, all the confusion, all the…" She sighed again. "I just can't be what OPUS wants me to be. And I don't want to work for an organization I don't respect."

"Then what will you do?" he asked.

"Take some time off," she said, having made that decision, if no others. "I don't want to rush into anything just yet. I just…I have a lot of things I need to figure out."

He said nothing in response to that, so Lila looked up at him again. The moment her gaze connected with his, he asked, "Am I one of those things?"

She had to be honest with him, she knew. More to the point, she had to be honest with herself. So she replied, "Yeah. You are."

His expression didn't change in any way at her revelation. He only studied her in silence, as if he were waiting for her to say more. She supposed the least she could do was give him an explanation. The problem was, she wasn't sure she had one.

Honest, she reminded herself. Be honest.

"I've never met anyone like you before," she began. "And I care about you in a way that I've never come close to caring for another human being. But it all happened so fast, Joel. And even though my life does kind of run at light speed most of the time, this thing between you and me, it's…it's…" She hesitated, trying to find the right way to say it. "It's too important for me to just sit back and let it happen, the way I usually do."

"Why not?"

She blinked at the question as if he'd just flashed a too-bright light in her eyes. Probably because that was how the question made her feel. Surprised. Disoriented. Off balance. "What do you mean, 'Why not?'" she asked.

He shrugged as if the question were a simple one, and never once looked away. "Why can't you react instinctively to what's happened between us?" he said. "It seems to me that's the one thing you *should* react instinctively to."

The answer to that should be obvious to him, she thought. It was, after all, so obvious to her. She couldn't react instinctively because… Because… Because…

"Because it's too important," she said again.

His expression softened a little at that. "Lila—"

"No, Joel, don't," she interrupted him, holding up a hand. "There's just too much going on right now for me to make sense of any of it. The man I've focused my entire existence on finding for the past two years is suddenly no longer my concern. I have a sister I met for the first time a couple of weeks ago, for just a few hours, that I need to get to know. My partner, my best friend in the world, is getting married soon and he's going to have priorities that don't include me, which is totally as it should be." She felt tears welling up and cursed herself for not being able to better control them. "And then there's you," she said softly.

His dark eyebrows arrowed downward. "What about me?"

She shook her head. "That's just it, Joel. I don't know about you. You're the most confusing thing of all."

He said nothing for a moment, and his expression never changed. Finally, very softly, he told her, "Then I guess I need to help you figure me out."

She forced herself not to look away when she told him, "No. I can only do that by myself."

His brow furrowed. "Just like you do everything else, huh?"

His remark confused her. "What do you mean?"

"I mean you think you have to do everything by yourself," he said. "It's not just the job—it's your whole life. You can't accept the fact that there are some things you do need someone else to help you with. And one of those things, Lila, is life."

She started to object—even though she knew part of what he said was true—but he hurried on before she had a chance. His expression cleared a little as he spoke, however, and he smiled, albeit a little sadly. Still, his voice was lighter when he told her, "But that's okay. For now. Go ahead and try to figure me out by yourself. In the meantime, let me help you out with something else you need."

The sudden change in tone, in him, confused her even

more. "What are you talking about?" she asked. "What else do I need?"

"Your partner's getting married this weekend," he reminded her. "You'll be getting to the church on time, after all."

"What does that have to do with something I need?"

He lifted a shoulder and let it drop. "You need a date, right? I mean, no single person wants to go to a wedding without a date. Everyone's in matchmaker mode at weddings, trying to foist you off on their nephew. Or their neighbor. Or their plumber. Or their barber. Or their nephew's neighbor's plumber's barber. Who needs that?"

She smiled in spite of her confusion, in spite of her tumultuous emotions, wishing all it took to make things right between them was attending someone else's wedding. And then she heard herself say, "Yeah, I guess I do need a date for that."

Joel nodded once, satisfied with her answer. "Then it's settled," he said. "I'll be your date for the wedding."

"But—"

"No, no, don't worry. It's no trouble at all."

"But—"

"I have absolutely no plans for the weekend."

"But—"

"This may come as a surprise to you, but I even own a suit."

"But—"

"And even more surprising, I know how to dance."

"But—"

"And I always bring a gift."

"But—"

"Still, Lila, there is something you should know about me," he concluded, sobering.

The expression on his face now made her mouth go a little dry, so very serious was it. Very quietly she asked, "What?"

"I love you."

Lila actually reared her head back involuntarily at the words, so overwhelming was their power. She closed her eyes, thinking it might take away some of their impact, but that only made them sink deeper. It wasn't that she was surprised Joel loved her. It wasn't even that she was surprised he would tell her. What surprised her was the absolute conviction with which he said it.

"I love you," he said again. And again the words, the feeling, went right to the bone. "And I will love you forever. But, Lila."

She opened her eyes again, looking at him.

Very softly he told her, "I can't wait for you forever. That's not the way I'm built."

She wasn't sure what else to say after that, so she told him, "I'll pick you up at your house Saturday morning. Eight o'clock. Pack for two nights in the Hamptons."

He nodded. "I'll be ready."

She nodded back, with less enthusiasm. She only wished she could say the same for herself.

JOEL SLEPT BARELY A wink Friday night. Which wasn't surprising, because he hadn't slept well all week. At least, not since returning to D.C. His house had become too quiet, too inhospitable, too empty. Which was strange, since it was cluttered with the remnants of four generations of Faradays, and never before had he found the place lacking in any way. On the contrary, Joel had always loved this house. Without Lila, it just wasn't comfortable. By Saturday morning, as he stood gazing out the living-room window onto the street below, he was beginning to wonder if his house would ever feel comfortable again.

And he wondered if Lila would ever be able to love him.

He hadn't seen or spoken to her since their return. They'd been separated the moment they debarked the plane to be debriefed individually, something that had taken up the rest of that day. As he'd risen to leave his debriefing, hoping to find Lila still around, he'd been handed a slim vellum envelope he recognized as official OPUS stationery. Inside had been a brief, handwritten letter from Lila telling him she would be in Cleveland visiting her sister for the rest of the week, but that she'd see him at eight o'clock Saturday morning, just as the two of them had agreed. The wording of the note hadn't exactly been formal, but neither had it been all that familiar. Just an announcement of her plans, and a reminder of the time, and a *Take care, Joel* before signing her name.

Take care, Joel. Yeah, he'd get right on that.

He told himself now, as he had told himself for days, that her trip had nothing to do with him. She would, understandably, want to see the sister she'd met only briefly before having to take off to find Sorcerer. But she'd left so quickly and abruptly. And she'd left without telling him goodbye. She'd left without telling him a lot of things he really would have liked to hear.

His thoughts halted right there, because a car pulled into a spot at the curb half a block up from his house, and he knew without question it was Lila. Sure enough, the driver's door opened and a blond head emerged, connected to a body that was petite and potent. Sunglasses covered her eyes, but nothing could hide her strength and determination, though the pale yellow sweater she wore over well-faded jeans went a long way toward softening both. As she made her way up the street toward his front door, she looked carefree and flirty and feminine. Unless he was just imagining that.

Then the knot in his belly cinched tighter.

He arrived at his front door just as she knocked, and he pulled it open immediately. She'd pushed her sunglasses to the top of her head, so the surprise etched on her face at his quickness was unmistakable. Likewise unmistakable was the way she smiled at him when she saw him—warmly, a little nervously, happily. He wasn't imagining that.

Nevertheless, there was another quick pull on the knot in his stomach.

"Hi," she said.

"Hi," he replied.

Neither seemed to have a clue what to do or say next. So Joel opened the door wider, stepped aside and invited her in, hoping none of his anxiousness showed in his actions or voice. He ran his fingers restlessly through his dark hair, tucking a handful behind one ear, then brushed his palm over the blue-and-white-striped shirt he'd tucked into his own reasonably reputable-looking jeans.

"Have you had breakfast?" he asked. "I could make more coffee, if you want some."

She shook her head. "I'm good, thanks."

She certainly was.

Even though he'd promised himself he would let Lila be the one to bring it up, before he could stop himself, he heard himself asking, "Did you have a good visit with Marnie?"

Her smile fell a little. "Um, yeah…Joel…about that…"

He immediately regretted saying a word. Holding up a hand in apology, he told her, "I'm sorry. I didn't mean that to sound the way it did. It's none of my business what—"

"No, I should have told you I was going to visit my sister in Cleveland," she said. She smiled. "My sister in Cleveland," she repeated. "I like saying that. It feels nice." Then her smile fell. "I'm sorry I took off the way I did. But I just…" She sighed deeply. "I just needed to get away for a few days, that's all."

"I understand, really," he said. And he was surprised to realize he did. "And I'm glad you had Marnie to give you a safe haven," he added. "We all need one of those." Though he wished Lila would see she had one in him, too.

"It really was a good visit," she said. "And it was nice to spend more than an evening with her. But kind of weird, too, you know?"

He shook his head. "Not really. But I can imagine."

She sighed. "It's just… It's just weird to know I have a family. I grew up telling myself it was okay that I didn't have one, even though everyone else did, because, hey, I didn't want a family anyway, so there."

Joel smiled, hoping it looked reassuring. "Just like the hurt little kid who says she hates the very thing she craves so no one will think less of her for not having it, huh?"

Lila nodded. "But even as an adult, I kept telling myself I didn't want it. I've always let that hurt little kid in me dictate how I felt about family. It's only been since spending time with Marnie that I've come to realize how incredibly desperately I've *always* wanted a family." She crossed her arms anxiously over her chest as she continued, "During those months I was in hiding, running from OPUS, I was completely alone. I didn't have anyone to talk to, no one to trust, no one to share anything with. For the first time in my life, Joel, I was actually *alone*. Completely alone. The way I'd always told myself I wanted to be. And it was horrible. I never want to have to live like that again. I never want to be alone."

He wasn't sure what to say in response to that, so he said nothing. Besides, she seemed to want to say more.

But she only sighed and drove her gaze restlessly around the room, until it settled on a painting that hung between the front door and window. It was the latest from Joel's thirteen-year-old niece, a watercolor titled "The Shoes My Mom Won't Let Me Have." It was executed in angry slashes of purple and gold that most art critics would probably have called "self-indulgent." Joel, however, thought the kid showed promise. Once she stopped being thirteen.

"You have some new art," Lila said.

He nodded. "Yeah, it was waiting for me when I got home from Cincinnati. There's a nice one from the two-year-old, too. It's supposed to be a dog, I think. Maybe a butterfly. Possibly a hamburger. Or else it's a depiction of man's eternal struggle with his inner Paris Hilton."

"Interpretive art, huh?" she asked with a smile.

"For lack of a better word—like incomprehensible—yeah."

She looked around the room some more, then back at Joel. "You have a nice place here, Joel. It's…homey."

He wondered about the rapid ricochet of changing subject, but decided to go with it for now. "It's okay, I guess."

"No, it's more than okay. It's really…cozy. The kind of place that would be nice for raising a family."

The knot in his belly went so tight then, it nearly cut off his circulation. "Maybe…"

"That was what you said you wanted," she reminded him. "Remember? That day we left for Cincinnati. Life with all the traditional trappings. You said the house could be a Tudor, and the dog could be named Pal, but that that was what you wanted. The whole suburban fantasy of wife, kids and riding mower."

Had he said that? he wondered. He thought back to the day in question. Strange. He supposed he had said that. He'd probably even believed it. Then. Now, however, none of those things showed up on his list of Things That Would Make Joel Faraday Happy. In fact, there wasn't even a list anymore. Because there was only one thing Joel Faraday needed to make him happy. Lila Moreau.

"I guess I did say that," he told her. "But things change, Lila."

"In just a couple of weeks?"

He nodded. "A couple of weeks is a long time. A lot can happen in a couple of weeks. You should know that better than anyone."

She looked at him in silence for a moment. "Yeah, I guess I should." She met his gaze levelly. "I'll never be the sort of woman who can live a traditional life, Joel. Even though I'm not sure yet what I'll do for a living now that I'm not working for OPUS, it will still be something…edgy," she finally said. "Maybe not dangerous, but I have to have something, some kind of adventure, some kind of excitement. Something unpredictable and…and breakneck and…and not routine. The life in the suburbs thing, the whole soccer-mom existence… That's not me. Ever. I know a lot of women—and men, too—are totally suited to that, and I salute them. But I'd suffocate if I had to live a traditional life in the suburbs. And I'd be a lousy mom."

He started to argue with her, but knew better. This wasn't a realization she'd come to easily, he knew. It was something she'd doubtless figured out a long time ago.

"So if you want kids," she began again, "I'm not—"

"I want you," he told her before she could finish. "And that's all I want."

"You say that now, but—"

"Because I know it's true. Look, Lila," he said, "you're not the only one who's had things to figure out. Maybe before I met you I had this vague idea of what I wanted my future to be. But now…"

He paused, drove his own gaze around the room, then looked at her again. "You could take away this house and everything in it," he said. "You can take away my job and tell me none of my work has ever mattered. You can tell me I'll never have kids or dogs or crabgrass or anything else in the traditional domestic-bliss scenario. Frankly, Lila, I don't give a damn.

"But take away *you,*" he said more softly this time, "tell me I'll never have *you,* and I just can't see any reason for wanting anything. Because you are all I want. You're all I need. When I think of the future now, it's full of uncertainty. But that wouldn't scare me if it weren't for the fact that, right now, one of those uncertainties is you. And that, Lila… That does scare me. It scares the hell out of me."

Her eyebrows had arrowed downward as he spoke, as if she wanted to believe him, but couldn't quite make the leap.

"I love you," he told her. "I want to be with you. I want to spend the rest of my life with you. Even if I have no idea what that life will bring. It doesn't matter what happens or doesn't happen. It doesn't matter what I have or don't have. As long as I have you." He inhaled another fortifying breath before voicing the last part, then added, "And as long as I know you love me."

This was her cue, he thought. If she was going to say it, it better be now. Because if she didn't say it now…

She nodded slowly, her expression filled with…something. Something pretty major, he could tell. He just couldn't quite say what. But all she said was, "We should probably get going. I promised Oliver we'd be there before dinner."

CHAPTER NINETEEN

IT WAS A GOOD THING the drive took six hours, Lila thought six hours later. Because it had taken every last minute of those hours to get her and Joel to a place where they were *almost* as comfortable together as they had been before.

Oh, who was she kidding? They'd never be that comfortable again. Not until she could acknowledge—to both herself and Joel—how she felt about him. The problem was that, even after thinking about it for days, and talking about it with Marnie for days, Lila still wasn't sure. Even the six-hour drive hadn't made things any clearer for her. It was wonderful to be with Joel. And when she was with him, she never wanted to be away from him. But she couldn't envision a future with him, either. Nothing would come into focus for her. As hard as she'd tried to figure things out over the past few days, in a way they'd become even blurrier than they'd been before.

But six hours in the car had eased some of the tension that had been present at Joel's house. Enough that they were able to at least pretend there was nothing unsettled between them. For now, Lila thought, that would have to be enough.

The Nesbitt estate was exactly the way she recalled it from her single visit there six months ago. Massive. Lavish. Excessive. Though, granted, at that time she'd been eluding the authorities, had arrived and left under cover of darkness and had been forced to limit her stay to about twenty minutes. She also hadn't been dressed appropriately for high society, wearing, as she had been that night, the oversize uniform of a security guard she'd coldcocked and half a pair of handcuffs. So she hadn't really had the chance to appreciate the full effect of the place. Now as Joel steered her car up the long and winding road that was the Nesbitt driveway, she took her time to enjoy the view. And the phrase that leaped first and foremost into her mind as she surveyed the house and grounds was *Holy crap*.

The Nesbitt home probably wasn't that much different from any number of other East Hampton estates, but since Lila's experience with such abodes was limited, she thought the house was amazing. Oliver had told her the place actually had a name—Cobble Court—and that it was worth a cool fifty million dollars. Which meant fifty mil was just a fraction of the wealth claimed by Desmond Nesbitt III, Oliver's future father-in-law.

She grinned as she thought about Oliver marrying into such a family. True, the Sheridans were no slouches when it came to money, but this… This went beyond money. With this sort of wealth came the potential for global domination, and Oliver just didn't seem like the type of guy who would be comfortable with such a thing.

Then again, his intended, the youngest offspring of Desmond and Felicia Nesbitt, wasn't much the type for such a thing, either, even having grown up in the lap of this sort of luxury. Or rather, this particular lap of luxury. It was just one of many things Lila knew Oliver loved about the woman, even if Lila had found Avery to be…oh, a bit neurotic. At least, she had been six months ago when Lila met her, a skinny, bespectacled computer geek who was confined to her home by agoraphobia and crushing panic attacks that assailed her whenever she tried to leave.

Oliver, however, had told Lila just a few days ago—when she'd called him to tell him she was leaving OPUS—that Avery had come a long way since November. Her agoraphobia was under better control, and she was actually able to make trips from the city to her parents' estate now without loading up on scotch first. And she and Oliver were able to go out within the city from time to time, to plays or restaurants in venues that were small and dark and fairly sparsely populated.

It was a huge accomplishment for a woman who'd spent years holed up in a Central Park condo, virtually never leaving it. And Avery, Lila knew, credited Oliver's entry into her life as being responsible for the majority of her progress. Then again, Oliver had come a long way, too, since Avery had entered his life. He'd been on the road to becoming a bitter, hardened tight ass before he met her. She'd opened him up a lot, had put something back into his life that had been missing for a long time. In a way, Lila supposed, Avery and Oliver had saved each other from lives that would have otherwise been empty and hollow and sad.

"Holy crap," Joel said from the driver's seat as the house grew larger the closer they came. "There really are people in the world who live this way?"

"What?" Lila asked, gesturing toward the palatial home. "Haven't you been to dozens of parties at places like this?"

He shook his head. "My family has money, sure, but…" He eased up on the gas and slowed the car, as if they were approaching some holy shrine that commanded obeisance. "But not like this. This goes beyond rich. This is that top one percent of the country's population that claims ninety-nine percent of its wealth."

"I always thought that was one of those urban legends."

"This place would confirm it as fact, I think."

Lila couldn't argue. The massive Tudor mansion looked like something from a Brontë novel, its beveled glass windows sparkling like diamonds in the midafternoon sun. The lawn rolled seemingly for miles, the kind of flawless green that comes only with a full-time gardener and chemical warfare on the weeds. Beyond the house lay a long ribbon of private beach fronting a wide pond, and there were doubtless views of the ocean beyond that from the upper floors in back. It was out back, near the water, that the double wedding of the Misses Avery and Carly Nesbitt would be taking place. Though had Mother Nature had the temerity to be uncooperative today, the festivities could have been moved inside fairly easily, along with the five hundred guests, because the house could have comfortably accommodated the United Arab Emirates.

Fortunately, Mother Nature knew better, and the blue May sky was streaked with gauzy white clouds, the sun glittering above it all like a newly minted coin.

Joel urged the accelerator toward the floor again, and the car began to pick up speed. "And here I was worried we might be crowding them by accepting their invitation to spend the night at the house."

Lila laughed at that. "Are you kidding? I think they're giving us our own wing."

And she couldn't help thinking as she said it that that was good, because she was hoping the night ahead would be a noisy one. And not just in terms of the wedding reception, either.

Okay, so maybe the tension between them was easing more than she realized. They—or, at least, she—still had a way to go.

"Come on," she said softly, smiling at him, "we don't want to be late. I am, after all, the best man."

He smiled back. "The best woman, too."

There was, of course, no way they would be late. The wedding was still hours away. But Lila wanted to enjoy every moment. She'd never been in a wedding before. Hell, she'd never been *to* a wedding before. She honestly had no idea what to expect, save the few dramatized weddings she'd seen in movies and on TV. And she really, really, really hoped that Oliver and Avery's didn't turn out like one of those. Especially the one on *Dynasty.* Then again, just a shot in the dark, but probably the Nesbitts knew better than to invite anyone from Moldavia.

Of course, it wasn't just Oliver and Avery's wedding. Avery's sister Carly was getting married today, too, to Tanner Gillespie, the man who had been partnered with Oliver while Lila was busy being a fugitive from justice. And as odd a couple as she thought Avery and Oliver were, from what Lila had gathered of the second couple via her conversations with Oliver, Carly and Tanner were even less suited to each other.

She was able to see for herself, since it was the latter couple

Lila and Joel encountered first, within moments of the elegant Nesbitt butler inviting them into the elegant Nesbitt foyer of the elegant Nesbitt estate. Never had Lila felt more *in*elegant than she did when she saw the elegant Nesbitt employee dressed in black tie and tails. Or, at least, something that sort of looked like black tie and tails. Only without the tails. And the tie was more charcoal. Joel seemed to feel the same way, because he suddenly ran a hand over his travel-rumpled clothing. Lila had started to mimic his action when an ungodly outburst from somewhere beyond—like maybe hell—halted her hand.

"Tanner!" something sounding vaguely human—though not quite female—screeched from somewhere deep within the bowels of the house. "What color is this?"

There was a soft reply that Lila couldn't hear, followed by a retort that was more than clear. "It is *not* petal-pink. It's almost apricot, or my name isn't Carly Nesbitt. And the roses are supposed to be petal-pink. *Not* almost apricot!"

"Excuse me, Miss Moreau and Mr. Faraday," the butler, who'd introduced himself as Jensen, said as he did a little half-bow thing. "There appears to be a problem in the parlor."

Then without awaiting a reply—which Lila wasn't sure, but probably wasn't proper butler protocol—he spun around and made his way toward the screeching. Lila and Joel exchanged a glance, smiled at each other and, it went without saying, followed him. They arrived in a room furnished in a half dozen shades of blue, with accents of ivory, and not another lick of color. Except for lots and lots of flowers that, Lila had to admit, looked more apricot than they did pink. Even the woman standing at the center of the room wore a white robe and had her hair wrapped in a white towel.

"She's right," Joel leaned in and whispered in Lila's ear. "Definitely apricot. Or my name isn't Joel Faraday."

The woman—who had to be Carly Nesbitt, Lila thought—snapped her head up to look at them and immediately narrowed her eyes.

"Damn," Joel muttered, straightening. "Busted. She's got good ears."

"Of course I have good ears," Carly said, dropping her hands onto her waist. "I'm a Nesbitt. Who the hell are you?" But before either Lila or Joel could reply, she made a not-so-soft tsking noise and said, "Oh. Right. Oliver's partner. Lila, right? Nice to meet you, heard so much about you. Blah blah blah. Now back to my problems." With the requisite pleasantries concluded, she did indeed go back to her harping about the roses.

"Carly."

The name was uttered softly from the opposite side of the room, and only then did Lila realize there was another person present besides her, Joel, the butler, Carly and Carly's ego. The man was dressed in faded jeans and an equally faded chambray work shirt, which, coupled with his pale blond hair, was in keeping with the room's decor. No wonder Lila had missed him. Although, looking at him now, she was surprised she had. And not just because she was Lila Moreau, ex-überspy. But because the guy—who had to be Tanner Gillespie—was gorgeous. Not gorgeous like Joel, mind you, but extremely attractive in a boyish, all-American kind of way.

"The roses will be fine," he said, his gaze never leaving

his fiancée's. "You're wearing white, remember?" He flashed
her a grin. "Not that you're entitled." A soft sound of outrage
escaped Carly, and she opened her mouth to say only God
knew what, but Tanner continued before she had a chance.
"White goes with anything."

He pushed himself away from the wall and strode across
the room. His eyes never left Carly, and she seemed to be
completely spellbound by him, because she stood there
silently watching his approach. He stopped only when his
body was flush against hers, then bent his head to kiss her in
a slow, openmouthed, full-tongued kiss, even though there
were others looking on.

Then he pulled back and continued to look at her.
"Besides, sweetheart," he said, "you're so beautiful, nobody's
going to be looking at the flowers."

Damn, Lila thought. He was *good*.

"Damn," Joel said softly. "He's *good*."

"Tanner Gillespie," Tanner said then, still looking at Carly,
but obviously talking to Lila and Joel. "Nice to finally meet
you, Lila. Heard a lot about you from Oliver. Heard even
more through the OPUS grapevine."

"Uh, nice to meet you, too," Lila replied.

"Oliver and Avery are out back," he told them, still looking
at his intended. "Not that I'm trying to get rid of you or
anything. But my fiancée and I have something we need to,
ah, discuss right now. In private."

Yeah, and Lila would just bet it wasn't the color of the
roses.

"I'll take you to Miss Avery and her intended," Jensen
offered, clearly realizing his services were no longer neces-

sary. Tanner obviously had everything—i.e., Carly Nesbitt—
under control.

Lila and Joel followed the butler down a hallway that was
roughly the same length as Versailles's Hall of Mirrors,
passed an endless assortment of rooms, each color-coded in
a different—but monochromatic—way than the one preceding it. Finally they arrived in what Lila supposed was a
garden room or something, because one entire wall was glass
and looked out onto the lush and inescapably elegant Nesbitt
gardens—all eight billion acres of them—behind the house.
The room itself was crowded with potted trees and ferns and
big leafy things she couldn't begin to identify, and furnished
with the sort of furniture that looked as if it was supposed to
be outside, but which probably cost more than all the bamboo
in China.

The gardens, clearly, would be where the dual nuptials
took place, since a sea of folding white chairs had been set
up for as far as the eye could see. At the farthest reaches of
the seating was a white pavilion of sorts, and even from this
distance Lila could see that it was encrusted with—well,
there was no denying it—apricot roses. On the nearest side
of the seating, however, stood two people with their backs to
Joel and Lila, whom Lila hadn't seen for some time. Her
partner Oliver and the woman with whom he was about to
join his life forever.

Forever. She waited for the ominous boom of thunder and
the violent crash of waves that should have accompanied the
word. Strangely, it instead evoked images of peaceful sunsets
and tranquil beaches. No matter what happened in the future,
Lila thought, Oliver would always have Avery there with

him. Be it joyful celebration or grievous loss, he would have a companion to share it all. So maybe in that way, *forever* wasn't such a bad deal.

Still, even though Lila knew how much Oliver loved Avery, there was a part of her that couldn't believe he was going to go through with this. She and her partner might have grown up in entirely different environments and lived through entirely different experiences, but she'd begun to think the two of them were pretty much alike. Oliver had always been as restless as Lila, as discontented as she, as dissatisfied with life as she. He'd never voiced a desire to find the right woman and settle down, had never seemed even remotely the domestic-bliss type. He'd always struck her as the sort of person who couldn't be happy unless he had a lot of action and adventure in his life.

Now Lila watched through the big window as Oliver draped an arm over Avery's shoulder and pulled her close. She watched as he dipped his head the not insubstantial distance to drop a kiss on the crown of her head. She watched as Avery looped an arm around his waist without hesitation, as if it were the most natural thing in the world for her to do. Standing like that, the two of them looked like one creature with two heads and four arms, an entity made doubly strong by having twice the strength and stamina, a being that just dared the world to try to smack it down, because it would give it right back double.

And that was when Lila understood.

It wasn't a life of action and adventure Oliver wanted. It was someone to enjoy life's action and adventure with. And what greater adventure could there be—and what better action—than to fall in love? And to stay in love. Against all odds. In a world full of flaws. Forever and ever and ever. Oliver had been restless and discontented and dissatisfied with life because it hadn't been complete. Something—someone—had been missing from it. Now that he'd found Avery, that missing piece had fallen into place and had made his life—had made *him*—whole. He wouldn't be settling down with her. Just the opposite. The two of them had a lifetime ahead of them filled with all kinds of experiences they couldn't even imagine at this point.

Lila snuck a glance at Joel and wondered if maybe, just maybe, she'd been restless and discontented and dissatisfied for the same reasons as Oliver. And she wondered if maybe, just maybe, she'd been drawn to Joel for the same reasons Oliver had been so drawn to Avery. The same way Avery was unlike any woman Oliver had ever encountered, Joel was like no man Lila had ever met. Since that first night she'd tried to handcuff him in his home, she'd experienced some of the greatest thrills of her life. There had been moments of heart-stopping excitement, of breath-stealing exhilaration, of mind-scrambling ecstasy. There had been discoveries of feelings she'd never known she possessed, and the exploration of desires she'd never dared acknowledge. He'd filled needs and satisfied hungers no one had ever been able to assuage—not even her. Joel Faraday had been—

Well. He'd been quite an adventure. And very exciting.

Before she was able to do more than stagger at all the revelations bombarding her brain, Oliver turned and saw her and Joel through the window and immediately lifted a hand in greeting. Avery turned, too, and smiled, and Lila was stunned by the changes in the other woman. Gone were the long, childish braids and the little black-framed glasses. She'd put on some much-needed weight that had rounded her body and face and buffed away the edges. The shadows beneath her eyes—and the shadows *in* her eyes—had vanished.

She looked…peaceful, Lila thought. She looked comfortable. She looked like a woman who had landed in the place she was always meant to be, and it was more beautiful than she'd ever imagined.

"Come on," Lila told Joel. "I want to introduce you."

Without even thinking about what she was doing—or why she was doing it—she wove her fingers through his and gave his hand a gentle tug. Then she continued to hold his hand as she led him to and through the open French doors leading out to the garden. The moment they were outside, Oliver's gaze, she noted, dropped to their entwined fingers, and a huge grin split his face. But he said nothing when Lila and Joel came to a halt in front of him and Avery. He only reached for her, without letting go of Avery, and pulled her into a fierce, one-armed hug. As always, Lila was startled by how incredibly handsome he was, with his jet-black hair and his pale green eyes. And as always, she decided this must be how a woman felt when she had an older brother she knew she could count on, no matter how much trouble she ever found herself in.

Wow, how about that? All this time she'd had a family without even realizing it. She'd just been adding to it lately. She snuck another peek at Joel, who had held firmly to her hand when Oliver swept her into his hug, and found him looking back at her with a soft little smile that sent warmth seeping into her every extremity. And she realized then that she could do a lot worse in life than to see him smiling at her like that every day.

"My second favorite woman in the world," Oliver said with a laugh, tightening his arm around her neck...at the same time Joel tightened his fingers on her hand.

Lila laughed, too, looping her free arm around Oliver's waist above Avery's—though not nearly as snugly as the other woman's was—and then pulled Joel in close, too. "Wow, I've come up in the world," she said. "I used to be number three, after Angelina Jolie and Carmen Electra."

"I have no idea who you're talking about," Oliver said.

Noting the way he was beaming, she replied, "Yeah, I can see that."

She disengaged herself from the group hug and moved closer to Joel. And if she ended up moving a little—okay, a lot—closer than she'd originally intended, it was only because the eight billion acres of elegant Nesbitt gardens were so crowded with all those chairs and pavilions and apricot roses.

"This is Joel Faraday," she said by way of an introduction. Still standing close. Still holding his hand. Still not caring what anyone—except maybe Joel—thought about that. "Joel," she added, gesturing first toward Oliver, then Avery, "this is Oliver Sheridan, and his soon-to-be wife, Avery Nesbitt."

Avery smiled, and Lila was again overcome by how much she had changed. Six months ago she would have been a flinching, cowering mess just standing this far away from the house. Even inside the house, Lila knew, Avery had had problems, because it hadn't been her condo in New York. But she looked and seemed as comfortable here as a woman would be when she was surrounded by all the things she loved best and needed most. Looking at Oliver, Lila realized Avery was just that.

"Good to see you again, Lila," Avery said. Then she smiled. "Thanks for using the front door this time. You scared the hell out of the dogs last time you were here."

Lila chuckled. "I brought them some gourmet doggy treats in the hopes that it will get me back in their good graces."

"Come on," Oliver said, tilting his head toward the French doors through which Lila and Joel had passed only moments ago. "We have a wedding to plan for. And you," he added, looking directly at Lila, "have a few responsibilities as my best man."

THE WEDDING WAS BEAUTIFUL, of course—and, inescapably, elegant—but the reception was even better. Mostly because it was considerably less elegant. Mostly because a full quarter of the guests were Tanner Gillespie's family—blue-collar laborers, every last one—who injected a lot more life into the party than the elegant Nesbitts could have managed on their own.

"It was an interesting courtship those two had," Oliver told Lila and Joel as the three of them stood in the elegant—and massive—Nesbitt ballroom, watching Carly and Tanner take their turn cutting their wedding cake.

Lila sipped champagne from an elegant crystal flute, being careful not to spill any on the sleeveless black gown she'd chosen for her best-man attire. Carly had insisted all the women in the ceremony have their hair done by her stylist, so Lila's had been swept up and artfully arranged by a guy named Eddie who looked like a dock worker and had hummed "I Feel Pretty" the whole time he was working on her.

"Yeah, I kind of guessed that," she said. "Though I probably would have used a different word than *interesting*."

"What gave it away?" Joel asked. "The fact that for their first dance as a married couple they chose the Talking Heads' 'Burnin' Down the House'?"

Oliver laughed. "That wasn't their first choice. But my new mother-in-law adamantly refused to have Jimmy Buffett's 'Why Don't We Get Drunk and Screw' played in her house."

Lila shook her head. "I'm thinkin' Tanner's family has done a lot to shake up the elegant Nesbitts."

"Whoa, yeah," Oliver agreed. "But then, the elegant Nesbitts have done their part to rub off on Tanner's family." He pointed at Avery's mother. "Felicia even got Donna—" now he pointed at the woman who had been introduced to Lila as Tanner's mother "—an invitation to join her gardening club. And Desmond-Three got Frank, Tanner's dad, season tickets to the Met."

"There's only one Met now?" Lila asked. "What happened to the rest of the team?"

Oliver leveled a look on her. "Smart-ass. The Metropolitan Opera."

"Ooooh."

"Anyway, they all get along surprisingly well now. Don't

think it was always like that, though. Tanner's family hated Carly for a long time."

Carly chose that moment to shriek in outrage, then shout something across the ballroom at the caterer about how the cake was *supposed* to be amaretto, *not* a proletarian chocolate assault on her senses.

"Imagine that," Joel said.

"And the Nesbitts weren't too crazy about Tanner, either," Oliver went on. "But they eventually realized it was her he loved, not her money."

"Go figure," Lila said. "Though I guess the money is a nice bonus." Still, seeing the way Tanner looked at Carly, it was clear the elegant Nesbitt greenbacks were not what he was looking forward to rolling in tonight. "They look really happy," she said, smiling. Then she turned back to Oliver. "And so do you."

He smiled back. "I never thought it could be like this, Lila," he said softly. "The way it is with Avery and me. It's just…" He sighed again, and, amazingly, it did nothing to detract from his manliness. "I just never thought it could be like this, that's all. You really should—"

Whatever he'd intended to say got cut short by the announcement that he was needed to cut his own wedding cake now. The three of them looked up to see Avery, a vision in soft ivory, waving to him from near the table, so Oliver said, "Later," and made his way toward his new wife without a single look back.

He really did look happy, Lila thought. He really *was* happy. The way she wanted to be happy, too. With someone in her life she knew she could count on, someone who would be there through good times and bad, someone who would love her and want her just the way she was, without expecting her to be anything else.

Joel didn't care about anything but her, she reminded herself. He'd told her so. The same way she'd discovered over the past couple of weeks that she didn't care about anything but him. She wasn't sure what she was going to do with her life without OPUS as a part of it. But that didn't scare her, because she knew she'd land on her feet. She wasn't sure what she would do with her life without Joel as a part of it, either. But that did scare her. Beyond words. Because without him, she would have nothing to hold on to, nothing to balance her, nothing to keep her steady.

Without Joel, Lila would have nothing at all. Without him, her life would be empty. Because without him, she had no one to love. And without love... Well, without love, what was the use of living?

No one could possibly know what the future held, she told herself. No matter how well they planned it. Which was all the more reason not to face it alone.

"What are you thinking about?" Joel asked her.

Oh, he did have such perfect timing, she thought. He'd come into her life right when it had begun to crumble, and had given her the hand she'd needed to hold on to until the earth began to steady under her again. And now he was asking her a question like that, right when she needed an opening to tell him how she felt.

She turned to look at him and smiled. "I'm thinking about how much I love you," she said. "And about how incredible our life together is going to be."

His mouth dropped open for a moment, then he smiled. "You love me."

"I do."

His smile grew broader. "You know, you say those two little words on a day like this, in an environment like this, the people who hear those two little words might think they mean something besides what you intend them to mean."

Lila tucked her fingers up under his hair and curled them around his nape. Then she pushed herself up on tiptoe and kissed him. He looped an arm around her waist when she did, and for long moments they continued to kiss each other, nothing too passionate, but nothing too innocent, either. When Lila finally pulled away, she lowered her arm to circle it around Joel's waist and nestled her body into his. Then she sipped her champagne as if nothing had happened.

So Joel leaned down and, moving his mouth beside her ear, whispered, "Tell me I didn't just daydream that you told me you loved me and then kissed me."

"Why? Did it feel like a dream?" Lila asked as she lifted her champagne for another sip.

He nodded, nuzzling her ear as he did. "Yeah, it did, actually."

"That's funny," she told him. "It was supposed to feel like your future."

He chuckled at that and tightened the arm around her waist. "*Our* future," he corrected her.

And for the first time since meeting him, Lila had to admit that sometimes when it came to correcting her, Joel Faraday knew what he was talking about.

EPILOGUE

LESS THAN AN HOUR'S drive from Christchurch, New Zealand, in the library of a posh Greek Revival estate that looked out over the azure Pacific, Elliott Wainwright IV—who had at one time gone by the name of Adrian Padgett, among others—looked at the overstuffed manila envelope that sat on his desk. It had arrived from New York this morning, having traveled halfway around the globe—much as Elliott had done two years ago when he left the United States for the last time—to find its way to him.

It was not a good sign, this overstuffed manila envelope showing up the way it had.

He hesitated before opening it, wanting a few more minutes of blissful ignorance in which he could make himself believe the significance of the package's arrival meant something else. Something happy. Something fortunate. Something besides what he was sure lurked beneath the innocent-looking manila.

He shoved his hands deep into the pockets of his beige linen trousers, ruining the line of the white linen guayabera shirt he wore with them. It didn't matter, he told himself. He and his wife, Delilah—who had at one time gone by the name Iris Daugherty, among others—had built a good life for themselves here. Even if what he suspected lay in the envelope was indeed inside, no one could take that away from them. They'd paid cash for the estate and had invested the remainder of their ill-gotten gains wisely enough that not only could they afford their current lifestyle quite well, they'd even been able to repay much of their ill-gotten gains. They were doing their best to amend their past wrongs as well as they could—provided, of course, they could live like a king and queen until they did so.

No matter what, the two of them were safe in the life they had forged here. Not only was their house excessive in its beauty and wealth, it was also excessive in its security measures, right down to the full-time security personnel and Doberman pinschers, many of whom had become pets—especially Elliott's favorite of the bunch, Pookie. So named by Delilah—let that be made clear.

As if conjured by the thought, Delilah entered the library then, all blond and tanned and beautiful and glowing. That last wasn't due just to the summer sun that left her formerly fair skin bronzed a golden cream, but was also a byproduct of what lay under the scantly swollen mound of her belly. At almost fifty, Elliott was about to become a father for the first time. The realization by turns delighted and terrified him. Fortunately, Delilah was more than ready for the baby's arrival. And fortunately for the baby, Delilah would be his—or her—mother.

"I saw Bryan bring up the mail," she said as she strode across the library toward him, the flowing fabric of her variegated pareu dancing about her bare feet. "I saw the package. Have you opened it yet?"

Elliott shook his head. "I'm not sure I want to."

"Maybe it's good news," she said. Though even she didn't sound as if she believed it.

"Or maybe it's the end of my world as I know it."

She thrust out her lower lip in an obviously childish pout. "Oh, don't be so melodramatic."

He sighed, then stepped away from the desk. "Fine. Then you open it."

She lifted her chin and smiled. "All right. I will."

That was Delilah, he thought with affection. She was always the strong one.

She lifted the manila envelope from the desk and, without hesitation, jammed her thumb under the flap and jerked it along the top with a faint but—Elliott couldn't help thinking—ominous *rrriiippp*. Then she withdrew the fat stack of papers from inside, taking a moment to read whatever the top page said. He tried to gauge the contents of that page by her reaction, but her face revealed nothing.

That was Delilah, he thought with admiration. She was always the self-contained one.

"Well, at least it's not a form letter this time," she finally said, looking up. "They addressed you by name and made some nice comments."

Elliott sighed. "But they still rejected the book, didn't they?"

She nodded. "I'm afraid so."

"Same reasons this time?"

"Pretty much."

"Tell me."

She glanced down at the cover letter again and read,

"'Dear Mr. Wainwright. Thank you for giving us the opportunity to consider your novel…' blah, blah, blah '…unfortunately doesn't meet our needs at this time…' blah, blah, blah… Ah, here we go. He says, 'Your writing is very strong, and your espionage novel is very compelling. Unfortunately, much of it is so far-fetched, we can't see it being palatable to our readers. The fictional spy organization you've crafted for the story, although intriguing, is simply too over-the-top to be taken seriously.'" She looked up again. "Well, there you go, Elliott. Your life with OPUS was just too far-fetched to be palatable and too over-the-top to be taken seriously."

He sighed heavily. "Note to self. Next time water down the reality of my experiences and make OPUS less OPUSy."

She smiled at him as she placed the manuscript back on the desk. "I told you no one would believe half the stuff OPUS had you doing. Or half the stuff OPUS was responsible for."

"At least my writing is compelling," Elliott said, taking heart.

"Hardly anyone sells their first novel," Delilah reminded him.

"Yes, but this is my third."

"Hardly anyone sells their third novel."

He chuckled at that.

"You'll just send it out again."

Yes, he thought, he supposed he would. Never let it be said that Elliott Wainwright IV—or any of the other men he'd been in his life—was a quitter.

"Besides," she added, threading her arm through his, "I have something that might cheer you up."

"What's that?"

She took his other hand in hers and opened it so that his fingers were splayed wide, then she pressed it against her belly, which was nearly the size of half a basketball. "Wait for it," she said softly.

So Elliott did. And after a few minutes he felt the flutter of something extraordinary against his hand.

"That's your son or daughter," Delilah said.

He shook his head in disbelief. They were procreating. In all his life, he'd never imagined himself capable of such a thing. He felt that familiar battle of pleasure and fear waging in his midsection, and was astonished to realize how easily pleasure won. Fear hadn't even put up a fight this time. It had just slunk away.

He remembered a time when he had wanted to rule the world. Because he had wanted to be important. Had wanted to be remembered. Had wanted to matter in the big picture. Whoever it was inside Delilah pushed against his hand again, and he realized he was important. He would be remembered. He mattered very, very much.

With his hand still curved over her belly, he leaned in and kissed her temple. "You saved my life, Delilah," he told her.

She cupped her hand over his cheek. "And you saved mine," she replied.

She curled her fingers over the back of his hand, and they stood looking out the window at the blue, blue Pacific, not saying a word. None was necessary. None could say what they both felt so deeply.

Life was good. For all of them.

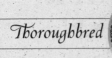 

Thoroughbred *Legacy*.

Launching in June 2008

A dramatic new 12-book continuity that embodies the American Dream.

Meet the Prestons, owners of Quest Stables, a successful horse-racing and breeding empire. But the lives, loves and reputations of this hardworking family are put at risk when a breeding scandal unfolds.

Flirting with Trouble

by *New York Times* bestselling author

ELIZABETH BEVARLY

Eight years ago, publicist Marnie Roberts spent seven days of bliss with Australian horse trainer Daniel Whittleson. But just as quickly, he disappeared. Now Marnie is heading to Australia to finally confront the man she's never been able to forget.

The race begins in June, wherever books are sold.

REQUEST YOUR
FREE BOOKS!

2 FREE NOVELS
FROM THE ROMANCE/SUSPENSE
COLLECTION PLUS 2 FREE GIFTS!

YES! Please send me 2 FREE novels from the Romance/Suspense Collection and my 2 FREE gifts (gifts are worth about $10). After receiving them, if I don't wish to receive any more books, I can return the shipping statement marked "cancel." If I don't cancel, I will receive 4 brand-new novels every month and be billed just $5.49 per book in the U.S. or $5.99 per book in Canada, plus 25¢ shipping and handling per book plus applicable taxes, if any*. That's a savings of at least 20% off the cover price! I understand that accepting the 2 free books and gifts places me under no obligation to buy anything. I can always return a shipment and cancel at any time. Even if I never buy another book from the Reader Service, the two free books and gifts are mine to keep forever.

185 MDN EF5Y 385 MDN EF6C

Name _____ (PLEASE PRINT)

Address _____ Apt. #

City _____ State/Prov. _____ Zip/Postal Code

Signature (if under 18, a parent or guardian must sign)

Mail to **The Reader Service:**
IN U.S.A.: P.O. Box 1867, Buffalo, NY 14240-1867
IN CANADA: P.O. Box 609, Fort Erie, Ontario L2A 5X3

Not valid to current subscribers to the Romance Collection,
the Suspense Collection or the Romance/Suspense Collection.

Want to try two free books from another line?
Call 1-800-873-8635 or visit www.morefreebooks.com.

* Terms and prices subject to change without notice. N.Y. residents add applicable sales tax. Canadian residents will be charged applicable provincial taxes and GST. Offer not valid in Quebec. This offer is limited to one order per household. All orders subject to approval. Credit or debit balances in a customer's account(s) may be offset by any other outstanding balance owed by or to the customer. Please allow 4 to 6 weeks for delivery. Offer available while quantities last.

Your Privacy: Harlequin is committed to protecting your privacy. Our Privacy Policy is available online at www.eHarlequin.com or upon request from the Reader Service. From time to time we make our lists of customers available to reputable third parties who may have a product or service of interest to you. If you would prefer we not share your name and address, please check here. ☐

BOB08R

#1 *NEW YORK TIMES* BESTSELLING AUTHOR
DEBBIE MACOMBER

What do you want most in the world?

Anne Marie Roche wants to find happiness again. At 38,
she's childless, a recent widow and alone. On Valentine's
Day, Anne Marie and several other widows get together to
celebrate…what? Hope, possibility, the future. They each
begin a list of twenty wishes.

Anne Marie's list includes learning to knit, doing good for
someone else and falling in love again. She begins to act on
her wishes, and when she volunteers at a school, little Ellen
enters her life. It's a relationship that becomes far more
important than she ever imagined, one in which they both
learn that wishes can come true.

Twenty Wishes

"These involving stories…continue the Blossom Street
themes of friendship and personal growth that readers
find so moving."—*Booklist* on *Back on Blossom Street*

Available the first week of May 2008 wherever books are sold!

MIRA®

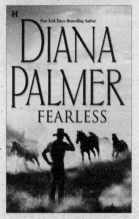